Blood Silver

The Yocum Dollar
by
Woody P. Snow

Denise
Hope you enjoy this
story —
Love Jay (woody)

Pen-L Publishing
Fayetteville, Arkansas
Pen-L.com

First Edition Printed and bound in USA
ISBN: 978-1-940222-22-6

Cover design by Adam Ritchey
Interior by Kimberly Pennell

Legends and yarns and folktales
are as much a part
of the real history of a country
as proclamations and provisions
and constitutional amendments.

– Stephen Vincent Benét

Blood Silver

PROLOGUE

The flat black thing turned out to be a laptop computer.

Clint Smith, twenty-seven, had run across all kinds of personal items before – eyeglasses, cameras, bikini tops, a deck chair once – but never a computer, one hundred and twelve feet below the surface, and he couldn't help but wonder, had it been thrown into the lake in a fit of frustration or accidentally dropped, much to someone's horror?

Maybe an unhappy wife, whose husband was supposed to be spending his vacation time focused on her, sneaked it overboard in the middle of the night.

He loved how a guy's imagination seemed so much freer down here than up in the dry world.

Maybe the water patrol had been swarming in on a terrorist. If his diabolical plans were on the hard drive, he would have had to make that computer disappear before "the man" boarded.

Clint was able to recognize the crooked "E" in the four-letter brand name because, even below the second thermocline, the ambient light on this day afforded a visibility of nearly seven feet.

Dewey Short, Duck Island, Breezy Point, Moonshine Beach – the spots most scuba enthusiasts stuck to – Clint and diving buddy, Daniel, avoided. Been there, done that.

Once, he was able to lift some risqué photos from an SD card out of a small Nikon he found. Would he be able to dry this laptop enough to peruse its hard drive? Maybe it held the world's only key to Einstein's unified field theory.

They had decided to dive the Joe Bald area in an attempt to locate the original confluence point of the James River and the White River before the lake was created, not for treasures necessarily but more to see if such a point were discoverable or discernible in some way.

When a river is dammed to make a fifty-three thousand acre lake, can a person come along seventy-some years later and chart that river's original course? Would it be possible for a scuba diver to pick his way back along the river's natural path from point A, the dam, to point B, where the two rivers originally merged into one? That's where the local history would really be, wouldn't it? And possibly, one or more of the legendary Yocum Silver dollars. Who knew? Clint didn't.

As a child, and to this day, he sometimes imagined finding one of the fabled trade coins. He had no expectation of ever actually laying eyes on one but a guy could always dream.

When his fingertips dipped into the silt to take hold of the laptop they touched the edge of a small hard disc. He pinched it immediately.

Coins possess a mystical quality that impels a human hand to behave that way, automatically clenching them, and that's what his right hand did, tightly. With his left, he tried to wave away the murk he unsettled and then dolphined himself away to find Daniel to whom he gave the sign for both to go up.

Standing in the boat with the disc in his left palm, he gently wiped the mud away with his right index finger. When it began to gleam, his pulse quickened.

"What is it?" Daniel asked, removing his tank.

Clint gazed away as though studying the condos across the lake on the hill-side, in the hundreds now, but he didn't see them. His mind's eye was peering through a hole in time to another world long since gone. "Take me in," he said.

"What?" It was only just past eleven. "Why?"

Clint lowered his bottom to the deck, folded his legs and studied the coin. "I've got to go visit my great grandmother."

"Now?"

"She's a hundred and two, Daniel." He looked up. "No time to waste."

y

Her name was Ruby Smith, but Clint, since the age of two, had always called her Gramma Yoka. She was by far the oldest resident of Lake Shore Assisted Living.

Tears welled as she held the coin in her hand and studied it. "Do you think it's real, Jerry?"

"I'm Clint, Gramma Yoka, Jerry's *son*. Jerry, your grandson, is your daughter Martha's boy, and I'm Jerry's boy."

She sighed, confused.

"Yes, I think it's real."

"Your Grampa got killed building that dam. Did you know that?"

She meant his great grandfather but there was no point in correcting her generational time warps today. "Yes, Gramma, I knew that. In 1955, right?"

"1955. Got caught in one of those gigantic cogs. Crushed the life out of him."

"I know," Clint said, nodding sadly. "He used to tell my dad, your grandson, Jerry, the story of the Yocum Silver Dollar and he, my dad, Jerry, your grandson, passed it on to me, the story, I mean."

She turned the coin over to inspect the other side. "Trade Coins," she said softly. "That's what they called them. Whose is it?"

Clint shrugged with a smile. "The way I see it is . . . well, as the great, great granddaughter of Arnold Yoachum, I think this coin belongs to you, Gramma."

"Me? What would I do with it?"

Clint pulled a chair up near hers. "Now this is just an idea that hit me on the way over, Gramma, but I was thinking you might want to donate it to the museum at College of the Ozarks."

"Ralph Foster's place?"

"Right."

"He's the same age as me, you know."

"Ralph passed away in 1984, Gramma, but the Ralph Foster Museum is bigger than ever. Here's what I think we should do. You donate the coin and we record you telling the story to go along with it."

"What story?"

"The story of the Yocum silver dollar."

"That was your grampa's story, Jerry, not mine, and I can tell you as sure as shootin' most folks never believed a speck of it."

Clint leaned in and put a hand on her shoulder. "They will now, Gramma. They'll have to."

She thought about it for a moment then returned her eyes to the coin. "It's pretty, isn't it, Jerry?"

"I'm Clint, Gramma. Yeah," he nodded. "It's pretty. It's beautiful."

PART ONE

It is not possible a land which has within itself everything to make its settlers happy can remain unnoticed by the American people.

—Moses Austin
1761–1821

CHAPTER 1

Cahokia, Illinois Territory
October 12th, 1813

His mother had given birth to three big sons with no need to bother a doctor, so his wife could do it too, he assumed. But tarnation, how long did it take? As an event, James, the middleborn of the three Yoachum boys, thought this would be a wonderful moment, but his wife, Ruth, was not enjoying it at all, nor had she been, not a second of it, since seven fifteen that morning, six hours ago, when she announced the baby was coming. The baby had not come and Ruth, God bless her, toiling to pass the new person into the world, had been suffering painfully the whole time.

James finally gave in to his younger brother, Solomon. "You're right, Sol, go get the doctor. Hurry."

Fifteen minutes later, to the sounds of a blood-curdling scream, the doctor burst through the door with Solomon on his heels.

"Get back, Jim," The physician ordered. "Stand away, both of you." He pulled the blanket aside that James had arranged for modesty's sake, then drew a sharp breath. "Good Lord."

"It's all right Ruth," James called to his wife, "the doctor's here. It'll go quicker now." He stared at the back of the doctor's head. "She's been hurting terrible, Doctor. What can you do?"

"I think I can save the baby," the doctor said.

"Yeah. Good," James said, and then thought for a moment. "Wait. What do you mean?"

"I think I can save the baby," the doctor said sharply. "Step back. Don't watch. Let me get this little thing out."

James, confused, turned to his brother.

Solomon's look was one of deep regret.

"Wait, hold on," James said turning back to the doctor. "If it's between the two of them, forget about the blasted baby. Save my wife."

"Too late," the doctor said. "Sorry. Now, please, shut up and let me work."

"Ruth?" James called nervously over sickening, sticky noises. "Ruth?" He could not fathom the doctor's words or the way he had spoken them, as if in anger. "What do you mean, too late? Too late for what? Ruth?"

Then there was that sound which had not changed in thousands of years, the first cry of the newborn as the doctor swung around with an eight-pound bloody mess and laid it in the crib, prepared weeks earlier by its mother, nineteen-year-old Missus Ruth Yoachum.

"Ruth?" James shouted.

The doctor reached into his bag for a clean cotton wipe, then looked up to James. "Mister Yoachum, your wife did not survive." He shook his head. "She should have, but this is no time to blame anybody."

"What are you talking about?"

"She should have had a cesarean days ago. Weeks ago. Surely you knew things weren't right."

James could not comprehend. "Ruth?" he shrieked, kneeling by her side. He studied her anguished gaze. Dark curls matted by sweat clung to her delicately featured face, her large brown eyes lifeless.

His younger brother stepped forward to put a hand on his shoulder. "She's gone, Jim."

James went rigid. What kind of doctor was this? She was alive when the doctor walked in, then hunched over her, and now, three minutes later, she was . . . dead? "I ought to kill you," he snarled, twisting toward the doctor.

"You think I'm the one to blame?" the doctor said. "What time did she go into labor? Huh? What time?"

As the doctor and Sol waited for an answer they saw a sudden change come over James as though someone had just blown out the candle that had lit his soul for twenty years, and then James Yoachum, the man, appeared nearly as lifeless as his lost wife. Quietly, barely breathing, he blinked and then walked out of his house.

Sol and the doctor went to the door and watched as James wandered away.

"She should have had a cesarean days ago," the doctor repeated.

"I don't understand" Sol said. "What do you –"

"That baby was never going to pass naturally through this girl." He turned back to tend to the wailing newborn. "She just wasn't built for it."

Sol sighed and stared at Ruth.

The doctor pulled the blanket over her face. "There's things need to be done here," he said. "We lost one and we got a new one, both need to be dealt with in a right timely fashion and I don't think your brother's in a state to do any of it."

"He'll be all right," Sol said.

"Let's hope so. In the meantime, I know people. You stay here. I'll send some women over and get the coroner to tend to Missus Yoachum."

Sol nodded, tears welling in his eyes. "Thank you, Doctor."

James was wandering the streets of Cahokia, Illinois, the bustling capital of St. Clair County.

People on foot and on horseback moved out of his way as they stared at the huge man with the yellow hair who was obviously not all right.

y

Around two that afternoon, Solomon spotted James on a barstool in the Dancing Fox Tavern on Water Street.

He paused in the door to study his brother, trying to calculate some measure of the whiskey he may have consumed.

He didn't look wobbly, but then James was nearly six and a half feet tall and did not go down easily for anything, including alcohol.

He had never been a drinker, not really, not after having survived childhood with a German father who drank daily and amused himself by shooting dogs. In the end it was an enraged dog owner that shot Heninrich Yoachum to death when James was fourteen, Sol, eleven.

Today was different. Sol could tell now by the way James swayed on the barstool, but who could blame the man? He had just lost his wife, Ruth, whom they had known, both brothers, since they were little and so yes,

James was drinking, pouring alcohol into his troubled soul, and Sol could feel his brother's torment as he watched him from the door, sitting there, deranged with the pain of unfathomable loss as the alcohol streamed its anesthesia through his veins.

Sol laid a brotherly hand on James's shoulder to let him know that he was there, standing by his side on this day of unspeakable heartache. But something needed to be talked about here, and it was an urgent thing and so he had to speak. "Jim?"

"Hey, little brother, pull up a stool."

"James, you have a son. You're a Pa now. I'm an uncle."

James stared ahead. "I don't want to be a pa."

Sol seated himself. "Well, you started out as a son, didn't you?"

No answer.

"Then worked your way up to being a brother, and you were always a swell brother, and now you've been promoted to being a pa." Sol's effort was to frame the rungs of life as a foregone conclusion of responsibility, but still there was no response. "It's terrible about Ruth but you got to come on now and take care of your boy."

James shook his head. "Just leave him be. He killed his own mother so it's natural that he not survive, you know, without a ma. That's just natural. It happens sometimes. A deer don't drop its fawn the right way, they both die. That's nature's way."

"But we ain't animals, Jim, and your baby is alive and kicking."

"I don't care."

"You remember Missus Hargas? Rachel Hargas? Had a baby about a month ago? Doc says she said she'd be glad to wet nurse your boy for you."

"Quit calling it my boy. It ain't my boy. I don't want the blasted thing."

Sol stood back, angry now. "Well, then why don't you just go home and shoot him? Shoot him right through his dark curly haired little head. You'll have to take good aim. He ain't no bigger than your foot and he squirms like a –"

A smashing right fist to the face put a stop to Sol's rebuke and knocked him to the floor.

James rose from his stool, and muttered, "Leave me alone." He paused to get his balance and then hobbled out the tavern door.

Sol rubbed his bleeding mouth but yelled loud enough for James to hear, "He's Ruth's son too, Jim. He's a Yoachum!"

CHAPTER 2

Passed out on a mud bank of the Mississippi River, James was booted awake by kicks to his rump with just enough force to make sure he came around.

He peered up to see a much smaller man about his age, well dressed, wearing glasses and sporting a countenance that made him look like the landlord of the river. "What?"

"Get up," the man said. "If you're going with me, get up now. I won't tell you again."

James rose to his knees to assess the gutsy pipsqueak. "Who the blazes are you?"

"I'm Henry Rowe Schoolcraft, sir, and if you're going with me I expect you to watch your language and behave like a gentleman." He pointed to a nearby lean-to. "Report to the quartermaster."

His head filled with the sludge of pain and confusion, James could only gawk.

Schoolcraft started to walk away but then turned. "Pathetic."

"What?" James said.

"You, my slow-witted friend. Are you signing on for the expedition or not?"

Across the river James could see the torchlights of St. Louis. Against that glow on this side, he saw silhouettes of men readying bundles, sacks and polls. There were keelboats, six or seven of them, at the water's edge. He nodded. "Yes Sir. I'm going."

"Be hasty then," Schoolcraft commanded. "We put in at first light."

Impressed by James's size, Schoolcraft assigned him to the rear boat to watch for any navigational problems that might be remedied by a big man before any loss of control.

James nodded as though he understood but wondered what he was supposed to do if a sack of whatever fell overboard from one of the boats. Jump in and swim after it or dive down to retrieve it from the bottom of the Mississippi? He wasn't going to do that.

He decided that if there were a problem he would shout at whomever he thought was responsible, and then order them to make things right. Besides, he wondered, why didn't they stock up on supplies in St. Louis? James had heard the population over there now was nearly fifteen hundred. He assumed Schoolcraft had specialized materials for whatever mission he was on. He wondered too, if he would actually stick with Schoolcraft, or just how long he would go along with the odd little fellow.

The contract he signed committing him for the duration of the expedition didn't matter to him. He knew that when he signed his name, it was just something to do. When you regain consciousness in the mud on a riverbank – sign a contract. Why not? What did it matter? Nothing mattered.

In a little over three hours the six boats crossed the Mississippi and were moored in the wooden slips, which were supposed to have been reserved for Schoolcraft, but other boats occupied two.

When James observed how Schoolcraft admonished the pier master and how quickly the latter struggled to correct the situation, he figured his butt-kicking new boss must be a man with connections. For the first time, Henry Rowe Schoolcraft impressed James Yoachum. He would again years later.

On shore, at around nine, along with a speech about responsible behavior, Schoolcraft handed out four banknotes to each man and then announced the roster for guard duty to his group of eighteen.

Six men would stay with the boats for six hours, then another six, and then the final third. They would start their journey North at five the next morning.

James, assigned to the last shift, reckoned he had till eleven that night to do whatever he wanted. And what he wanted was to drink again, to fill his brain with alcohol's dominion over comprehension, because his mind was starting to ask questions and he didn't want questions. How can a man comprehend the incomprehensible? Better to drown the impulse. He wanted numbness.

y

By noon James straddled a stool at the bar in a smoky, brick-walled tavern full of French fur traders. As he neared the bottom of a glass of bourbon the bartender stopped.

"What?" James asked.

"Monsieur," the bartender said, "that is your fourth. You will pay now, oui?"

James reached into his pocket, withdrew one of the banknotes he'd been allotted at the pier and smacked it down. "One more, bartender. I've got new money right here."

The bartender shook his head. "No paper," he said. "Coins only, s'il vous plait."

James felt flimflammed. "What's wrong with paper money?"

The bartender shrugged. "It is . . . paper."

"Yeah, but –"

Interrupted by a hand on his shoulder, James turned to see Schoolcraft. Ah-ha, he thought with a smile, the well-connected pipsqueak who had berated the dock master. He would kick this annoying, French, coin-grubbing bartender's pompous tail. "Set him straight, Boss."

"Mon ami," Schoolcraft addressed the bartender. "It is not just paper. My employee here holds official U.S. Treasury notes from the National Bank of St. Louis. It is legal tender."

The bartender surveyed the important-looking fellow, then asked, "Your official U.S. Treasury notes, they are promises, oui?"

"That's right," Schoolcraft said. "From the St. Louis National Bank."

The bartender reached under the bar then placed two empty glasses before them. "For that," he said, you get the promise of two drinks."

"Now see here," Schoolcraft rebuked, "this is legal tender in all of the United States."

"But you are in Missouri, Monsieur." The bartender shrugged. "Missouri is not a state." He nailed his eyes to James. "You will pay now Sir, and then you and your sophistiquee friend will leave."

"Now see here," Schoolcraft said again. "Do you know who I am?"

The bartender pointed for them to turn and look. A distinguished man in his mid-forties sat at a table in the back corner. "Do you know who he is?"

They didn't.

"Colonel Pierre Menard, the propietaire. He accepts paper money from no one." He spread his hands in a gesture of condolence. "Je regret."

"The lieutenant governor of Illinois?" said Schoolcraft, his face brightening. "He'll accept treasury notes from me." He was mistaken.

The Colonel was sorry but there was nothing to discuss, and he wanted them out of his tavern.

Ill-natured for a lieutenant governor, Schoolcraft thought, especially when Menard ordered his security men to "jeter les clochards out into the street."

They were about to do that, and had gone so far as to grab Schoolcraft by the arms to jerk him out when James stood up.

A man of his measure in an obviously unpleasant mood brought a sudden reconsideration of the matter. They could stay but they would not be served for paper money.

Schoolcraft was enraged. "Let's go find a civilized establishment," he bellowed for the room to hear.

Outside, as Schoolcraft tucked his shirttail back into his britches – it had gotten yanked out by Menard's men – he said, "Down the street, there."

James withdrew the other three bills from his pocket, crumpled them into a wad and dropped them to the dirt street.

"Mister Yoachum," Schoolcraft said, "Those are official redeemable notes. Those men in there, they're ignorant. Pick up your money and we'll try that hotel down there." He pointed. "I need a meal and I'm sure you do as well. I'm buying."

James did not look to see the hotel, and he wasn't listening. He was turning away, his money left in a clump on the street.

"Wait, Yoachum," Schoolcraft said. "You signed on for five hundred days. You're going to see things that no other white man . . . . Where are you going? You signed a contract. Yoachum! You all right?" Schoolcraft knew that he wasn't.

James walked away, going somewhere else to get to somewhere else, on his way to somewhere else, of which he had no vision, for which he had no plan, and no concern. His mind felt like an expanding bubble trapped within his skull and about to burst. He wondered if it would blow his head open. It didn't matter.

CHAPTER 3

Had James been listening to the tavern chatter, and had he understood French, he would have picked up on the scuttlebutt about a new organization called The Committee for Public Safety, as worries about British-Indian attacks were spreading in Missouri Territory due to the ongoing War of 1812. He would have learned that a man named William C. Lane was politicking to be the first mayor and was building the first brick house in the city.

He wouldn't have cared. He didn't care about anything except getting away from reality.

For days he walked roads, paths, and some natural passageways, straight into the late sun, so he assumed he was headed due west. He did not realize that being October, this would actually lead him Southwest.

At night he would find a creek, drop to his knees and drink from cupped hands, then fall over onto his back and stare up at the stars, trying not to see his wife's anguished, lifeless face. How she had suffered those last, what had it been, five hours, six? He couldn't remember but it was terrible. It was worse than terrible and he had kept thinking that it was natural, and that it would be over any second but it wasn't. It had gone on and on and on. Now she was dead. How could that be? Was it his fault? The doctor had intimated that it was, hadn't he? He sank into sleep as autumn leaves fell onto his face.

Morning after morning, some part of his mind would struggle to keep him in slumber because awakening was so merciless. But awaken he would.

He would shiver, rise and move on, unaware of his beard growth and of his weight loss.

James would like to have had some venison or some turkey or a boar, all of which he saw frequently but had neither the skill nor the ambition to even try without a gun. A gun. That would be grand.

There was still plenty of carpetweed everywhere but with nothing to boil it in, the raw chewing was punishing. There were several varieties of chickweed, dandelion greens and every spring-fed stream he ran across had an abundance of watercress, which he devoured by handfuls.

So James sustained himself, but the part of his mind he managed to cling to for survival purposes was eroding. He knew that. Whether he wanted to survive or if he deserved to, he wasn't sure.

One morning, weeks after walking out of St. Louis, or maybe it was months – it was getting very cold – James, coming over a ridge, surprised a brown bear some fifty feet away. Beside a stream, it was eating something it had caught, then suddenly sniffed and rose up to stare at the human. Had James been frightened by this sight, which a normal man would be, he would have ducked back behind the ridge and peeked to eyeball the creature to be about eight feet, weighing maybe seven hundred pounds. By this point he was nothing close to being a normal man and continued his walk as if the ursine behemoth were no more than a squirrel.

The bear began to unleash a thunderous roar but stopped short of the crescendo and gazed curiously at the white, hairless biped coming at him, directly, no hesitance.

"I want some of that," James said. "Whatever you're having there, I want some."

The bear sensed that something was out of order, and then made a threatening lurch forward with another ferocious howl.

James kept coming.

As if the bear instinctively diagnosed madness in the skinny interloper and didn't want to deal with whatever that might mean, the animal dropped to all fours and sauntered away.

James sat where the bear had been and gnawed the flesh from the carcass of a half eaten muskrat.

y

A few weeks later, it must have been December by now or later because it was snowing and the flakes were sticking to James's long scraggly beard, he came to a bluff which offered no way to descend.

He figured it was about three hundred feet high as he sat and stared out through the now swirling snow. What he saw below appeared to be an expansive valley but he knew he would never get there. He had reached the end of the line and if he stayed here, just sitting here on this amazing bluff, he would freeze to death, no question. Could he turn around and find shelter or build some? He could try but what would be the point? He was tired. He was sick. He was done.

He thought about his wife again and wished he could tell her good-bye. No. Hello. Would he see her in heaven? If Catholicism were legitimate she would be there, having been a Bible believing member of Cahokia's Church of The Holy Family.

She had tried to get him to attend with her, and he did once, but found the rituals of the liturgy too abstract for his appreciation. Ruth never nagged though. She never nagged and that made him suspect that maybe he was a callous man and he didn't want to be, so he had been planning to go with her again and start attending regularly, after the baby came. Now he repented not having told her of this decision.

If suicide was a sin, he figured it was because it was murdering somebody but he wouldn't be doing that at all. Who could blame him for expediting the inevitable? With only his ragged flax linen shirt and britches, he was going to die. Of course he was. Wouldn't it make more sense to just throw himself off the bluff and get it over with?

He leaned into a crawl position and worked his hands and knees to the edge of the bluff to look down.

A blanket of snow covered everything now but there was a dark streak. A river maybe. He would love to have seen it in the summer. But it was winter and it was cold. So cold, he could, if he should so choose, just lie back and shiver himself to death, but dang it, he didn't want to be found that way by anybody, as a fool who just sat there and let himself turn into a snowman. There would be more dignity in flinging his body off the cliff and to just disappear in the swirling snow.

With the last of his strength he stood and began to prepare for his exit from this world. "Dear Lord, I've lost everything, I can't go on. I'm sorry for the bad things I've done. I hope this is all right with you, what I'm doing here, but there's no other choice if I don't want to get ate by crows and such, and I don't so . . . bless me father for I have sinned. Amen, and here we go."

He looked down again and then decided it would be best to back up and get a run at it. He stepped back about twenty feet and told himself it was time. It was time to take the big leap.

But something was wrong. His legs refused to go along with the plan. He couldn't do it. Hot tears brimmed in his eyes with the stabbing guilt that now he was a coward. He had never suspected himself of being one before. He wiped his face with a tattered sleeve and decided to look down one more time, over the rim. It only made sense to determine a course. He hadn't chosen his trajectory. That was the problem.

Carefully he moved three steps forward. On the fourth, his foot slid out from under him. He landed hard on his backside and was impelled by the gravity of the sloping ledge, over its edge. He screamed.

A jumble of rock outcroppings protruding from the face of the cliff could have ended James Yoachum's story in an instant, but he fell through only air, snow, and a myriad of outreaching juniper branches growing from the cracks in the rocks.

His fall ended feet first, crashing through ice, his body plunging into bone-skewering water, the physical shock of a lifetime.

When a foot touched the river's bottom he instinctively shoved down to thrust himself up, to rise, if possible, back above his airless, frigid hell, well aware that this was not heaven and that he was not dead. Not dead, unless . . . maybe this was hell. If it was, it was not the traditional one because it wasn't a lake of fire. It was a river of ice and, dear Jesus, he wanted out of it.

As his head popped up into the snowy air he gasped with pain and began to paddle his way out of the water. Working his way atop the mantle of ice, he managed to crawl to the other side of the river.

Disappointed to be alive, it would be only minutes before that situation was remedied. James knew that.

He only wished that he could feel warm one more time. A man shouldn't have to die cold, although he reckoned that millions had, probably, over thousands of years. A real man should die fighting for a just cause.

Was there a reference in the Bible to anyone having froze to death? He would ask Ruth. He closed his eyes and waited to go, then fell unconscious under a snowfall that seemed impatient to make him disappear.

CHAPTER 4

James Yoachum regained consciousness three days and ten miles from his jump, or from when and where he had planned to jump, but slipped and fell instead.

He was sore and disoriented but he was warm, and that was good enough for now.

As he lay in some kind of dark smoky enclosure lit by flickering fire light, he tried to knit his last fragments of memory into some kind of conscious tapestry. He wondered why he wasn't dead. He certainly should have been.

He tried to sit up but was pressed back down from behind by a pair of tender hands on his head accompanied by what sounded like a child saying, "Nelema. Nelema."

James rasped, trying to use his voice for the first time in weeks or longer. "Nelema?" What was that word? Who was with him?

The child said, "How do you talk? French, English –"

"English," James croaked.

"Good," the young voice said. "I know this." She thought for a moment. "Nelema mean, 'not now.' Not now for you to stand. Not strong."

"Where am I?" James asked.

Sitting on a walnut stump a few feet from James's feet was the girl's chief who gave her a nod.

"You are with Lenape," she said, looking back to James.

"Indians?" he asked.

"The whites call us Delaware. Name of mine is Mekinges. What is name of you?"

James was mystified. "The Delaware Indians?" He tried again to raise himself, but was stopped.

"Not yet. Not yet," Mekinges said, sliding around beside his shoulder with a clay bowl. "You weak. Need strong." She lowered the bowl with one hand, reaching under his head with the other. "You put this," she said, and held it to his mouth.

James was startled by her appearance, older than her voice, thirteen or fourteen, with lustrous black hair, delicately sculpted features and a wide smiling mouth. He did as she said, partly because of the distraction of her beauty, but mostly because he was starved.

He noticed as he sipped that Mekinges was dressed in a fringed deerskin dress adorned with silver ornaments, which also, in smaller form, had been threaded somehow to encircle her neck and dangle from her wrists.

As he sipped the last of what tasted of sassafras and deer meat, he could not help but stare at the girl.

"More?" she asked.

"Please," he whispered.

She smiled as she passed the bowl to someone for a refill, and nodded. "Please," she said. "Yes. Is a good say. Long time since my English."

After the second bowl she laid his head back onto the mat of corn husks and James started to fall back to sleep.

"Not yet," she said. "Name of me is Mekinges," she said again. "Yes?"

"Mekinges," James repeated.

"What is name of you?"

"Jim Yoachum."

She smiled, satisfied. "Jimyocum," she repeated as if one word, then nodded. "You sleep now, Jimyocum."

y

He was awakened about every six hours by the touch of Mekinges who would say, "Jimyocum, time for food. You eat and get big for woapank."

"Woapank?"

"Woapank mean . . . hmmm . . . day that is come next sun."

James managed a smile. "Tomorrow?"

"Ayyy," she shrieked, then giggled. "I know that one. I forget. Yes, tomorrow."

When he was next awakened, it was by an icy blast of air, which caused him for a moment to dream he was back on the bluff about to slide over its edge again. He bolted up to find himself staring into the eyes of the Lenape Council who were fascinated by his size, and by his beard and the curious straw color of his hair.

As he rubbed his eyes to clear the cobwebs, he counted eight, each wearing a turban of otter hide, all seated on stumps of various heights. Small silver attachments on their shirts gleamed in the firelight.

The man in the middle had an imposing appearance with a resolute countenance that made James realize immediately that this would be the man he would be answering to.

With another gust of frigid air from the outside, Mekinges appeared, pulled the door-flap shut again, then walked around to sit by James.

James sensed that she was there to help him somehow.

"Jimyocum," she said, pointing to the chief, "This man is Kikthawenund. He is Captain of our village and he is Mekinges's father."

James studied the chief and saw a face that radiated the charisma and energy of a natural born leader. "Your father?"

Mekinges nodded. "He want to know why you be here and when you go away."

"Where am I?" James asked.

"You are with Lenape," Mekinges answered. "This place here," she raised her hand to indicate the room, "is long house, like Haudenosaunee, but we have just one. Many wigwams all around."

It was a long house, James could see, maybe a hundred feet long with high slender poles arched over the top. By the warmth he guessed that the outer layer was made of animal hides. There was a door at each end and three evenly spaced smoke holes in the ceiling, although they did not seem to him very efficient.

"So, I'm in a Delaware Indian village and your pa wants to know when I'm leaving?" He looked at the tribal elders, each stone-faced.

Mekinges nodded. "Yes."

James said, "Tell him I can leave right now." He started to get to his feet. "Tell them that I am grateful for . . ." His legs shook. He collapsed back onto the mat, hunched over his knees.

15

Mekinges wanted to assist him into a more comfortable position, but resisted. "Kikthawenund want more of your say," she said. "Why are you here with no more white peoples?"

James looked up. "Tell Kitha . . . Kiktha, what?"

"Kikthawenund."

"Tell him, why I am here is nobody's business but mine."

Mekinges was taken aback. "Not understand, Jimyocum," she said uneasily. "The Captain have . . . uh . . . sick inside for whites come here."

James shifted to a seated position and looked into her eyes. "He's worried, you mean?"

"Yes," she said, pleased with another English word. "Worried. My father is worried. Where are your peoples?"

James lowered his head to think about this and realized that his Indian saviors had reason to worry. They probably suspected that he was an advance man for an onslaught of white intruders who would swarm in, petition the Government for another forced relocation of the natives, and destroy what they had here.

In Cahokia he had heard tales from a few English-speaking Cherokee, of broken treaties and terrifying raids. He'd heard about the cruelty of the Spanish, the burning of villages and worse.

He'd never had a part in that sort of thing, but how would they know? They couldn't know that, and yet they saved his life. Even with their suspicions, they had saved his life when in good conscience they could have let him be. Let him die. Why hadn't they?

He would learn later that a hunting party did not have the authority for such decisions and would by Lenape standards of conduct, all life being sacred, save whatever living thing they could, although Kikthawenund, Mekinges's father, The Captain, admittedly would have left him at the river to die.

Now he felt guilty and for some reason somewhat ashamed. He lowered his head. "Tell your father that I am alone."

Mekinges nodded as if suspecting as much and translated James's statement to her father who seemed doubtful and demanded more.

"Kikthawenund want to know why," she said. "Why you come to Lenape land alone? Are you trouble-man who run from white law?"

How could he answer without breaking down? He didn't want to cry in front of these people but the numbness had abated and he felt so raw that he could cry, if he let himself; he could cry like a lost child and why should he care what they thought? Nothing mattered. Then he thought, maybe they had a right to know. He was the trespasser. He was on their land.

"No," he said. "I am not a bad man. I walked away from the white world because of pain in my heart. Understand?" He patted his chest. "I only want to be alone and I will walk away as soon as I am able. I am sorry to bring you this bother. Thank you, thank you, for your help, Mekinges. You are kind people. I will leave soon."

Mekinges translated for the council.

y

The council accepted James explanation. The elders decided that should they let him go now, given his condition, he would only freeze to death again in a day or two. Since there had been no reports or signs of other white men in the area, he could stay until the weather warmed enough for a safe journey to somewhere else. What would be the point of saving his life and then sending him out to lose it? He obviously had no survival skills and was not even smart enough to know that. Kikthawenund told his daughter that since the man seemed to have the intelligence of a pinecone, what harm could he do?

CHAPTER 5

Spring

When the weather warmed in that year of 1814, James did not leave the Lenape village. He wasn't asked to. Apparently other whites had not followed him, so there was no worry on that account and he had become such a crowd pleaser that everyone enjoyed being around him. Everyone except Kikthawenund.

The council of elders reasoned that since Jimyocum seemed sincere in his efforts to learn the ways of the Lenape, it would be wise for them to learn from him. If there should come a time when whites might provoke a confrontation – it had certainly been known to happen – wouldn't it be beneficial to understand their language? Jimyocum could teach them.

Besides, he was a huge man, six inches taller than their tallest brave and his strength, once he regained his health, was almost mystical. He could carry three deer at once on his shoulders.

And the kids loved him. They squealed with delight the first time he carved a yo-yo and demonstrated its amazing ability to fall down and then back up again, over and over.

The shaman was alarmed by this magic at first but James showed him how to carve one, and with a length of twine from deer sinew, the anti-gravity secret of the flick of the wrist, where upon the Shaman himself took a shine to the white giant from the river.

As it turned out, only one person took seriously the challenge of learning English. It was Mekinges. She couldn't get enough.

The elders all said they should learn it, that they would learn it when time permitted, but being in their fifties, most of them, they could never quite find the time.

New things are awkward when you're set in your ways, a general human disorder, Mekinges noticed. She shared the thought with James.

There were a few though, mostly kids, who did take some interest, and would from time to time ask James to teach them phrases that they thought were funny. "The owl shat in your eye."

James was as eager to learn Mekinges's language as she was his, and so they spent many hours huddled together murmuring, often giggling.

This behavior dismayed the girl's parents who sometimes worried that Jimyocum had cast some kind of spell over their otherwise sensible daughter. He was all she could talk about.

It was also disturbing to some of the braves, potential mates in the other two clans, the Wolf and the Turkey, who were watching Mekinges mature into a desirable woman and coveted her for their own.

"Well," the consensus was, "he will leave to be with his own kind sooner or later."

But one night James had a dream in which the whole world spoke Lenape and he, the white giant, could understand everything clearly. The dream impressed him so much that it stayed in his mind for days, weeks, and months.

1818

James had been living with the Lenape for a little more than five years.

As simple as they had first seemed, he learned they were a complex people, proud to talk about their exploits as hunters or fighters, but muted when it came to internal matters of joy or sorrow, even though those strings were as deeply interwoven with the fabric of the heart as with any other people in the world.

They would risk unflinching openness to protect friends and family with heartfelt compassion and noble feelings. Whenever they could they enjoyed games, races, and tests of strength, all regulated by complicated rules.

The Lenape of both sexes delighted in ornaments, especially silver gew-gaws attached, along with colorful plumage, from their turbans to their belts.

Men removed all facial hair and the women often colored their faces with red ochre. Tattooing was common to both sexes. Older men wore their hair long but warriors usually had a scalp lock, greased to stand erect. The council of elders wore only a single eagle feather, which designated their status as a sachem.

James deduced that the men kept their faces smooth because their beards grew so thinly. His did not. If he didn't shave everyday, which he hated having to do, there would be a full beard within two weeks, a straw-colored beard, which made him stick out even more as an odd duck.

He was twenty-six. Mekinges was nineteen. She was tall now, and slim but with eye-catching breasts. She had a delightfully generous smile and hair as black and as shiny as obsidian.

Although the Lenape had no names for the months, all were raised to study the orbital phases of the moon as thoughtfully as any astronomy scholar of the time, and had a name for every phase.

The full moon to rise tonight would be the Pink Moon, which James, had he been caught up on such things, would know, meant mid-April. He could have guessed as much but he didn't care. It was spring. It was springtime in the Ozarks. What fine-fettled man could ask for more, especially when sitting beside the most beautiful maiden in the village?

Snowy Egrets glided up and down the river. Redbuds of every hue between orange and purple filled the low woods between the white outbursts of Dogwood blossoms. In the high woods billions of baby leaves sprouting from the oaks, maples and sycamores brushed the horizon with an exquisite feathering of a thousand shades of green.

Children played outside wearing only breechcloths.

Those over the age of ten were in learning circles, some chipping away at chert to make scrapers, spearheads, knives, drills, arrowheads and gravers, some carving bone for needles, fish hooks and skewers, their work checked and critiqued by supervisors.

The Shaman, with his own advanced class, scraped powder from deer antlers into a boiling vat, then held up a dead skunk to squeeze the anal scent gland, its contents dripping into the pot.

James wondered for what possible purpose, but did not ask. He still had much to learn.

Most of the women were planting what they called the three sisters; corn, beans and squash, as they did each year when oak leaves became the size of a squirrel's ear.

Corn, planted along the strip of land between the river and the wigwams, was the most important. It could be ground into corn meal. It could be fed to stock and the shucks were useful for mats, brooms and mattresses. The cobs could be burned for fuel or carved into pipes for the men, or dolls for the little girls.

The women who were not planting were making clay pots, weaving rush mats and bags, and making baskets.

It all suddenly amazed James. Everything did. The first twenty years of his life were so far behind him now that he would not allow himself to even think of them.

These wonderful people, The Lenni Lenape, the ancients, the original tribe of all Algonquin-speaking peoples, had taken him in. They were his life now, his fortune and his future.

It was springtime in the Ozarks. Anything was possible and it filled him with an exuberance he had never known before.

y

The stumps upon which he and Mekinges sat this fine spring afternoon, were the same as those he noticed when he first met the council of elders in the long house, a structure first conceived by the Iroquois, or "Haudenosaunee," Mekinges had told him – People of The Long Houses – but adapted by the Lenape.

They were practical, James thought, these stumps scattered around the village. Of different heights, the short fat cuttings of walnut trunks were movable and served well as stools and worktops.

He still lived in the long house and helped with its maintenance. When the elders needed privacy he would go to the other end or find something to do outside.

By Lenape standards it was a large village, nearly a thousand wigwams, stick-erected domes covered by elm bark and skins, inhabited by the three major Lenape clans, the Turtle, The Wolf and The Turkey, stretched willy-nilly along the river.

On the pitaiwagawan, front porch, of Mekinges's parent's home, she and James played a game of jackstraws while purportedly teaching each other new words. The object of the game was to take turns picking up a stick from a jangle of them without moving any of the others. The running total looked about even, but they weren't counting or paying attention to who might be winning. They were focused on each other, whispering, and laughing.

James would point at something for the Lenape name and Mekinges's translations would fly from her sensual mouth like small invisible birds.

James stuck out his tongue and pointed.

"Wilanu," she said trying to grab it with her fingers.

He raised his buckskin shirt and pointed to his navel.

She giggled. "Wilhwi."

He paused, looked around and then pointed to her breasts, individually, the left one, then the right. She was fully dressed, but that didn't block the spear of panic that struck his gut when he looked up, his forefinger still pointing, and saw her father in the door glaring down at him. His pulse quickened with guilt.

"Nunakána," she said as she watched the color drain from his face. She turned, looked up, and laughed. "Nux," she said to Kikthawenund, "Yushe lëmatahpi," which James knew enough to mean, "My father, sit down here."

Kikthawenund grunted, "Mata." He stepped from his wigwam, and walked away.

James sighed, glad to still be alive, but she could see he was disheartened. "Walk with me, Jimyocum," she said, rising from her stool.

As they walked through the young corn stalks toward the river James said, "five years, five years, and he still hates me. Ahpu hàch ila kèski luwhëlit shwilait?"

"No, Jimyocum," she answered, and he loved the way she spoke his name, "There is no warrior here who can call you a coward. Not even my brothers."

"Do I not keep the long house clean and strong?"

"You make long house better all the time, but . . ."

They had reached the river. "But what?"

Otters, unheeding, played fifty feet away, as they lowered themselves to sit on a limestone outcropping.

"You should make own wigwam."

James thought about this, then smiled and shook his head. "No, Mekinges," he said. "I've got a better idea."

"What?" she asked.

James watched a Great Blue Heron land on the opposite bank, then turned to her. "You'll see."

She enjoyed his playfulness but did not take the bait. "Good," she said. "I wait. Then I see."

They sat in silence for several minutes as they watched a very elderly beaver struggle against the current to reach some apparent obligation upstream. They hoped the old fellow would make it.

It was time, Mekinges thought, to try to explain her father. "Father not hate you, Jimyocum. He is captain and worries much time for village to keep safe. White peoples, all his time, bring double-cross."

He fixed his eyes on hers and scratched the stubble on his neck.

"Father's mother live by great water."

"Your grandmother. In Delaware."

"Father born there but White law then make Delaware go east to Ohio. Father have wife there."

"Your mother."

"No. Wife . . ." She held up one finger.

"Wife number one. His first wife."

She nodded. "White law makes our tribe move again all the time but wife stay, so he get next wife in Indiana. I born in Indiana where they make Lenape go to school, where I learn English talk, but not my brothers."

James nodded. "Winona is your mother, right?"

"No, wife number two my mother. She die. Then father have four sons and little girl, me, and so my mother's sister take him for her husband."

"Winona's your Aunt?"

"It does not matter to Lenape. She is my mother now. We all family."

James nodded and prodded her with his eyes for more.

"Then the Governor there, Henry Harrison, break four treaties, signed by Indians. The Treaty of Greenville, the Treaty of Fort Wayne, the Treaty of Grouseland and . . . I not can think of." She smiled apologetically.

James was more than impressed. "That's all right. Go on."

"Brothers of Shawnee, Tecumseh and Tenskwatawa, say all Indian tribes should be as one to fight the white double-cross, so Harrison try to pull apart the Indian tribes, the Shawnee, the Miami, Kickapoo, Chippewa, and, uh . . .

other ones . . . others, yes, wait . . . the Pottawatomie, and . . . I don't know now. But there was big fight from Shawnee and many Shawnee was killed."

James was astounded. "Tecumseh," he said. "I've heard that name I think." How could this girl of nineteen have this knowledge?

"Governor, Henry Harrison, he write good words on paper but made Lenape shut their eyes and double-cross our peoples. He say we own all land at White River, that it be for Lenape and he would give his own monies for to buy things to be civilized and said he make this promise to president of America."

"Stop. Wait," James said, awed by her erudition. "The names of the treaties, the names of the tribes and the governor . . ."

"Yes?"

"You remember these things?"

Mekinges laughed, "No, silly man. In Indiana Father make William Patterson read his writing many times to elders so they could keep it in their . . ." She pointed to her head.

"Their minds," James said, "so they could remember it?"

"Yes. Remember. That is hard word."

"Who was William Patterson?"

"I don't know."

James shook his head trying to place the name, William Patterson. He knew nothing of the treaties she mentioned. How could he have? He'd had some schooling, but as an Illinois farm boy was taught only of the greatness of American pioneers, like Daniel Boone, and the savagery of the red-skins, like Tecumseh, who reportedly tried to scalp William Henry Harrison, which he had believed. That was it! That's where he'd heard those names – in school as a boy and he had believed it. Why wouldn't he have? But now, this recounting of the Indian side of history, these events Mekinges had just unfolded, they sounded credible. He could imagine the corruption, the sly coercion, the treaty breaking, the double-crossing. It all rang true. Still, how could she know?

Mekinges, as if reading his mind, pinched his arm and said, "Father tell same story on night of every Beaver Moon to all who come to the long house. He always makes me and my brothers be there for this. Father puts the writings out on table and tell us stories so we not ever forget. He wants nobody ever forget. He make me be there, so I hear this many times."

"The writings?"

"Yes."

There were writings? James wondered. "He has documentation of this? Of what you just told me?"

"He has papers of writings but cannot read, so he tell what he . . . what is word?"

"Remember."

"Yes, he tell what he remember from William Patterson, so everybody will remember. Remember is hard word for me."

"He has papers?" James pressed disbelievingly.

"Yes."

"Who was William Patterson?"

"I don't know. I say that already."

"But he has a copy of his papers?"

"Yes."

"Could I read them?"

Mekinges thought for a moment, then smiled. "I will tell Father you can read English. He could be glad to hear the words again." She nodded. "I think yes."

"And this governor . . . Harrison?"

"Yes."

"He flat out lied and cheated?"

"He double-cross."

James shook his head. "Wonder what ever happened to him? I hope he got scalped. The Government," he huffed like a curse.

"The Government," she repeated to stitch the term into her brain. "And whites ask why Lenape not be like them, civilized."

"Oh, sweet princess, you people are more civilized than anybody in America."

She assumed it was a compliment, smiled and continued. "At Anderson, our people bring animal skins for trade of food and cloth. One day, whites say no more animal skins. Must have money."

James shook his head. "Money," he grumbled, "the root of all evil. I hate money."

"The . . . Government," she said again trying to comprehend its magnitude. "Does the Government own all land everywhere?"

"They think it's God's will," he said. "Something called Manifest Destiny, if I remember right." He shrugged. "Although, there have been bloody wars over that question, which I guess you just told me about, at least one example."

"What?"

"The Shawnee battle?"

"Oh. Yes, the Tecumseh war. Many peoples killed. The Government then say we must be like white people or leave." She put her fists together in a ball, and then slowly pulled them apart. "This people," she said, nodding to her left fist, "follow father to go away."

"Half," James said. "Half the Lenape left with your Father."

"Yes," she said, smiling. "Half to Missouri and so . . ." She spread her arms. "We now here. We like. Is good place, yes?"

"Yes," James affirmed. "This is a very good place and I want you to tell your Pa that I will help him keep this place safe for his people. Would you do that?" He spat into the river. "Damned Government."

"Damned Government," she echoed with a smile of pride for her white giant, and then spat into the river like he did. She giggled, wiping her chin. "Yes, I will tell. I will say you are great brave for Lenape."

The sun was nestling in behind the treetops now and the 'Pink moon' was rising.

"Do you think that will help your folks to accept me? Do you think they will ever accept me?"

Mekinges leaned over and kissed his ear. Her lips were warm and soft, and as he felt the soft curve of her breast press against his arm, his heart quickened. His face turned red.

"I accept you, Jimyocum," she whispered. "Ejaja."

"Ejaja?" He didn't know that one.

She kissed him again. "Yes," she whispered. "Ejaja. Wherever we go."

They looked around, saw no one, and then put their arms around each other to physically share the enchantment of tòkaniloku, the gloaming.

y

The next morning James was honored by The Captain with a presentation of the writings, which he was to read aloud, but only for a small group, five of Kikthawenund's most trusted confidants.

James figured that this was in case the papers turned out to be a load of hogwash. That would embarrass the chief who for years had guarded them as important historical documents. Maybe this wasn't such a good idea. What if Kikthawenund did get embarrassed and became enraged?

Mekinges assured him that they only wanted the truth of the writings no matter what. "Do it," she said.

They gathered at the river near the giant Willow. James unrolled the parchments. He looked them over and then began to read with Mekinges interpreting.

April 5, 1805

To William Wells Agent of Indian Affairs from William Patterson Indian Chief

Friend and Brother! I am sent by the chiefs of my nation to speak these words. Our minds are troubled concerning the visit we made to Governor Harrison last summer at Vincennes. Our chiefs was told by the Governor that he would give them an instrument of writing that would show that the country on White River belonged to the Delaware and that he would give them money out of his own pocket to become more civilized. The Governor then wrote two papers which he told our chiefs contained the words he had just spoken to them and that he wished them to sign them both that he would send one to the President of the United States and one they could keep for themselves, in order that the good words he spoke be kept in remembrance by the white and the red. Our chiefs cheerfully signed these papers.

Friend and Brother! You may judge for yourself how our chiefs felt when they returned home and found that the Governor had been shutting their eyes and stopping their ears with his good words and got them to sign a Deed for their lands without their knowledge.

Friend and Brother! The chiefs of my land now declare to you from the bottom of their hearts that they never sold Governor Harrison or the United States any land at Vincennes last summer.

Friend and Brother! Our chiefs place confidence in you to take immediate steps for bringing a fair understanding and that you as soon as possible inform our great father the President of the United States how Governor Harrison has imposed on his Red Children.

Friend and Brother! My chiefs declare to you that they did not sell the land and they knew nothing about it and are not willing to sell the lands on the Ohio from the mouth of the Wabash to Clark's grant at the Falls and that they consider it out of their power to do any such thing without the consent of the other nations in this country.

Friend and Brother! My chiefs wishes you to prevent this land being settled by white people which would violate the articles of The Treaty of Greenville.

Friend and Brother! These are the words that was put in my mouth by the chiefs of my nation in order that I might deliver them to you.

Signed, William Patterson.

y

James, moved to tears by the writing, looked up as Mekinges finished the interpretation. He wiped his eyes while the others watched her.

Kikthawenund was nodding. It was as he remembered it; proof positive that white men could not be trusted.

CHAPTER 6

The Delaware Nation did not know the year of 1820 was significant historically. Missouri's enabling act was passed and submitted to Washington, its first constitution was adopted, and its first gubernatorial election took place, none of which was known or cared about by the inhabitants of the nearly two million acres promised to the Delaware Indians by the U. S. Government in the treaty of St. Mary's.

Between going on hunting parties and helping with the pigs, James spent his spare time felling trees and hewing the logs with blades crafted by his own hand, to build the only cabin in the village.

He chose a spot on the upriver edge of the village that he thought would be good for both sunlight and drainage, got it approved by the council of elders and slowly but surely, day by painstaking day, erected a mud-chinked cabin with notched corners.

Another novelty about the house was that it had the settlement's only window, a feature he thought would impress Mekinges.

For the most part, his neighbors thought this was a silly idea, even after all the difficulty of creating it, especially since it faced north, a fact James had neglected to take into account until Mekinges asked one day why he thought all the wigwam doors faced south. "Your house hole will face the winter wind."

Children loved it though and delighted in hopping through it, in and out.

The cabin itself was impractical according to Kikthawenund. What if they should have to move because of something, anything, a flood, perhaps? This river was known to flood every seven years or so. How foolish to have a home that took so long to build.

Mekinges passed this along to James and he admitted that although her Pa had a point, his house would be better protection for her against dangerous animals. "Wild elephants, for example," he joked. "They could trample all over your wigwams."

She didn't get it. Not even a smile. "For me?" she asked.

He looked into her eyes. "Why do you think I built it, Mekinges? I want you to live with me there."

They were on their way to a place in the woods that Mekinges warned him was confidential and must never be spoken of.

"I want to live there too," she said, "but that is not our way for wikindewagan."

He stopped. "Wikindewagen. Is that the word for marriage?"

"Husband and wife?"

"Yes! That's marriage! How do we do it?"

She took his hand to lead him on. "How do we do what, become wikinditschik? Married peoples?"

"Yes," he said with pretend exasperation. "What are we talking about here?"

She laughed.

They entered a clearing where several men were working around clay kilns with hammers and chisels.

Three eighteen-inch silver bullion bars were stacked on a limestone ledge.

The workers turned with alarm until they recognized The Captain's daughter. She would not be here had he not told her to come.

"Silversmiths," James muttered, indifferently. "I knew they had to be around here somewhere, but I want to talk about us, Mekinges, this marriage idea." He sounded like an adolescent whining for honey, but was simply focused on the question, what must I do? "You know darned well I built that house for you. Your pa can mock me, the other braves can mock me, but –"

"Shh," she said, hushing him with a hand to his mouth. "Not now." She spread her hands. "You must look. See what is here but never speak of it."

"Well, it's hardly a secret. The whole tribe wears silver jewelry, armbands, and such. It had to come from somewhere."

30

"Not come from here. Just make here."

"Where's it come from?"

"Father only trust you for here first. He say whites kill for silver."

"But I'm the only white around."

Mekinges shrugged.

"Fine," James said, in a huff. "I've seen where they make it, and I'm not going to kill anybody, and I will never tell a soul, and I don't care where it comes from, and I don't even want to know, and how do we get married?"

Mekinges laughed, then turned with a furrowed brow. "Father say whites are coming from the east."

They walked back the way they came. "Well, maybe some French fur trappers," James said. "They're like mice to cheese, but I don't think they're a threat for the village. They've been through here many times, I'm sure."

"You give mother gift."

"What?" James asked.

"For marriage," she giggled.

He stopped. "Wait. What? I give your mother a gift?"

"Is our way."

"But how?"

"You leave gift on pitaiwagawan."

"The front porch."

"Yes, at night. If mother take gift by high sun next day, we will be married, and you be in Turtle Clan."

"Just like that? That's it? What about your father? He'll have to approve."

She shook her head. "Fathers have no say in this. My father was in Turkey clan till he marry mother."

It was too good to be true, James thought. All this time he'd been worried about the father's consent when neither he nor Mekinges had to have it.

The Delaware tribe was matrilineal, tracing their lineage through the maternal line, granting mothers the authority to approve marriage. It was Winona he had to please. How could he do that?

"What kind of gift can I offer her, Mekinges?"

"Mother say she want horse."

James felt his elation drain through the souls of his feet. "A horse," he said flatly. "You're serious?"

Mekinges smiled.

31

"Where am I going to get a horse?"

She pinched his arm to get him walking again. "Two day walk to north, flat land there – many horses."

"I've got to catch a wild horse? How am I supposed to do that?"

Mekinges gave an exaggerated frown. "Do you not wish to have me, Jimyocum?"

"You know I do."

"Then you will find a way. Bring horse to her wigwam door and go away. If mother take this gift, she will bring me next night and give me to you. Then I will come in your house and we be wikindithik."

James nodded but had a troubling thought. "What if Winona does not accept my gift?"

Mekinges shrugged with a teasing smile. "What if you can't catch horse?"

James loved that look. She was so beautiful, yet so rascally. He wanted to grab her, squeeze her and kiss her, but they had reached the edge of the village by his cabin.

People were still coming by to inspect it, share their opinions and gossip.

"Oh, I'll get a horse, don't you worry," James said. "I'll get the finest horse your ma's ever seen."

y

Mekinges had spoken true. James did come to a flat plateau fairly twenty miles north of the village, and there were horses, sure enough, maybe twenty by his reckoning, at least that he could see from where he had stopped to climb a tree. How had she known?

To his angst there were also people, and judging from the three cabins and wagons he spotted, they were white people. This was not good. James was unaware of the treaty of St. Mary but he felt in his gut that the plumes of smoke from burning brush piles were made by such encroachers as gave his future father-in-law the 'big worry.'

Manifest Destiny? Could white people go wherever they wanted and do whatever they wanted, anytime they wanted? Take whatever they wanted?

Did they think these horses were theirs? If so, what if he got caught and accused of being a horse thief? He remembered that even in Illinois, that would be a crime right up there on the list with murder, and with no legal system to speak of in these parts, there would be no trial.

James had brought a braided leather rope. His plan was to mosey slowly, unthreateningly, into the grazing drove of equines and befriend one with carrots. He would talk to it, throw a carrot down, then another, as he got closer and closer, then close enough to stroke the animal while he gently worked a loop around its head.

Patiently, he inched his way toward the horses. All but one matched his pace in moving away. Oh, but that one was the one he would have chosen, a magnificent chestnut stallion with a black mane and tail, maybe eighteen hands from fetlock to withers, with a white blaze and three white socks.

To his delight, the carrot plan worked. The stallion, not skittish like the others, all mares he noticed, seemed to pay him no mind until he was right next to it, where upon it looked at him with a calm curiosity.

"Hello, big fellow," James said in as friendly a tone as he could, then offered another carrot, which the horse, stretching its neck, accepted with a nip of its lips. James stroked the animal as it chewed, and then gently slipped the rope's loop over the horse's head. The stallion behaved as though it was just another day, and all it wanted was another carrot. "I've got him," James thought. And he did. His plan worked perfectly. All he had to do now was lead the beautiful stallion back to the village and present it to Winona.

On the journey back, James would be kind but firm to let the horse know that it was in responsible hands. He wrapped the rope around his wrist securely so as not to slip from his grip should there arise some resistance in crossing a creek, or some such thing.

The instant James gave a tug, the horse bolted. It galloped through its group of mares, all of whom followed, and then ran, dragging James through brush, thistles and sumac, over stones, through blackberry bushes and saplings.

James imagined that if he could stand the pain and just hold on – he had no choice – the stallion would tire and he, the man, would be the victor.

This fantasy may have panned out had the rope stayed snug around his arm and the turf not have become so rocky, or he may have been dragged to death.

As valiant was his effort, James's head met with a protuberance of rock, split his brow and rendered him unconscious, just as the rope separated from his hold and departed with his perfect gift horse.

y

James did not know how long he'd lain there when he came to, or why his body ached from head to toe, especially his head, or why his right wrist and hand were raw and swollen.

For several minutes he lay trying to figure out where he was and why. He also did not realize that his face was caked with blood from a gash on his forehead. When he sat up things began to come back to him. He'd had the horse of his desire and let it get away. "Damn."

Now what? He could walk to one of the cabins and ask for help. "Yeah, sure," he said aloud. The thought of having to report that to The Captain snuffed out any such notion immediately. Why would he seek help from the people about which he was going to have to warn Kikthawenund? Besides he didn't need any help, or so he told himself.

He would find his way back to the tree he had climbed when he first reached this clearing. There, he had a sack with more carrots and a pouch of water, the latter being needed urgently. His mouth and throat were desiccated.

Until he made it onto his feet he hadn't realized how sore he was. It hurt to walk, but he had to. The sun was getting low and he would not be able to find his spot in the dark.

Luckily, through the high brush at least, the stallion and his dragged body had made a kind of path for him to follow back. He calculated by the distance of the tree line that he'd been drawn about a quarter mile.

As physically wrecked as he felt, the bigger pain was in his heart. He had failed, the consequence of which he found unbearable to ponder. "No," he thought, "I cannot go back without a horse."

James caught a glimpse of something on the ground about fifty feet from the woods, a black something, an animal something, but he could not tell what it was. He paused and then approached cautiously.

He recalled his brother, Sol, telling him – what, seven, eight years ago? – that wolverines had made their way down from The Great Lakes and had been killing cattle in Illinois. He didn't believe it then, but what if? Or maybe it was a black bear. Prudence was warranted, whatever it was, since he was feeling a current lack of wherewithal to engage in any kind of confrontation.

He heard a deep dry cough.

It was a horse, which lifted his spirit quick and high, but then again what did he have here?

An elderly, sick, black mare laid on its side, despondent and feverish with a considerable amount of mucus draining from its nose. What was wrong with it? Colic? Distemper? Worms, maybe?

It didn't matter. It was a horse. If he could keep it alive and somehow lead it back to Winona's wigwam, everyone would know that he tried and how could it be his fault if the mare died afterwards?

He wanted to sit beside the mare with encouraging words, but instinctively knew, maybe because of his own thirst, that the animal needed water. He certainly did.

He found his cache of supplies, grabbed the pouch, and made his way back to the creek that he remembered some five hundred yards away. He sucked up water for himself, then filled his pouch to return to the wretched mare, which to his gladness, drank eagerly.

That night and all the next day, James sat with his horse, talking, singing lullabies, massaging its flesh, and sharing carrots. He thought the horse seemed to especially like his rendition of the song, Meet Me by Moonlight Alone, so he sang that one several times.

There was no way he could have known, but a horse doctor would have diagnosed the mare as suffering from Equine Influenza, which usually, if tended to in a stable and kept safe from predators, a horse could pull through after a week's time. With this particular horse though, out here on the prairie, it would not have survived had it not been for James.

On the morning of his quest's fifth day, the horse rose to stand on all fours, seemingly grateful to its savior. James did not even have to tug the rope. The mare followed him.

y

On the evening of his seventh day away, James, exhausted and weak from hunger, and sore from his bruises, lacerations and cracked ribs, paused in the woods to marshal his fortitude. He was determined to walk proudly. He straightened his spine and took an evenly paced stride into the village.

He had no idea that to the gawkers who watched him pass by, it looked as though James had gotten into a fight with the scrawny mare and the mare had kicked his "wasitia."

Up ahead he heard Mekinges squeal with delight. "Ketëlsin. Ketëlsin." She ran to him. "You did it. You did it."

Together they led the horse to the wigwam of Kikthawenund and Winona, both standing in the door, the father scowling, the mother smiling.

At that moment James's knees buckled. He fell to the ground and lost consciousness.

Kikthawenund rolled his eyes.

Winona made her way over, knelt beside him and sent Mekinges for the shaman.

PART TWO

"White Chief, may the sun shine upon you and defend you. Your magic powers are well known to us and we seek your friendship. At first, we committed the error of thinking of resisting you, but only foolish men persist in their errors. Wise and rational men know when to change their mind. We are here to wish the palefaces a happy stay and help them, whatever they need."

– The Cacique of Tali

CHAPTER 7

The 1500s

In the year 1533, after his role in the slaughter of thousands of South American natives, and the plunder and decimation of the gold-affluent Inca Empire, Hernando Desoto, under the command of the ruthless and remorseless Colonel Pedrarias Dávila, developed a lifelong thirst for wealth and fame.

By the year 1535 he had amassed so much booty, he decided to return to Spain to settle down and marry the Colonel's daughter, Doñ Ysabel, who had waited for him for sixteen years.

He could have lived a long and noble life then, but got restless and envious when he began hearing the glorious reports of Ponce de León's adventures.

In 1538, de Soto paid, from his own coffers, the cost for a return voyage to the new world. He took three ships loaded with saws, axes, shovels, hammers, falconets, powder kegs, swords, lances, four hundred men, and one woman pretending to be a man.

His title was Governor, which is what his men called him, and his flagship was the eight-hundred ton San Cristóbal.

After a rest in the Canary Islands and then Cuba, the expedition made its way up the gulf side of Florida and finally landed in a massive bay, which de Soto named, "Bay of the Holy Spirit," which later was known as Tampa Bay.

During his time in Florida, while the number of his hogs increased from thirty to three hundred, he lost one hundred and two men to either sickness or arrows from the natives.

On June 15th 1539, de Soto left half his group behind, and headed north with ninety cavalry, eighty infantry, an alchemist, his page, Ribera, and his chamberlain, Fuentes.

By May of 1540 he reached what today is Savannah, Georgia and then trudged on through what is now South Carolina, North Carolina, and then Tennessee.

They measured their journey by leagues, the distance a person could walk in one hour.

Along the way he tried to befriend the locals. More often than not they cooperated and gave him gifts of food and hides.

When a cacique, leader of the locals, disappointed him in some way, the Governor would capture a few of the tribe's members, cut off their right hands and noses, and then send them back to their cacique with the message that this would happen to him if he didn't change his way of thinking.

Almost invariably, the cacique would send back a conciliatory message, such as: "I have determined to conform my wishes to your will, and hold as right all that you might do, believing that it should be so for a good reason, providing against some future event, to you perceptible but to me concealed; since an evil may well be permitted to avoid another greater, that good can arise, which I trust will be so."

In one village de Soto preached the gospel of the great Lord, "who had made the sky and the earth, and man after his own image; that he suffered on the tree of the true cross to save the human race. Since he rose from the grave on the third day, his divinity is immortal. And that having ascended into heaven, he is there now with open arms to receive all that would be converted to Catholicism."

He then directed his men to build a lofty cross of wood on the highest spot in the village.

A day after the cross was erected an unusual lightning storm occurred, convincing everybody, the Indians, de Soto's men and de Soto himself, that he was truly a special man in the eyes of the Lord.

As the word spread and got embellished in its dissemination, de Soto managed to convince the natives that he was immortal like a god.

Although some did not believe it and his party fell under attack seven separate times, de Soto was well trained and well armed. He was a brilliant tactician who, along the way, even though outnumbered, managed to kill most of those who dared to confront him.

By May of 1541, the Spanish cavaliers became the first white men to see the Mississippi River, and cross its breadth, some thirty miles south of where Memphis is today.

Heading west he was greeted with beans, maize, walnuts, dried persimmons, fish, skins and shawls. He was taught the trick of ensnaring rabbits and given directions when he had a question concerning his journey's pathway.

The Indians didn't want him around but they were afraid to displease him and so offered everything they could to help him move along.

When the Governor asked a chief named Quiguate which way would be most inhabited, the chief said going south would lead to the most people but there was a large province to the northwest near some mountains.

De Soto and his alchemist calculated that the hilly region would make a difference in the soil, and that silver and gold might afterward follow. They went northwest.

Early July, Desoto entered the Ozarks, a track abounding in picturesque valleys and caves, replete with varied mineral resources, and "surely," he thought at long last, "silver and gold," the object of his relentless quest.

In a severe rainstorm, which his men joked about being like the one they used to convince the Indians that the Governor was a god, they took shelter in a cave. It was de Soto's lucky break.

While his men explored the cavern's passageways, his alchemist detected ore with a vein of silver, and proudly reported that it seemed to be abundant.

So gladdened by this charmed discovery was de Soto, that he and his remaining ninety-five men decided to erect a log fortress atop the hill above the cave, within walking distance to a very fine river.

The problem was that this enterprise would require intensive labor and his men were not fit for the task. They were weak and weary. Their horses were no better.

Slave labor was in order now because it was required on behalf of Spain. It had worked in the past, in South America. He knew how to do it. After all, he was a god.

With the tricks of his trade, he enslaved fifty local natives, and, with all the brutality of his former Colonel, forced them to dig the ore and smelt it into eighteen-inch ingots, all the while excavating a new tunnel as they followed the vein. They stacked the ingots along the tunnel wall.

The Spaniards considered the natives to be little more than beasts of burden and whipped them to work harder, harder, and harder. At night they chained them to prevent escape.

The idea was to extract the ore, smelt it, then send the precious metal back to Spain where de Soto imagined he would again be glorified. It wasn't gold but it was the next best thing.

Although the natives had their suspicions that de Soto was no god, they did not rebel until he and forty-five of his best hunters headed out one morning to procure a supply of meat.

Upon his return late afternoon, he found his overseers and guards dead and neatly laid side by side. The fortress had been ransacked. The Indian slaves were gone.

Having only those forty-five men left, all of whom were spooked by the remains of their fellow conquistadors, and tired and hungry, de Soto decided to wait till midnight and depart the area as stealthily as possible.

They dragged the bodies of their slain companions into the cave and prayed for their souls as they attired them in full-dress uniforms. Afterwards they camouflaged the entrance as well as they could and left under that night's cloak of darkness.

It was de Soto's plan then, to get back to the Mississippi where he had men waiting, where he would rest, reconnoiter and then return for the silver the following spring.

Don Hernando de Soto died of typhoid fever in the spring of 1542 on the west bank of the Mississippi at the southeast tip of what is now Arkansas, the remains of his remains resting today on the bottom of Lake Chicot.

His men kept his death a secret in hopes that the rumor of his immortality would not be dispelled.

PART THREE

Suppose a white man should come up to me and say, "Joseph, I like your horses. I want to buy them."

I say to him, "No, my horses suit me; I will not sell them."

Then he goes to my neighbor and says, "Pay me money, and I will sell you Joseph's horses."

The white man returns to me and says, "Joseph, I have bought your horses and you must let me have them."

If we sold our lands to the Government, this is the way they bought them.

– Chief Joseph, Nez Perce

CHAPTER 8

Summer 1822

James and Mekinges, sleeping peacefully on their wood-framed bed of corn husks, were startled awake by gunfire. They bolted up and scrambled to the window but could see nothing.

"You stay here," James commanded, as he threw on a deerskin shirt and pants. He slipped his feet into his moccasins and ran from their cabin, Mekinges at his heels.

Another shot rang out, and then a scream. They followed the sounds to the river.

Kikthawenund and others stood in a circle around seven men on their bellies, hands and feet bound, side by side. They were dressed in dyed cloth and cowhide boots.

"White men," Mekinges whispered.

"What is your father doing?"

Kikthawenund held a flintlock pistol. He was studying it.

James thought it looked to be the common work of a blacksmith. He watched as Kikthawenund took careful aim as if to fire a lead ball into the head of one of the captives. "No," he cried and ran to The Captain. "Mekinges, tell him to stop."

Kikthawenund fired the gun, its ball entering the dirt an inch from the man's ear, then looked up, not surprised to see his son-in-law and daughter, nor the others who were gathering to discover the source of the terrible noise, the gun fire and the screams. Kikthawenund stepped back and nodded. He'd been waiting for them. He needed answers. He wanted them now.

James took a deep breath and in a subdued voice asked his wife to ask her Pa, "What in blazes was going on? Who were these white men? Where'd they come from?"

Mekinges put a calming hand on James's arm and asked her father to tell her what was happening.

"Did I hear English?" one of the prisoners asked. For that, he got a kick in the ribs from one of the elders.

"No, stop," James said.

"N'wischasi," Mekinges repeated in Lenape.

Kikthawenund stared hard at James. "Kuwaha hèch n ask`nu?"

"No, Captain," James answered. "I don't know him. How would I . . ." He froze then as he looked down on the man who had spoken. "Well, I don't know. Maybe I did meet him once." He turned to his wife. "Ask your father if I can talk to them."

She gave his arm a teasing pinch. "That's what Father is wait for."

James knelt near the head of the talker. "Schoolcraft?"

The man turned, dumbfounded. "Yes! Yes, that is my name, sir. How do you – ?"

"Not now," James said. "What are you doing here?"

"My colleagues and I are on an expedition to record a profile of the physical constitution of the geological formations and soil in this area. Nothing more, Sir." He twisted his neck and saw that James was struggling with that answer. "Minerals, Sir, I am documenting the rocks and minerals of the Ozarks."

"Why?"

"I've written one book on the topic already, A View of The Lead Mines of Missouri, published in 1819?" He spoke it like a question, as though James might have heard of it.

"We don't have a library," James said, humorlessly, as he considered two key points; One, the year, 1819? How could that be? The second was the word 'minerals.' He would ask about the year when or if he got a chance. The immediate danger was in that word – minerals. "Listen to me well,

Schoolcraft," he said softly, "I am going to try to save your life but I will most certainly fail if by minerals, you mean, S-I-L-V-E-R, and I beg you not to speak the word out loud. Do you understand?"

"Do I know you, Sir?"

"No. Is that your gun The Captain has?"

"Yes, he got them all. We each had one, only as a last resort for protection. We mean no harm to anyone and I have an extensive record of fine relationships with many Missouri natives. My wife is half Ojibwa."

"You'll probably have to spend the night here like this. I'll talk to the council and tell them you're harmless and maybe, maybe, they'll let you go in the morning. Do you remember the word I told you not to mention?"

"Yes, but why? I can assure you, there is none to speak of in Missouri despite all the rumors. Minor traces maybe mixed in with some galena."

James rose to his feet. "Good luck," he said as he turned back to Kiktha-wenund, who was waiting for answers.

Would there be a way to explain Schoolcraft's interest in minerals without endangering these men's lives? He thought not. He looked back to the scholar. "Schoolcraft, could you possibly be doing anything else? Studying birds, mapping rivers, or . . ."

"Of course. I have the topographical chartings in my bag."

Mekinges pointed to a pile of confiscated travel gear at the base of a nearby Sycamore.

James nodded. "I should address the council of elders," he said to Mekinges as more people gathered, intrigued by the excitement.

James could see that The Captain wanted answers immediately but he held firm while Mekinges interpreted his request for the council members already present.

James wanted them away from the white men and took it upon himself to ask two braves to guard the men while he headed up the hill toward the long house. He was out of line for sure. It was disrespectful for him to behave as though he had any authority, but he concluded that at the moment it was the best move he could make. Let Kikthawenund get angry with him instead of the white strangers, at least for now. Tomorrow is promised to no man.

y

It was the middle of the night but the circumstances of the moment necessitated urgency in the minds of all who followed James into the long house. Torches were lit as the councilmen took their seats.

James, not wishing to appear as though he thought he had any towering wisdom, also sat.

Mekinges remained standing, her hand on his shoulder, to interpret her husband's words for all to hear, sentence by sentence.

James cleared his throat. "It is bad that these white men have come to our land, but they did so with no want for anything from us. They are not from the Government. They are on their own, visiting many tribes to understand the needs of the red people, and making friends as they follow the rivers to draw them on paper. The rivers, I mean."

Mekinges rolled her eyes as she handed him a leaf of paper taken from Schoolcraft's bag.

James looked at it, a rough sketch of the southern half of Missouri with some thirty different squiggly lines. His heart sank as he worried that they would never understand it, until he noticed on the right side of the page, a top-to-bottom heavy line that could only be the Mississippi, and in fact was labeled, Miss. He pointed this out to Mekinges and said, "big river, five days east."

She remembered that river and smiled. She took the map to her father and pointed to it. In Lenape, she asked The Captain if he remembered that river. "Kithane," she said. "Big river."

Of course, he remembered the Mississippi River and as he studied the parchment and began to grasp the concept, he recognized other rivers on the cartogram. He nodded, amused by the absurdity of such a project, and yet seemed impressed by the transcendence of the work. He could see those rivers as if from a cloud in the sky.

He could see them and was familiar not with all of them, but certainly with some. But what was the point? Why would anybody do this?

Others stood to gape over his shoulder till Kikthawenund decided he had better explain what it was they were viewing.

It was a good moment, James thought, and so used it to inform them that the white men tied up at the river were friendly to the Indians, and that in fact, their leader, the one who spoke, was married to an Ojibwa woman.

Although The Captain insisted there could be no reason for such research other than eventual incursion, the council, in the end, sided with the shaman who trusted Jimyocum's judgment.

It would be wrong to kill the trespassers at this time, but justified if they should ever be caught again on Lenape land, which, after all was promised them by the Government.

James breathed a sigh of relief, slipped out of the long house, and returned to the captives as the sun began to kindle a new day.

He found them in a new configuration, tied in a circle around the sycamore tree. Apparently the guardian braves, of whom there were now twenty, being both curious and industrious, had needed something to do. Not only had they rearranged the prisoners, they also ransacked all their travel bags. One brave looked as though he were reading a Bible. The captives appeared none the worse.

James knelt beside Schoolcraft. "Mister Schoolcraft?"

The man turned his head, seemingly unperturbed. "Good morning," he said. "I remember you now. The man with the money problem in St. Louis?"

"Yes," James admitted.

"You abandoned the expedition."

James stared. This man had the nerve of a banty rooster.

"Well, so did most of the others, that same day," Schoolcraft said. "As soon as I paid them, three fourths of them I never saw again." He nodded toward his men. "You remember Mister Ebenezer Brigham here, from Massachusetts."

"How would I –"

"And Mister Pettibone there, he was also with us in St. Louis. The others are Mister Holt, Mister Fisher and –"

"Damn it, Schoolcraft," James interrupted. "It doesn't matter who they are. They're intruders like you."

"By the way," said Schoolcraft, "that French bartender was right. The Bank of St. Louis collapsed. So did a second one. The paper money was worthless. Missouri is now the only state in the union without a credible bank. Nothing but wildcat notes and shinplaster."

"Missouri's not a state."

"Yes it is. It wasn't then. It is now. The slavery sympathizers won. Your governor is Alexander McNair."

"No." James couldn't believe it. "When?"

"Just last year. 1821. Illinois too. 1818."

"So this is . . ."

"1822."

"Impossible."

"Schoolcraft smiled. "Time is a tricky dog, my friend, to be sure. Here one day, faithfully by your side, the next day, gone." He sighed as James considered the metaphor. "I can't remember your name."

"No matter," James said. "I think I can save your life but you'll have to promise to leave immediately and never come back."

"Yoachum," he shouted. "That's your name. Am I right?"

James rolled his eyes. "Do you not understand the danger you're in here?"

"We have survived the hostility of the Osage and the Pawnee, so at this juncture, although respectful, I am not afraid. By the way, I should tell you that because of the treaty of St. Mary's, thousands more Delaware will be coming here soon.

James sighed sadly. "Then my father-in-law is right." He shook his head. "You people have no shame."

"Your father-in-law?"

"Mister Schoolcraft, do you wish to live today, or to die?"

"How did you ingratiate yourself with this community, Yoachum? These are the Delaware, am I right?"

"The Lenape."

"There are lots more on the way, you heard that, right?"

"White people?"

"Well, yes, white people, of course. The Louisiana Purchase has been terribly mishandled – opened a floodgate – but no, I mean more Delaware are coming. They're coming here. Soon too, I think."

It was nonsense. James ignored it. "I'm going to direct these braves to untie you." James signaled the braves who bent to loosen the bindings. "If you wish to survive your invasion of this land, you will rise to your knees and bow to them three times, as a sign of apology, then run to the east as fast as your little white legs can carry you."

"What about my men?"

"I told the elders that you would go back to the east and warn other whites not to come here." James was making this up as he went along but he thought he was right.

"I won't leave without the rest of my party."

James shrugged. "Then you won't leave."

"You can save my life but not my colleagues'?"

"I'm sorry."

As the ties were loosed from his wrists and ankles Schoolcraft said, "I regret having to tell you this, Yoachum, but President Monroe has already issued a proclamation that Missouri land can be sold as soon as it's surveyed."

"Surveyed for what?"

"Borders, boundaries, county lines."

"But this land was promised, promised, to the Indians forever."

"So you know about the Treaty of St. Mary's?"

James shook his head.

"Yes, well, the red population may be allowed to remain here but – I'm sorry Yoachum – white settlers are already on their way from Tennessee, Kentucky . . . from everywhere, bringing families, horses, chickens and cattle."

"But why?"

"Human nature, I suppose, but I promise you, Yoachum, that one of the missions of my life is to help the Indians protect their own ways as integration with the homesteaders is forced upon them."

"It's never worked before, has it?"

Schoolcraft thought for a moment. "It can work, and I'll do all I can to make sure that it does. I made that promise to my wife and I make it now to you."

"I should kill you this moment," James said.

"No, you should not, and if you did, it wouldn't make a whit of difference. The expansion of the frontier is underway. The world is enlarging."

"Not for the red man. It's getting smaller."

Schoolcraft nodded with empathy. "Well, I am on your side, I give you my word on that. Now, please, release my men."

"No."

Up the hill, looking down, the elders stood watching.

"If you don't want your life to end this morning, you will bow three times to the elders – you see them up there – then turn and run to the east."

"My men?"

"I'll do what I can."

Schoolcraft seemed comfortable with that answer. "Good. I trust you. Is there anything I can do for you?"

James thought about that. "Well, if you ever come across a man name of Solomon Yoachum, please tell him that his brother is all right."

Schoolcraft nodded. He turned and bowed three times to the elders, then rose to his feet and ran eastward into the woods.

His captive men watched with bewilderment as he called back, "It'll be all right, men."

The remaining captives, James saw, did not take comfort in that. Fear clouded their faces as they looked to him with pleading eyes.

"You fellows stay quiet and pray to your God. I'll see what I can do."

He could have let them all go. He could have, but he was enjoying a peculiar sense of power, a control over this tiny sampling of white men, the people who had devastated the lives of so many Native Americans, and he wanted to prove to The Captain that he was not a pushover. If Schoolcraft was right about the eventual onslaught, could his prisoners be some kind of hostage bargaining chip? Probably not. And he would have to tell Kikthawenund what Schoolcraft had told him. Their world would be changing again.

CHAPTER 9

June 1823

A tall, broad shouldered man, thirty-four year old William Gilliss halted his steed as he approached a fork in the river. He had a square, ruddy face with prematurely graying curls. In his company were six other whites on horseback and six Negro slaves on foot. He twisted in his saddle to proclaim, "This is the place."

It was mid-afternoon so there was daylight enough to reconnoiter casually, inspect the site and establish a guarded perimeter.

What resistance they had encountered to reach this point they had finagled their way through, with promises of peace and gifts of hemp seeds, flax linen, ribbons, trinkets, and whiskey.

In the morning, Gilliss would send one white and one black back to Potosi to report to the Colonel that they had found the ideal spot for their planned frontier trading post.

Unbeknownst to them, another report was already being sent to someone else. Kikthawenund.

Although the whites observed no evidence of Indians as they took their measure of the place, they were in fact surrounded by Lenape braves, and could easily have been sent to the afterlife within minutes.

y

That morning, a year ago, when James confided to the council what Schoolcraft had told him, that the whites were coming and that there was no way to stop them, Kikthawenund, although appalled, began to appreciate and respect his son-in-law's insight and frankness. Maybe he wasn't as dumb as a pinecone after all.

James had told him about the cabins he had seen on his trip to procure the horse for Winona.

After days of discussions and arguments, the council conceded to the reality of the situation, and decided that the Lenape would simply have to adjust to the new world order. It had never worked out for them before, but maybe this time. What else could they do?

September

The final touch of a splendid log and rock building went up with ropes as slaves raised a huge colorful sign, MENARD's TRADING POST.

Standing back near the tree line, watching with pride as the painted wooden emblem was hammered into place above the doorway, Gilliss was startled by a voice from behind.

"Menard's trading post?"

He swung around to see an Indian. No, not an Indian; a huge white man dressed as one. "What the hell?"

"You are building on land that belongs to the Delaware Nation. You are not welcome here."

"You're a white man," Gilliss said.

"I was only born so. Lënape ta ni."

Gilliss gawked at the unusual person. "Excuse me?"

"I am Delaware."

Gilliss extended his hand. "I'm William Gilliss, here under official authority to establish a trading post for all the people in this area."

James ignored the hand but studied the man, a thick fellow of about 180 pounds with a round reddish face. "Whose official authority? The Government that promised this land to the Lenape?"

Gilliss suddenly saw a dozen braves standing behind James in the shadows, weapons at the ready. "Can we go inside and talk about this?" he asked, fear seeping into his voice.

James made a pretense of considering the invitation but it was what he'd been sent to do. He finally nodded.

ɣ

Inside the building, workers were crafting long plank tables along the walls, above which shelves of various heights and lengths were affixed. An assortment of new wood barrels were scattered around, and near the door a counter top with various scales and measuring devices stood ready for business.

James insisted the door remain open. He didn't have the authority to order a massacre but Gilliss couldn't know that, and again James enjoyed some small sense of power.

The two men sat across from each other at a rectangular table in the middle of the room while Gilliss decided to tell his guest all about himself; that he'd been a ship builder and then a carpenter hired to strengthen and enlarge the post at Toledo, then made his way to Kaskaskia Illinois just a few miles down the Mississippi from St. Genevieve. "And then when I heard that the Delawares had come here," he said, "I knew it was my next logical move."

James stared bemused by the torrent of information, which although somewhat interesting, had no relevance whatsoever to the moment at hand.

Gilliss assessed the vacant look. "Well, the point is," he said, "I am a very good builder and what I'm building here, the Indians are going to love. Think about it," he said. "There'll be medicine, iron tools, salt, flour, cloth –"

"And white laws for Indian ways. No."

Gilliss sighed. "Pierre Menard owns this store. Do you know who he is?"

James remembered the name. "The Illinois politician with the unfriendly tavern in St. Louis?"

"Politician, businessman, fur trader. He operates the trading house of Menard and Valle in Ste. Genevieve, and he's the agent for the Department of Indian Affairs for this area. The reds love him – call him a great white father."

"No they don't."

"Yes they do."

"No, they don't."

"Besides, no disrespect, but I'm supposed to be talking with your chief. Captain William Anderson, right?"

"Nope."

"What's his name?"

"Kikthawenund."

Gilliss nodded. "I think that's him. Yeah. His English name is William Anderson, right?"

It never occurred to James that Kikthawenund might have an English name, but he remembered being aware that some prominent natives did from time to time take on such appellations as a means to integrate with the whites who were going to run them off anyway. He had sometimes wondered about the use of the term, captain. That was an English word, wasn't it? It wasn't a Lenape word. He didn't want to think about it now. He was irritated by this man's sudden white-assed insouciance. "Outside you had fear, Gilliss," he said. "I saw it. Now, inside, you feel safe?"

Gilliss stared. "What is your name?"

"My name is James Yoachum and I can, with a wave of my hand, have this place burned to the ground."

"Mister Yoachum, we expected trouble from the Osage, not the Delaware. Stir up trouble if you wish but I tell you, Sir, much of this land has already been deeded to The Atlantic and Pacific Railroad Company by an act of Congress."

"That's ridiculous."

"We're here to help people, Yoachum. White and red."

James glanced at the working slaves. "Not black?"

"Anybody with money to spend."

James puffed air mockingly. "And how do you suppose people are going to get this money?"

Gilliss spread his hands, palms up. "Mister, it's a trading post. We pay money for skins and furs. Buck skins. One buck, one dollar. Then they can buy whatever else they need, right here. That's how commerce works, in a cycle."

James rose with as threatening a grimace as he could muster. "That's how tornadoes work." He shook his head to indicate the futility of talking with a white man, and then walked out the door.

y

Upon reporting his dialogue with Gilliss to his father-in-law, The

Captain (Captain William Anderson?) invited James to attend a meeting of the elders the following morning.

James had learned over the years that one philosophy central to the Lenape's decision-making process was to always consider the consequences for the next generation.

After four hours of discussion, much of it heated, especially from Kikthawenund, who had seen it all before, it was decided that they would, for the time being, ignore the trading post and just avoid that area. "Besides," some asked, "what if?"

Iron tools? That would be good. Cloth and flour in exchange for buckskins? That would be good, and so easy. What if? What if the time had come for peaceful and prosperous co-existence? It was being forced upon them anyway, as before, but maybe this time, maybe this time. Besides, what would a rebellion bring but a war, which they knew they could not win.

Kikthawenund's argument was that the best way to deal with an infestation was to crush its head before its body could grow. Stomp out the little fire before it becomes big and burns your life to ashes. He lost that argument.

James saw both sides and was glad that he was not asked for his opinion. He didn't have one. He didn't know. He was happy with the way things were but maybe the elders were right. It would be exciting, he thought, to have a few luxuries, like salt and cloth and iron tools and . . . who knew what else?

CHAPTER 10

January 1824

January of '24 was unusually sharp-edged. The temperature did not rise above freezing for five unrelenting weeks causing the expected amount of discomfort and ailments.

Twelve babies died, and nineteen old people. That was about normal for winter but now Winona was sick.

The shaman did not think her illness was weather related. The cold didn't help of course, but he felt that her affliction was something that had gotten inside her as though from a tick, although it was not the right time of year for that. Maybe she had eaten some contaminated food, but then no one else was suffering similarly.

James slept in his cabin alone while Mekinges stayed with her parents to help with her mother's infirmity.

It was the middle of the ninth night now and something, only the Great Spirit knew what, awakened him, told him to rise, and go to them.

When he entered The Captain's wigwam he could see that several others had also gotten the calling, including the shaman who was backing away from Winona's prostate body, shaking his head, mumbling, "Ktmakienhin." N'schielendam. N'schielendam."

The shaman thought Winona was beyond his help and he was sorry. He was so sorry.

James knelt by his mother-in-law's bed. He put a hand to her face and then grimaced. "High fever," he said to Mekinges. When he repeated it in Lenape, "kshëlexin," for his father-in-law, he noticed tears, luminescent from the firelight, rolling down The Captain's noble face. James hadn't known this was possible. He had never seen tears on a Lenape face.

Two other women in the wigwam that James assumed were close friends or relatives began to weep. He wondered, was this it? Would they all just sit here now and wait till Winona gave up the ghost? "No," he said. "What about Menard's?" He looked to his wife.

She looked to her father.

"They've got medicine there," James said.

Kikthawenund, nodded. "Alàpsi," he said, his voice cracking.

Mekinges hugged James. "Father say go fast."

"Whose horse? His or mothers?"

"Kikiyonënana!" The Captain said. "Alàpsi."

"Of course," James said as he rushed out. He would take The Captain's horse and he would hurry, but what were his chances, really?

Now he had gotten Kikthawenund's hopes up, got the man depending solely on him, James, for help, and the odds were, although he would try as hard as he could – he didn't really even know what he was doing – the odds were that his mother-in-law would die and it would look like it was because of a failure on his part. The better part of him decided this was selfish thinking, that he should shut up the inner voice, and focus on getting this horse to the other side and back on a zero degree, night ride, seven miles through the forest.

y

The trading post was a compound now with cabins, outbuildings and stables but James saw light from not a single torch or lantern anywhere.

He dismounted, ran to the door of the store and pounded. He beat on the door until he decided to kick it down, and then there it was, a flicker of light, a lantern coming his way.

The door was opened by twenty-year-old Joseph Philibert, whose first words were, "You have got to be Jim Yoachum, the giant white Indian."

James pushed his way in and lunged for the heat of the pot-bellied stove. "I need medicine," he said. "Please, it's an emergency. Where's your medicine?"

"What's wrong?" Philibert asked.

"Sick woman. High fever. I've got to hurry."

Philibert scratched his head, looked around the room. "Ah," he said, "over here." He went to a large trunk near the door, found a key under the counter and unlocked it. "I'm afraid all we have is laudanum and" – he raised a blue bottle to read the label – "some salicylic acid. We're supposed to get some quinine in but –"

"Which one?" James demanded.

Philibert looked up. "Let's take them both. No charge if you'll let me ride back with you."

James thought he couldn't have heard right. "What? Why?"

"My name's Joe Philibert," he said as he put on a coat. "Let me throw a bridle on my horse, and we'll get going."

James followed Philibert out the door to an enclosed stall beside the store and noticed the young man had that short wavy hair, like the Frenchmen he remembered back in Illinois.

"I was going to have to ride out and find you anyway," Philibert said.

"Again, I ask, what for?"

Philibert swung up onto his mount, bareback, same as James. "We can talk later. Go, Mister Yoachum. I'll be right behind you."

James would liked to have had the time to explain to this bold fellow that if he came into Winona's presence and she died, the Lenape may very well connect the two occurrences, and he, Philibert, would be obliged to pay the balance for the life lost.

Dawn was breaking by the time they entered the village. Philibert reached into the pocket of his coat as he followed James into the wigwam.

The entry of another white man would on any other occasion have been highly alarming, but Kikthawenund, his mind mired in trepidation, seemed to consider the outsider as a ray of hope.

Philibert held up the two blue bottles. "Which one?"

Since James had heard of laudanum at some point or another in his life, he chose that one and then handed the bottle to the shaman who had no idea what it was or how to administer it.

He supposed that since he had diagnosed the illness as being an internal evil, it should be given orally, and so filled a wooden spoon and tipped it into Winona's mouth. Because the situation was so dire, he conjectured that a triple dose was in order and gave her two more spoons full.

Would it work? How long would it take? Nobody knew, but it was something. It was something, and James was just glad that Winona was still alive. His trip to the store had taken hours – he didn't know how many – but he had succeeded in a mission of hope on a dark winter's night. No other brave in the village could have or would have made that run to the trading post.

Kikthawenund commanded the two crying women to shut up. He wanted quiet now.

James, however, needed to talk with Philibert and told his wife. They would speak softly.

Mekinges asked her father who replied, "Kehela." (Of course)

The two men scooted around to sit as far back as possible.

Mekinges joined them. She wanted to hear what mystery the white stranger might have to discuss.

"You should slip out now," James told Philibert. "Get on your horse and don't look back."

"I told you, I have to talk to you."

"You did, but I can't imagine what about, and I can assure you, Philibert, that your life is in danger here. Do you not understand that?"

Whether he did or did not, he ended up staying until the sun had climbed halfway to the top of the sky, although in the sealed wigwam the illumination of the day remained outside.

James decided that whatever it was Philibert wanted to discuss couldn't be good and so he ignored the man other than to hush him when he tried to talk.

Mekinges pinched his arm. "Let him speak."

James snorted and stared; trying to imagine what possible business the stranger could have with him. "What is it?"

"There are over a thousand more Delaware on their way here," Philibert told him. "They're traveling with a fellow named James Wilson, a white man appointed by Pierre Menard. He's the man who –"

"I know who he is," James blurted too loudly.

"Menard, you mean."

"Who hasn't heard of that snoot?"

"His son, Peter, and I were friends in Kaskaskia."

"So?"

"Well, anyway, by all accounts, you are the man chosen to help their arrival go smoothly. You'll work with Wilson to, you know, make sure that the new ones settle in with . . ." He gestured toward Kikthawenund "Captain Anderson. That is him, isn't it?"

James lowered his head with an intense whisper. "First of all, no, that is not him. His name is Kikthawenund. Secondly, I don't know who Menard thinks he is but I can assure you that he cannot choose me for anything."

"It wasn't him."

James was confused. "Who then?"

"Somebody name of . . . School . . . something." He twisted his lips. "Schoolguard?"

James shook his head and sighed. "Schoolcraft."

"That's it. Anyway the Government is going to help financially. Pay a monthly sum to each registered Indian family."

"Pfff," James spat. "A monthly sum of wildcat money, not worth a fart. I've been down that trail." He rolled his eyes.

"No, I think they'll be paid in silver."

James swung a hand across Philibert's mouth. "Don't say that word out loud or you will surely suffer."

"Why?" asked Philibert, muffled by a huge palm.

James ignored the question. He had one of his own, a more urgent one, he thought, and it too was a 'why' question. He lowered his hand. "What is this about being registered? Is the Government planning to track down every living Indian?"

Philibert pursed his lips, uncertain.

"Why?" James demanded.

"Maybe for the census."

"What's that?"

"The census. It's what they do to count everybody."

"Why?"

"So they'll know how many people live here. I read in a St. Louis paper that the census in 1818 for Missouri was almost seventy thousand people. I think it was eleven thousand for slaves."

"And Indians?"

"I guess they don't know. All I know is, I got a post from Menard, and he told me to get this information to you. I guess the Indians trust you, so that's why they need you to help."

"I'll do no such thing. Listen, Philibert, what these people believe in is the land. The land is their faith. When you pierce their land you pierce their soul."

Philibert had no reply. He rubbed his eyes, took a deep breath and looked around. "Sorry about the woman."

At that moment, Winona coughed.

Everyone moved to her side.

She was gleaming with sweat, a good sign according to the shaman.

Winona's eyelids fluttered, then opened. When she saw their faces looking down at her, she seemed embarrassed, but gave a weak smile. The fever had broken.

Kikthawenund turned to embrace James. Then, astonishingly, he embraced Philibert. "Thank you," he said in English.

Winona was conscious and talking now. She was, in fact, blathering, saying queer things. She said her horse had come to her and carried her to the afterlife, but then they decided to come back. She smiled and said hello to her sons, each one, Sarcoxie, Shawnanuk, Pushkies and Secomdyan, none of whom were there.

Kikthawenund did not seem concerned.

CHAPTER 11

February and March that year were as gentle as January had been harsh.

Because the laudanum seemed to have done the trick, and the white stranger was credited for bringing the cure for Winona's illness, Kikthawenund's distrust for any and all things from the white world began to soften to the point where he agreed with the other elders that it would be worth experimenting in trade with Menard's Trading Post.

One buck skin was worth one dollar and a dollar could buy things that Native Americans never dreamed of – little things like coffee and sugar, tobacco products, needles and thread and blankets and, oddly to them, jars of honey in the winter. Unheard of. They could have stored honey themselves, of course, they knew that, but honey was to be enjoyed on the evening of that day's procurement. It was a summer treat.

Also considered a luxury, bear's oil and buffalo marrow, which they could purchase by the pound. And they could sell or trade their own produce by the pound, so many pounds adding up to bushels. They could see the scales. Beans, sixty pounds per bushel. Strawberries or blackberries, thirty-two pounds per bushel.

y

James Wilson, as it turned out, was an investor in Menard's business ventures and so was most happy to guide the fresh arrivals of Delaware to their new home in southwest Missouri, as agreed to in the 1819 Treaty of St. Mary's, and of course he urged them all to settle near the post 'for their convenience.'

The Delaware land grant was described as seventy miles East to West, forty-four miles North to South, which encompassed all the land of present day Barry, Green, Christian, Lawrence and Stone counties, for a total of 1,971,200 acres.

If Wilson could persuade the reds to live collectively, he could keep an eye on them and have a continual supply of hides and pelts to ship eastward to the warehouse, The House of Menard and Valle in Ste. Genevieve, which, for him, would be a lucrative enterprise by any man's reckoning.

He built a home on the banks of a sizable stream that flowed into The White River. That tributary became known as Wilson's Creek.

Many of the new Lenape arrivals erected cabins and wigwams around the post, which became known as Delaware Town to the pick-up and delivery workers that traveled in and out of the grounds on cargo wagons.

In the belief that Kikthawenund was the infamous Captain Anderson from Indiana, his settlement was called Anderson Village.

Those same transporters had a covert little trading post of their own, unstructured, just outside of Delaware Town, where Indians could trade for spirits – mostly corn whiskey, brandy and hard cider.

While this was regarded as a frontiersman's most risky and infamous sin, there was no viable law enforcement to prevent this supplementation of the cargo carrier's meager wages and the ease of the trafficking made it a matter of common logic to them.

The Indians, those who had registered, were indeed receiving silver coins from the Government – called "eight-reales," five per family, monthly – by way of the trading post, although no Indian doubted that this operation wasn't fishy, somehow.

The United States had not made silver dollars since 1803. The eight-reales were minted in Mexico. Sub-agents on four-horse buckboards protected by armed guards brought in the allotments.

Kikthawenund badgered James to try to explain to him why anyone would be entitled to money just for registering. He feared that the prospect of government allotments for people who did nothing would eventually bring out the worst in them.

James said he didn't know. It didn't make sense. If anyone should need money for some reason, they could do the work to kill an animal, skin it, and sell the hide to the trading post.

Kikthawenund advised his people against the registration process but the temptation of free money was too much for many to overcome.

Very few Lenape partook of intoxicants, but other tribes in the area did, especially the Osage.

The Shawnee, Kickapoo, Pinakashaw, Peoria, Wea, and Pottawatomie were all settling now in Southwest Missouri and things were looking pretty good for everybody, even Kikthawenund had to admit.

The only problem, as he saw it, was that more and more white settlers were moving in also, homesteading on what was supposed to be Indian land.

CHAPTER 12

Spring 1824

The construction went on around the trading post, with bunkhouses, a livery stable, a blacksmith's shed, a tan yard, a slaughter yard, various barns and corrals with for sale signs for cattle, hogs, and chickens.

To his dismay Kikthawenund, when he saw the post, figured there must be fifty permanent whites now, in this one spot, and at least as many blacks. But they were employed. They were all doing something – building, cleaning, tanning, raking, grooming livestock – they all had something to do, all but the Indians. "What were they doing here" he wondered, "just standing around, drinking, smoking, snickering and fraternizing with ne'er-do-wells from other tribes?"

He could not pick out any Lenape in the red-skinned cluster, he was glad of that, but he recognized the fashions of the Kickapoo and the Osage, and it occurred to him that he might be seeing a vision of the future. An easy life for Indians would lead to their ultimate humiliation. Could the Government's craftiness be that farsighted?

He learned later that the name given the young Indian idlers was "post rats." He didn't like it but he understood it.

James, Mekinges, and Winona were already in the store when Kikthawenund came through the door and looked around. He did not let his astonishment show but it was like a bolt of lightning from another world. Gleaming metal hatchets and axes, hammers, sickles, buckets, hoes, rakes and things he did not know.

James was at the counter with a stack of beaver pelts as William Gilliss counted.

After making a note on paper with a wooden graphite pencil, Gilliss looked up. "How's thirty dollars? Sound fair?"

"We don't want your money," James said as his wife and mother-in-law brought items to the counter, a rake and a hoe, sacks of salt, flour and beans, a box of needles with thread, and a spool of ribbon. "Just add the cost of these supplies and let me know if I'm short of pelts or . . ."

"Oh, I'm sure you're fine," Gilliss said. He was quiet as he tallied on a sheet of paper. "In fact, I owe you nine dollars."

"Can we have credit for that for next time?"

"Sure," Gilliss said. "But, well, just wondering, why don't you want the money? They're silver coins."

"We don't need them," James said and then wished he hadn't.

There was an awkward moment of silence as Gilliss eyed the silver adornments worn by his red customers, their bracelets, armbands, and hair fixtures. He said, "Well, no," I guess you don't." He was about to ask about it but caught a look from James that made him hold off.

James had to say something. Acting defensive would only stoke the man's imagination. "I know what you're thinking. The silver doodads? The Lenape came here with a good bit of silver from Indiana." He wanted to slug himself for the pitiful explanation.

"Oh," Gilliss said. "That would explain the beautiful pieces they wear."

Again, uncomfortably, they stared at each other till James motioned to Kikthawenund that they were free to go.

"Mister Yoachum?" Gilliss said.

James, halfway out, turned.

"In the interest of friendship, I should tell you that others have noticed, if you catch my meaning."

And there it was. Others have noticed. James wondered what to say. Of course others had noticed. It was one of the first things he noticed when he regained consciousness in the long house eleven years earlier. "Well," James said, "then be a friend to them as well, if you catch my meaning."

Gilliss nodded as though he did but it was more of an eerie feeling than an understanding. "Good day, Sir."

Outside, as they bundled their purchases on Winona's little mare, a buck-board of new white arrivals down the road distracted them.

The Captain shook his head and mumbled, "N' schawussi, kpahi. Peltowak."

"What?" James asked.

Mekinges said, "Father say they are coming and he does not know how to shut the door."

James dipped his head. "Tell him that should he give the word, we can pull this foul weed before it spreads." He watched the new white arrivals climb down from their buckboard, then shook his head. "Everybody wants to be Daniel Boone."

"Who is Daniel Boone?" Mekinges wanted to know.

James was about to answer but got a slap on the back, accompanied by a cheerful voice.

"Daniel Boone wasn't half the man of James Yoachum. Jimyocum, the white Indian."

They turned to see Joseph Philibert. Kikthawenund's face lit up with a smile as he explained to Winona that this was the man who brought the medicine that saved her life, then extended his hand for a shake, white man style.

Philibert clasped The Captain's hand with a bow then turned to James. "Have you heard they're changing the name of this place?"

"I don't know what you mean," James said.

"This river. It has a new name."

"The Lenape call it the White River."

"Yeah, well . . ." Philibert lowered his voice. "Indians don't get to name rivers, I guess. Just the Government."

It was an insult, James thought, and why was the man grinning? "Look, Philibert —"

"Joe," Philibert said. "Call me Joe."

James sighed impatiently. "Joe, we appreciate your friendship, what you did and all . . . that was something, riding out with me that night, but we don't care what you call the river." He turned to help his mother-in-law onto her horse. "Good fortune to you, Sir." He nodded to The Captain.

Kikthawenund took the reins of Winona's horse to lead them away.

"And to you, James. You did a great job and your government wants to salute you."

James turned with a look of puzzlement. "What do you mean?"

Philibert giggled like a girl and covered his mouth to hold in his secret.

James shook his head, took his wife's hand, then followed her parents off the trading post grounds.

y

Halfway back to their own neck of the woods, bandits with pistols sprang from the trees.

James counted six. They were white, probably in their twenties except for one older fellow, maybe fifty. A grizzly looking character, he did the talking.

"You reds sure do have a lot of pretty silver jewelry." He waited for them to panic but they didn't.

James looked to Kikthawenund, who shook his head sadly.

"Take it off," the leader said, stepping close to point his gun up under Winona's chin. "All the silver. Do it or else."

Winona rolled her eyes as her family feigned ignorance.

The grizzled mugger suspected then that the reds did not understand English, and yet he spoke it again. "You understand sign language?"

"I do," James said.

"Good; a smart Indian." He cocked the hammer of his pistol. "What do I mean by this?"

"If I read your white sign language right," James said, moving closer to the man, "it means that without that gun, you're afraid this old squaw will hop off her horse and kick your chicken ass up through your fat mouth. Am I right?"

The gunman was taken aback just long enough for James to snatch his gun and thump him to the ground.

When the man looked around for help he saw his partners being dragged into the woods, a pinecone shoved into the mouth of each. One Lenape brave stood waiting for him. "I'm sorry, I'm sorry," he pleaded.

James looked down. "What?" he shouted. "Better talk louder. We don't speak English."

The man was dragged away with his cohorts, never to trouble another living soul.

James turned to his wife. "Tell your pa, it's time that –"

She interrupted. "It's time you know."

He nodded.

Kikthawenund nodded.

Winona nodded.

It was time James knew the secret of the silver.

CHAPTER 13

April 1824

Kikthawenund recommended to the council of elders that James be included among those who were trusted with the secret. No objections were raised. He'd been among them for more than ten years. Jimyocum was tried and true.

The following morning, The Captain, James and Mekinges set out on a six-mile tramp into the forest in a direction James could never remember treading before, probably because of the formidable density of the thorny underbrush.

Kikthawenund knew a passageway through it.

They were not alone, James knew, flanked on both sides by guardian braves moving through the thicket as unseen as the breeze.

It still marveled him how these braves had mastered the trick of blending in with the very air. Would he ever be able to do that? He suspected not, inasmuch as he stuck out like a sore thumb, one of the unfairnesses of his life. He tried once to darken his hair with walnut goo but looked so ridiculous he became the butt of many jokes.

As they walked, Kikthawenund told the story of the silver with his own vocabulary as Mekinges put his words into English.

"Three hundred years behind us," she translated, "the soldiers of Spain come here to take the heads off of people who live here to make sacrifice to the walking tree."

"The walking tree?" James asked.

"Yes. There was a walking tree, the spirit of Manitowuk, who take care of everything that live here. Give food to hungry, and shelter all living peoples and animals in time of trouble. The Spainers think, 'We must sacrifice to this walking tree so it will let us do whatever we want to do.'"

"They sacrificed human heads? What did they want to do?"

"What they want to do was steal silver from the land and move it to the east to the big river, and then to the great water to take their stealings to their own home."

"They did not know that spirit of Manitowuk, the walking tree, would think this was not good. It was bad. The walking tree was very troubled. The Spainers was cruel to the peoples here and slaved them for work to steal from the earth."

"Who lived here then?" James asked.

"Choctaw," Kikthawenund answered.

"Choctaw," Mekinges said. "Flatheads."

"What?" James asked.

"Choctaw make their babies' heads flat right here." She pointed to her forehead. "They think it look nice." She giggled as she imagined it.

Her father continued, Mekinges translating for him.

"One day the walking tree call all the animals to follow him away – only time walking tree ever speak. All animals went away with the walking tree and the Spainers had no meat, so they followed far to the next river, two days away. But then the walking tree tells all animals to run back to their home. When the hungry Spainers get back to their camp, they see all the slaves was gone and their peoples was dead."

"Well, wait. All right," James said. "The Spanish guards were dead when the hunters came back?"

"Yes."

"How did they die?"

"Choctaw," The Captain said, sliding a finger across his throat.

"Choctaw," Mekinges repeated for her husband, copying the neck cutting motion.

James imagined it for a moment, then asked, "What happened to the walking tree?"

Kikthawenund answered.

"Father say, the walking tree maybe still be here, or maybe go to help other tribes. Walking Tree will walk again whenever the Great Spirit say."

"This would be a good time, I think," James said as he noticed they were now walking through an expansive stand of peach trees. He wanted to ask about the peaches but was too keen to hear more of the story. "So, all right. But . . . I don't understand. Do you mean the secret of the silver is three-hundred years old?"

Mekinges shrugged.

Kikthawenund thought that enough of the legend had been told.

They stopped at a clearing. The Captain pointed. "Talattauwoapin," he said.

James looked and saw . . . nothing. Why didn't his father-in-law just come out and speak English? He certainly seemed to understand it.

Mekinges said, "Father say, 'Look at this place.'"

James looked. Beyond the clearing he studied a vine-covered step, maybe twenty feet high, to a larger hill behind. Then five braves appeared from nowhere and came forward from the hill to greet their Chief.

At the foot of the rise, as the braves pulled the vines away, James could see a rockslide indentation, what could have been an opening at one time but was covered. Then he looked to the ground and saw a dark hole, three feet wide, with a wooden ladder descending into its depths.

Kikthawenund explained through his daughter that after the bad encounter with the Spaniards three hundred years ago, the Choctaw had sealed the obvious entrance to the cave and dug a less conspicuous one into the flat ground, one they could easily cover.

The guards lit torches and handed one each to the three of them.

Kikthawenund led the way. It was fifteen feet to the bottom where a sloping passage led to a junction room.

James and Mekinges followed.

In the junction room there were two passages, to the left and right of the main opening.

The Captain led them to the left, which sloped upward and explained that the other passage led to water, spiders, and white frogs.

After thirty feet they came to another junction room. Kikthawenund chose the difficult passage first, a narrow, four-foot high mud-floored crawl.

The next room was high domed. James, glad to be able to stand straight again, saw a large flowstone block in the center. The Captain led them around it.

James liked the way the walls seemed to sparkle as their torchlights passed by.

The air was cool and there was a slight breeze, which he guessed meant that there was another opening somewhere. Was anybody guarding that one?

Kikthawenund pointed to an obviously man-made shaft with wooden beams and then proceeded into it, its length about thirty feet before they came to another chamber, an even larger one. He stopped at its entrance and turned to mutter something to his daughter just behind him.

James was behind her. "What did he say?"

"You are schachachgapewin," she said. "You are honor-promised, that you will never tell what you see here."

James nodded. "Committed," he said.

"What?" she asked, not knowing the word. "Com . . ."

"I'm committed," he said. "I make a commitment. That means I give myself to this promise, that I will never tell anybody what I see here, on my honor."

Mekinges smiled. "Yes. You make commitment."

"I do. Ejaja."

"Ejaja," she said with a chuckle. "You have commitment for ejaja. That is good." She looked to her father.

Kikthawenund rolled his eyes unamused by their banter, then gestured for James to extend his torch to the far wall.

When he did he was flabbergasted. Their flames illuminated a wall of silver ingots, eighteen-inch bars, three inches thick, waist high and stacked uniformly for a length of what he guessed was thirty feet.

"Good Lord, Captain," he said. "You may be the richest man in the world."

Kikthawenund responded in Lenape.

Mekinges interpreted. "Father say, many peoples die with the way you think. Man not rich by silver or horses. Man only rich from Kishelëmienk, Creator of us all. Rich is in heart."

"God, you mean," James said.

Kikthawenund nodded.

"But why the big secret? It's yours. You've got guards. There's so much you could do with this kind of wealth. You could buy the trading post a thousand times. Maybe ten thousand."

The Captain moved toward yet another passageway as he mumbled again in his own tongue.

"Father say, you know the answer to your own question but you must see for yourself."

Ten feet later they were in a small dry room.

The Captain held his torch out low.

What James saw then took his breath away. Human remains. Thirty, maybe thirty-five, draped in formal Spanish raiment.

They moved close for a better look.

Nothing in his past could have prepared him for the wonder of this spectacle – skeletons arranged in a neat row against a cave wall in conquistador regalia as though someone had dressed them in their Sunday best to enter the afterlife. Oddly shaped helmets cradled each skull. Puffy sleeved shirts and trousers of gaudy colors, still vivid, adorned each skeleton, with breastplates resting on their once-muscled chests.

"Pawallessit," Kiktahwenund said.

"Rich men," Mekinges said.

James nodded. "I understand. They died because of the silver."

They stared at the three-hundred-year-old bags of bones for a quiet time till The Captain said, "Whites coming all around." He was suddenly speaking English. "I must trust you, Jimyocum. You will protect the silver."

"What?"

Kikthawenund turned to leave.

James said to his wife, "Me, to protect the silver? What does he mean?"

Mekinges shrugged, then pinched his sleeve to tug him away to follow her father back through the tunnels.

James looked back over his shoulder trying to imagine what their lives must have been like, those whose remains had lain in this secret darkness for hundreds of years. He could wonder about that later. A more pressing matter had just arisen.

CHAPTER 14

The Lenape Council of Elders agreed with Kikthawenund that a white man's-style house be built over the entrance to the cave of silver.

James would be in charge of one hundred men to fell the trees, split, hew and fashion the wood to his specifications.

Having watched him erect his original cabin for Mekinges, and having seen and marveled at the craftsmanship of Menard's Trading post, the imagining of such a project seemed conceivable and doable.

Although he had used oak to build the village's first cabin, it had taken him all summer, partly because he had done it on his own with only occasional help from Mekinges's brothers, but also because the wood was just too hard.

Mekinges suggested that, since there were so many mature Junipers around the cave's hill, he should consider that kind of wood. "It has a good red color and it smell nice."

James wondered why he hadn't thought of that for his first house. "Of course," he shouted, smacked his head and then embraced and kissed her for being so smart. "We could take Cedars out of these woods by the hundreds and it wouldn't even be noticeable."

"Noticeable?" she asked.

"I mean the forest won't even miss them. In fact, it would be good for the forest, I think. Give the other trees more room to fill out."

Mekinges smiled, pleased with their mutual decision.

"And you have to make other decisions too, Mekinges."

"Me?"

"Of course. It will be your house. I want to make it like you want it."

"I don't understand."

"Remember the white man's maps, the drawings of the rivers?"

She nodded.

"Tomorrow, I will go to the trading post and get paper and pencils and we will draw a map of how you want your house. I wonder if they'll have a ruler."

"Father is our ruler."

"No, I mean something to measure with. It's like a flat stick with . . ." Well, he would have to show her. She couldn't understand it now but James knew that she would.

And she did, two days later as they sat outside their cabin playing with the pencils and paper, laughing, James showing her how to draw a tree, a funny face and a pig wearing a feather headdress.

"Now," James said, "Let's draw our new house." He drew a straight line at the top of the page with a little circle directly underneath. "You know what this is?"

She stared at it. "No," she answered, disappointed in herself.

"This line is the hill. This little round spot is the hole into the cave."

"Yes," she squealed with delight. "I can see that."

Using the line of the hill as the back wall he drew a rectangle over the circle, his thought being that the further back the hole would be, the better.

"That is our house?" she asked.

"Yes."

"Is big house."

"Why shouldn't we have a big house? It will be safer and The Captain has given us a hundred men to build it."

She nodded. "You are right. Let's go show Father."

"Not yet," James said. "We need to make a map of the inside of the house."

Mekinges shook her head, not comprehending.

"You're going to want rooms in the house, Mekinges, a bedroom where we'll sleep, a front room where we will visit friends – that room should have a fireplace – and a room for eating, and a front porch, of course, where we can sit in the evening and watch the stars come out."

Mekinges eyes got moist. What kind of man had she married who could think of such things?

"So we will draw these plans for the inside of our house and then show them to your pa and to all the braves who will be our builders."

Y

James decided that the back wall against the hill should be the first order of business and then a wood plank floor, which proved to be a disagreeable task for the builders because of his insistence that the boards be smoother, smoother, and smoother.

They had worked around the cave entrance, which James decided they could design later, and then laid in the cedar logs for the other three walls.

Every three or four days the Council of Elders would appear to judge the workmanship and shake their heads with wonderment. Jimyocum certainly seemed to know what he was doing.

Kikthawenund would say, "I told you so," and then find James to express his approval of the project. Just how much this meant to James, The Captain probably did not know, but Mekinges did, and would thank her father for his encouraging words to her husband.

During the process James observed which workers had a natural talent for carpentry and which ones did not. He would use the gifted ones for the inside walls, the fireplace and the special project of designing a floor door above the cave entrance.

On the afternoon of the sixth week from start to finish, James sent a messenger to Kikthawenund to bring as many people as he trusted to come for an announcement, and bring food.

Two hundred people made the trek and gathered around the front porch where James asked his wife to give a short speech.

She protested, insisting that speeches were a man's job, but he persevered, and Mekinges stood high on a stump to proclaim that their house was finished. In her own tongue she thanked her father for believing in her beloved Jimyocum. She thanked and congratulated the elders and all the workers. "The white people are coming all around us," she continued in Lenape. "It is not right but it is true. Sadly, according to my husband, white people have as their most important calling, the pursuit of wealth . . . silver. Will we let them have it?"

"Atta," the crowd responded. "Atta, atta."

"We may not know what double-cross is coming next from the white people. I like to think that we will be fine here for the rest of our lives but my husband and my father think it is only a matter of time before we are betrayed again."

The throng grumbled.

"But if this is true, you may rest assured that our silver is safe under this house from now on, for many generations, for our children who may need it. My husband gives his word on this as a Lenape brave."

The crowd cheered and began to chant his name. "Jimyocum, Jimyocum, Jimyocum."

"And now, let us make games and songs and cook food to eat for our good spirits."

As the party ensued it became obvious that more than a few had brought alcohol for the get-together as the feasting and singing got louder and louder with dancing, feats of strength, and improvisational speeches that started getting bold and silly.

The Captain didn't like it but he allowed it. It was, after all, a special day.

James thought it was wonderful and said so. "Wulelendamen."

As the party proceeded into the night, some drifting away, some finding a place to sleep and some passing out, Mekinges took James by the hand and led him through the house to the back room. She lit a lantern. There was no bed but she undressed seductively, and then laid herself upon the floor door, naked and smiling with outstretched arms.

It was the proudest moment of his life. James undressed and lowered his body down to make love to his amazing wife.

CHAPTER 15

June 1824

On the first Monday afternoon of the month, the 7th, William Gilliss walked warily toward the young rabble of what the whites called 'post rats,' who on this day were collected around the blacksmith's shed, watching James Poole hammer molten iron.

They were drinking and smoking, as usual, but none as yet had caused any problems for the post other than making some Anglo passersby nervous.

Gilliss did feel some unease but spread his arms, palms up, and approached with a smile on his face to indicate that he was a man of good humor.

He invited the redskins into the store for peppermint sticks and tobacco or even pickles if they wanted, no money required.

The biggest of the group, an Osage boy of about seventeen, named Ketonga, convinced the others that if this were a trap, they were numerous enough and strong enough to fight their way out of it. "It could be fun. Who's too chicken?"

Inside, they were gestured to sit on the benches at the long table upon which sat bowls of white peppermint sticks, which they were urged to try.

Nervously – it could be poison – they did, and they liked it. They liked it a lot, but, some thought, wouldn't that be the smartest way to dispense poison, to make it delicious?

Also present were James Wilson, Joe Philibert, and three slaves, who caught the stares of the young reds. Till now they had only seen black-skins from a distance. Now they were corralled within four walls, the Negroes with their strange hair, staring back.

Gilliss called one of the Africans to join them and be seated next to Ketonga, who then began to quiver. A few of his friends nervously chortled at his sudden discomfort.

This particular black man, Duke, had at some time in his life learned enough Algonquian to, after a time, convey to each of these rogues from various tribal nations that there was to be a large, important pow wow on Friday, four suns from now, June 11th, right here at the post.

Gilliss laid a Spanish silver dollar in front of each Indian.

If each of them would take this message to as many of their own people as they possibly could within the next three days, there would be two more silver dollars per person. "This is very important," he said, "and there will be a big feast."

The boys looked at each other and nodded. Sure. Why not?

Gilliss had decided that it would be better not to mention that the new white settlers in the area were also being invited. That task would be up to Philibert and half a dozen select slaves.

In the meantime other slaves would build and set up a speaking platform with tables and benches to surround it.

y

They drifted in from all directions, mostly in groups of six to ten elders from the nearby nations, Shawnee, Kickapoo, Seneca and Pottawatomie, and white settlers from various factions who thought, who were hoping, that this would be a meeting to discuss what to do about the Indian problem.

Old Missouri names were represented. The Ernshaws, Friends, Pattersons, Pettyjohns and others, including angry squatters who had been displaced by the Delaware, as well as some Boonslick immigrants.

The whites knew they were in for a disappointment when the first man to take to the raised platform was John Polk Campbell, a Federally-appointed sub-agent who had complained to Missouri politicians about the outlaw character of the white locals who used Indian land without paying rent while charging them extravagant prices for corn.

For this occasion Campbell was only there to be sure that those in attendance were aware of his presence and that his eyes were upon them. Although he was the primary law officer in Southwest Missouri, he, himself, was never certain of his exact jurisdiction and he was continually seeking clarification of his official capacity when wrongs were committed against the Indians.

He also wanted to get a good look at the new residents of the trading post area. He didn't.

The hundred or so new white arrivals, living in squalid conditions behind and down the hill, had been warned by Gilliss to stay away from this affair if they didn't want trouble with him. They didn't.

It was a disappointing turn out with fewer than ninety of the established Ozarks inhabitants and no one at all from the Osage nation.

The Delaware contingent, for which the front bench had been reserved, consisted of James, his wife, her four brothers, and her father and mother. They were seated so close to the stand, they couldn't see who else was there with similar positioning around the sides of the stage.

When John Campbell stepped off, Joe Philibert suddenly appeared and stepped forward to tell the story of the night he first met James Yoachum.

Although Kikthawenund still held a favorable attitude toward the young Philibert, he could not for the life of him figure out why he would be recounting the story of that night, in front of a hundred strangers who couldn't be less interested without being unconscious.

Philibert concluded his remarks; "And that was my first encounter with this remarkable man, James Yoachum." He paused for some hand-clapping or some cheers or something, but had to go on without them. "And now our special guest, the honorable Henry Rowe Schoolcraft." Still, there was no applause.

James groaned. "Oh Lord, please, deliver me from this man."

"Ladies and gentlemen, honorable red brothers and sisters," Schoolcraft began, "it is an honor to be among you today. During the presidencies of Jefferson and then Madison, this country's native people were forced to sign no fewer than fifty-three treaties for land cessions.

"And now with the settlement of the Louisiana Territory, being so sudden and so disorderly, one would think that our red community could be again overwhelmed." He paused to clear his throat. "I would tell you of my first meeting, with James Yoachum, or my second, but both times were . . . are . . . an embarrassment to me. Suffice it to say that James Yoachum is one of those rare individuals whose singular presence creates new realities where he trods." He paused to look around. He got only one response; a proud smile from Mekinges.

"Today we are met at the cutting edge of the frontier of America, which could be chaotic and bloody were it not for the likes of this man. I have come down from my work in Michigan for this occasion to acknowledge that I owe him my life, as do five old companions, whom I shall ask to stand now."

Five men stood and were introduced by Schoolcraft.

"Mister Brigham, Mister Pettibone . . ."

Kikthawenund leaned across his daughter and said to James, "You saved their lives?"

James shrugged. "They think I did."

". . . and lastly, Mister Fisher," Schoolcraft announced with a hand stretched toward them. "Thank you for coming, gentlemen."

The men tipped their hats to James and then reseated themselves.

"A friend to all peoples, it gives me great pleasure to honor the first white man in this region with this official proclamation. From this day forward this beautiful river flowing beside us will forever be known as . . ." pause for effect ". . . The James River."

Surely somebody would applaud now, and finally there was one who did; Mekinges and then another, her mother.

Kikthawenund stared at James with a bemused smirk, then shook his head, bewildered.

"This is not my doing, Captain," James said.

As the smell of roast pork began to tantalize the nostrils of the so-far-unimpressed crowd, two blacks on the roof suddenly appeared, grabbed the edges of the tarp covering the sign and raised it to reveal what apparently was to be a wonderful surprise. The name, Menard, had been painted over to now read, JAMES RIVER FORK TRADING POST.

There was some scattered applause for this, but most were headed for one of the five roasting pits, where far too much meat for the number present was ready to be served.

Five turned out to be a good number, as the different factions stuck with and lined up behind their own kind at the serving stations. Who wouldn't take advantage of a free pork meal with sides of 'corn in the ear' and pickles?

Before Gilliss knew it, the new arrivals that had been ordered to stay away were in the serving lines trying to look unnoticeable. They were hungry. Their kids were hungry.

Kikthawenund wanted to leave. That was fine with James but as they stood to go they were accosted by none other than Schoolcraft, himself, along with Campbell, Wilson, Gilliss, Philibert and a Lenape chief.

Schoolcraft extended his hand for James. "Congratulations, Yoachum."

"For what?"

"The rest of us here will someday be forgotten but this river will bear your name forever."

"James?" James asked.

"That's right."

James nodded to Wilson, the man who had named the big creek after himself. "Isn't your name James?"

Wilson shrugged with a reassuring smile. "This one's for you, my man."

Mekinges spoke up. "Then how come you not name it Jimyocum River?"

James hushed her with a pinch to the bottom.

Kikthawenund would have walked away then but felt an obligation to stand silent and wait to learn of the fellow chief, which Schoolcraft knew should come next.

"Captain Anderson?" Schoolcraft intoned.

"I am Kikthawenund."

"Yes, Sir. I want you to meet George Ketchum, the leader, captain and chief of the new Delawares in this area." He turned to Ketchum. "George," he said, "this is the great Captain Anderson, whom I know you know from your people's history, who preceded you here years ago, made an alliance with the Cherokee and made this a safe and prosperous land for the Lenape nation."

James was puzzled then by the fact that his father-in-law did not refute the name by which he was introduced.

Kikthawenund nodded to his fellow chief, some twenty-five years his junior, and Ketchum nodded back with a bow. "It is a great honor, my chief. Ahkënutàm. Chulenènsàk asuwàk."

Kikthawenund nodded with gratitude and then invited George to his village.

"Òpànke?"

The Captain shook his head. "Naxa wiks."

James felt the need to interpret for Schoolcraft. "No, not tomorrow. Three weeks from today."

The young chief nodded.

"James," said Schoolcraft, as the others turned away to chat with George Ketchum, "we will probably not see each other again."

"You promise?" James asked.

Schoolcraft chuckled. "I'm on an amazing expedition up around the great lakes of Michigan and it's going to take years, I think." He dipped his head. "I wish you could be with me."

James was touched. "Thank you, Schoolcraft. Thank you. You're a remarkable man."

"Nah, just curious." He shrugged. "Curiosity is my malediction and my zeal, but I love writing about my observations and, well, they make books of my writings, publishers in New York, and it pays handsomely. By the way, do you have a Bible that doesn't belong to you?"

James's eyes rolled toward heaven. With a guilty grin, he said, "Yes."

"Do you read it?"

"I do. I read it to my wife."

"Good," Schoolcraft said. "And tell me something else. How old were you when we met?"

"How old were you?"

"Twenty, I think."

"Born in 1793?"

"Yes."

"Me too."

They shook hands.

"One more thing," Schoolcraft said, "I did find a Solomon Yoachum in Cahokia, Illinois." He studied James. "Your brother?"

"Maybe." James dropped his eyes to the ground. "It doesn't matter."

"I gave him your message, that you were all right."

James tried to imagine that meeting but resisted asking about it. "Thanks. That's good. That's good. Thanks."

"Now listen, if I ever do get back to the Ozarks, you must tell me about . . ." he lowered his chin and raised a palm beside his mouth to shelter his words ". . . the silver."

James withdrew his hand from their shared clasp and lifted his eyes to the hills. "All right," he said finally, and then nodded. "Mister Schoolcraft, you come back in one hundred years and I'll tell you then all that I know about that." He smiled. "But you won't believe it."

Schoolcraft peered into James's blue eyes, then returned the nod. "I'm going to hold you to that, Jimyocum." He offered his hand again with a smile. "A deal's a deal."

They shook again. "Wëli kishku," Schoolcraft said, surprising James with the Lenape phrase for, "This is a good day."

When James and The Captain turned, they saw that Winona, Mekinges and her four brothers, Sarcoxie, Shawnanuk, Pushkies and Secomdyan, were, in a verbal sense, chewing the ears off of George Ketchum, who, with wide-eyed bemusement, was scratching his head but smiling.

"Òwiyee," Kikthawenund barked.

"Not now," James repeated in English. To Ketchum he said, "George, my chief says you may bring as many of your people who want to come three weeks from today. There is much to catch up on for everybody."

"Thank you," Ketchum said. "How should we find —"

"Just follow the river," James said, pointing northwest.

"The James River?" Ketchum asked with a sly grin.

"I don't know what to say about that," James answered. "It's ridiculous."

Ketchum spread his arms, palms up. "Whites. They name cities, roads and rivers after us, then drive us away, but we can name nothing." He turned to go. "Three weeks then," he said.

"Naxa wiks," James affirmed and then offered his hand. Dang, he thought. Why was he doing this white thing? He hoped Ketchum hadn't noticed.

He had. The man turned back as though he had committed a social oversight. He reached for James's hand and pumped it. "The civilized way to part company," he said.

CHAPTER 16

July 1st, 1824

Nearly two hundred of the new Lenape arrivals followed Captain Ketchum to Anderson village for a reception party that made the one three weeks earlier seem feckless.

There were old games to play and new ones, hand games and stick games. There were target competitions, wrestling, and clothing and tool comparisons. There were stories and songs to swap all day long, and there was dancing.

The elders mostly watched and napped through the day with plans for a serious, quiet meeting after the sun went down.

James thought he might be invited to sit in on that meeting but since he wasn't, he gave himself and Mekinges enough daylight to make it back to their new home six miles away. The teeming thickness of the forest along their southwest route would be a grueling proposition in the dark.

George Ketchum's Lenape name was Kakeewha. He and Kikthawenund developed a friendly bond almost immediately and talked, along with the other elders from their groups, about how things in Indiana had changed and what the new Lenape families might expect in the Ozarks.

One thing Ketchum told Kikthawenund was that there was another Captain Anderson that had come with them. A brave whose real name he did not know had named himself after the original Captain Anderson in idolization, but enjoyed being mistaken for him.

Kikthawenund thought this was amusing. "Two Captain Andersons," he said with a smile. "Ten would be better." They laughed. "Less pressure on the first two."

Ketchum had brought with him a copy of the 1818 Treaty of St. Mary's which now, six years later, with all the white people he saw in this area, he deemed as practically worthless.

Kikthawenund showed him the letter from William Patterson, which, as it turned out, Ketchum could read for himself.

"Things seem relatively untroubled here, now," Kikthawenund was about to say, when suddenly there it was, trouble, a scuffle just outside the longhouse door.

Four braves brought in a white man, a tall strangely familiar-looking white man.

The braves apologized for the interruption but explained to Kikthawenund that the man was caught prowling around the village. They needed to know what to do with him.

The man, about six-foot-two, was blond haired and blue eyed. "Anybody speak English?"

Kikthawenund studied the man for a moment then shook his head with a sigh. "Kpakho," he said with a wave of his hand.

The braves obeyed and dragged that man back out to 'lock him up.'

Ketchum smiled. "Kèku hèch lakeyu?" ("What tribe is he?")

"Xahowehòsihàn." ("That's not funny.")

"Wimahtësa?" ("His brother?")

"Weitët èt," Kikthawenund answered. "Nkanshelìntàm." (I guess it's possible, but it's a surprise to me.) "You see? You see?" he continued in Lenape. "Who knows what double-dealing these people are capable of?"

"I like your son-in-law," said Ketchum.

"Well, I do too, and my daughter thinks the moon rises from his ass. But, a brother?" He rolled his eyes. "Let me tell you, I have four sons and each one is as different as the seasons." He shook his head. "This could be very bad."

"How so?"

Kikthawenund was not ready to share the secret of the silver. He shrugged and then, not so deftly, coiled the conversation back to how the new arrivals might bond with the old, for a stronger Lenape Nation.

CHAPTER 17

The next morning Jim and Mekinges were asleep on their bed.

By now, James had the beginnings of a barn and had been collecting and storing, in a dry corner, goose and turkey feathers to make a feather mattress. He reckoned it would take about fifty pounds to do it right. He had explained this to his wife, by handing her a rock, which he estimated to weigh about a pound.

"Fifty?" she asked with a doubtful smile. "Fifty times the heavy of this rock will take more feathers than the stars."

"No, it won't," he had said. "We'll get there. And then you'll stitch the feathers inside a canvass covering, and it'll be like sleeping on a cloud."

Mekinges laughed. "You have slept on a cloud?"

"No, but, well, you know." He gave her a grin. "No, I guess you don't, but you'll see. Just wait."

Déjà vu. She remembered these words from before, that evening on the river, when a better idea than a wigwam had popped into his head. It took him all summer to prove it but he did. He proved it. She had waited and watched and then had seen, along with the rest of the village, and that cabin was still standing firm, used now by The Captain for small private meetings.

"All right. I wait and see, but sleep on a cloud? You are a silly man."

In the meantime James had built a wood frame and filled it with pine needles and corn husks, over which they had spread a large buffalo hide.

The sun was already up. These days they slept late, their only duty being to be there, above the cave of silver.

Since food was brought to them, James didn't have to hunt or trap and Mekinges was able to order things from the trading post including an iron kettle, which they hung in the fireplace for cooking. Also, seasonings and spices. She had the time now to practice cookery like she had never imagined possible.

Other than that, there wasn't much to do except enjoy themselves and play games with the guards. There were usually four but who knew for sure? From time to time, with James's blessing, one or another of the guards would provide them with corn whiskey. James surmised that the Indians were buying the liquor from the floating gift shop, highly illegal, but he promised not to tell. Neither he nor Mekinges liked the stuff but James drank some every now and then to alleviate the boredom. And sometimes he thought that it gave him better insight to difficult Bible passages.

Entwined in each other's arms, Mekinges was awakened by the howl of a wolf, which she knew was not a wolf but a signal from one of the guards. Then came a rapping on the door, which ordinarily the Lenape would not do.

Mekinges bolted up and shook James.

"What is it?" he mumbled.

"I don't know."

"Go see," he said.

"You go see," she ordered, pinching his arm. She arose from the bed to grab a dress. "I woman. You man. I fix breakfast. You fix danger."

"Danger?" he asked yawning.

"Wolf call mean trouble."

James twisted himself from the bed, grabbed some pants and a shirt and tottered to the front room. When he opened the door the sight of two braves holding his brother, Solomon, dumbfounded him.

"Jim?" Sol said.

"Sol?"

They fell into each other for a semi-embrace. Sol's hands were tied behind his back.

"Good lord, you got old!" James said. "What in blazes are you doing here?"

Sol leaned back and smiled. "You've changed a lot too," he said. "I understand you're an Indian now."

The comment sounded crude to James. He shook his head, his mind suddenly jumbled.

"And you're famous now, huh?"

"What?"

"The James River? The James River Fork Trading Post?" He nodded, smiling proudly.

James took a breath to compose himself. "What are you doing here, Sol?"

"Guess who's there right now? At the post. Can you guess?"

As Mekinges stepped up behind, she heard him say, "No, I don't want to guess. Sol, you can't be here."

"But I am here. Or I should say we're here."

"He look like you," Mekinges whispered.

James turned. "Well, he's not like me and he can't stay."

"Yes, I can," Sol said. "I've already got a job. The blacksmith, James Pool, needs help at the post. I showed him what I could do yesterday and he's tickled to have me. Hired me on the spot."

No reply.

"So, don't you want to know who's with me?"

"It doesn't matter, Sol. I'm sorry." James looked at one of the braves, raised his hand with a flip. Sol was yanked away. James closed the door.

"Oh, c'mon, Jim," his brother's voice faded away.

Mekinges put a hand on his shoulder. "He your brother?"

James turned. "How'd you know?"

She rolled her eyes. "Easy to see. Who is at trading post?"

"Nobody."

"I think maybe somebody."

"I thought you were making breakfast. I want some chicken eggs."

"I love my brothers. You not love yours?"

James sighed. "I love only you."

Mekinges opened the door and shouted to the braves in Lenape, "Take him back to the trading post. Tell him I will visit soon."

James reclosed the door. "No, you won't. You will not go visit him."

"Yes, I will," she said resolutely. "I need to know what is truth about this."

CHAPTER 18

Delaware Town's ghetto was a shamble of hovels erected by a small group of entrepreneurs, who saw so many dreamers streaming into the Ozarks they seized the opportunity to offer lodging to the newcomers who were drawn to the post as a starting point.

For weeks the new arrivals could only house themselves in shacks and tents until the smell itself drove some away to try their luck at squatting. Some turned around and went back east, Osage Indians killed some, and some were able to find a place to build and farm, the bigger the family, the better. The term, squatter's rights, was beginning to be bantered around.

Although the Pre-Emption Act of 1841 was years away, the word, purportedly put forth from the governor's office in St. Charles, was that there was plenty of room for everybody, the rich and poor alike. It was hearsay that spread like a prairie fire.

How official this so-called housing project was, Gillis could not or would not say but Government money was paid to the builders and the new comers were made to pay a registration fee for their lodgings, as pitiful as they were.

Although he wrote letters of protest to Washington D.C., John Polk Campbell, the Federally-appointed agent, was seemingly powerless to control the influx, suspecting collusion between Gillis, Menard and the governor.

The settlement, as H. R. Schoolcraft had mentioned, was too sudden and too disorderly.

Governor McNair's opinion was that it would all work out because civilized farmers and industrialists could work together to strengthen the great new state of Missouri, and so the squatters came to take their chances.

Philibert, having seen the yellow-haired brother released by the Lenape braves at the edge of the post grounds, ran to Sol to inquire about his well-being.

"I'm fine," Sol said.

"Are you really his brother? Jim Yoachum's?"

"The younger one, yes."

"What are you going to do?"

They walked to Sol's tent. "I'm going to wait. One of the braves made me to understand that his wife would be coming to see me. Are there any interpreters here?"

"Mekinges? She speaks English. But she won't come alone, you can be sure of that."

"Mekinges," Sol said slowly. "What a pretty name."

"Your brother, and about a dozen Indians you won't see, will be coming with her."

"You think?"

"As sure as the bees do buzz, my friend. She's Captain Anderson's daughter."

y

It was nearly noon by the time James and Mekinges appeared at the edge of the grounds. Philibert and Sol were there to greet them.

"I knew you'd come, Jim," Sol exuded, "I knew you would. And you are Mekinges?"

"Yes."

Sol held out his hand. "I'm your brother-in-law, Sol Yoachum. It is so good to meet you."

Mekinges smiled.

"Well, come on, come on. You've got to see some people. You'll want to hold your nose. We got a tent in the shantytown about five hundred yards behind the store. It stinks like heck and it's noisy, but we are so happy to be here. What beautiful country this is. Oh, Jim, are you going to be surprised!"

As they followed Sol past the store, Mekinges looked up at her husband. "He talk more than you."

James grunted.

"You mind if I join you for the reunion?" Philibert asked.

"No, of course not," Sol said. "Not at all."

"What reunion?" James asked as his eyes fell upon the pathetic living quarters his brother seemed so cheerfully leading them to.

There were crying babies, a few drunken old men playing cards, and at least one woman obviously trying to sell herself. The stench was nauseating.

Sol led them past five dismal shacks and then a few tents. "We've got the tent on the end. Works out just right. Smells better and we've got a good view. I had five horses when I got here. Had to trade two to Gilliss for supplies. The man drives a hard bargain, doesn't he? But I've got a lot of credit on his books now." He stopped. "Well, here we are." He turned with a broad smile. "Ready?"

"For what?" James asked.

Sol pulled back the tent flap and called in. "Hey, everybody, come on out and say hello to my brother and his wife."

A small pretty dark haired woman of about thirty stepped out looking frazzled and spiritless.

Behind her a tall girl, about fifteen, with light brown hair, demure and shy, appeared with a half smile. Her eyes locked on Philibert and his on her.

"Where's Jake?" Sol asked.

"Out playing somewhere," the woman said. "Where've you been? We've been worried sick."

"Long night, Sweetie," Sol said. "I'll tell you about it later." He turned to shout, cupping his hands around his mouth. "Jacob? Jacob? Come back to the tent. Jake!" He turned back to James and Mekinges. "Jim, Mekinges, I'd like you to meet my beautiful wife, Mary Yoachum, and my lovely niece, Perninia. This is brother Jesse's girl, Jim. Ain't she a beauty?"

"She sure is," Philibert said, quickly regretting the breach, but Perninia's smile broadened.

"Jesse's coming," Sol said. "He would be here but he has to sell the farm first. He's having trouble selling it. But he'll be here. Sooner or later, he'll be here." He paused to study his brother's face. It was as unyielding as stone.

Mekinges was cordial. With a smile she stretched her hand to Mary and said, "It is nice to meet you, Missus Yoachum. We are family now, yes? Welcome."

Mary hesitated then took the proffered hand. "Thank you."

"And you, Perninia. You now my . . . . What is word, Jimyocum?"

James rolled his eyes. "Niece."

"Niece?" she intoned. "Like nice. You be our nice niece."

"Here he comes," Sol pointed to a path emerging from the woods.

They turned to see a youth of eleven gamboling their way.

As the boy got closer, James's heart skipped a beat. He stared in astonishment at the boy's dark curly hair, his eyes, his mouth and the contours of his face. He was seeing a ghost.

For a moment he was swirling with Ruth in a dance, and they were laughing and music was playing and the night was wonderful and she was pregnant and their world shimmered with joy.

Pregnant. Well, that didn't work out so well, did it, thanks to this adolescent who had the nerve to be prancing to him now, and how could anyone look so much like someone else? That wasn't normal. It was wrong. He didn't know why it was wrong exactly because his mind was a sudden muddle of roiling vexation.

"Come here, Jake," Sol said. "It's time you met your pa. Come on, come on."

James couldn't believe the gall. He grunted, turned and walked away, back up the hill toward the post.

The boy trembled as he watched his father leave him . . . again. He couldn't remember the first time but this time he felt it, and it was deep and it was devastating as he watched his father's form diminish in the tear-blurred distance.

The boy had dreamed of this moment all his life, Sol knew, and everybody near him saw that his heart was crushed by the unfairness of the ruthless rebuke. Without a word Jake turned and ran back for the woods.

Mekinges shrugged apologetically. "Jimyocum is hard man for first times, but I will try for him."

Mary didn't understand.

Sol did, and nodded his appreciation. "Don't worry about it," he said. "He'll come around."

Mekinges started to follow her husband, then turned back. "You have way to carry your things?"

"Yes Ma'am. Still got the buckboard. I wasn't about to sell that, and I've got all my smithing tools."

"Let Jimyocum be mule. I will help." She turned and walked up the hill.

"Me too," Philibert said. "I'll help."

"Sol, what's going on?" Mary asked.

"Not sure," Sol said, "but they want to help us. It will be all right, don't you worry."

Philibert wanted to stay for a conversation with Perninia, but he knew the compulsion was inappropriate. "Wouldn't be right," he said to himself. "Not now. Not yet." He followed Mekinges.

"Help us with what?" Mary asked.

"To move, I think."

"Move where?"

Sol shrugged. "Any where's better than this pig sty." He sighed. "I'd better go find Jake."

"Your brother broke his heart, you know."

"Yeah. Jim's in a state of a shock I guess. We kind of sprung this on him. It'll take a little time but his wife called him a mule, so it'll be all right." He kissed her cheek then trotted away to find his nephew who needed consoling.

He could use some himself, but from whom? His brother didn't want him here, his wife hated it here and now this, with the boy he loved like a son, stung and hurting from the rejection of his own father, a painful thing for anybody but especially a boy as sensitive as Jake, for whom his heart ached. Sol had always relied on his own sanguine personality, his ability to find a positive angle on almost any situation, but sometimes he questioned God's rationale in allowing cruelty to beasts and children, the most undeserved of such infliction.

PART FOUR

"Where today are the Pequot? Where are the Narragansett, the Mohican, the Pokanoket, and many other once powerful tribes of our people? They have vanished before the avarice and the oppression of the White Man, as snow before a summer sun."

—Tecumseh Shawnee

CHAPTER 19

July 1825

From an eagle's point of view, there were two houses now, James's, butted up against the hill, and Sol's on the other side of the natural rocky clearing, with a corn field, about two acres, just to the west where last year there had been a thicket of thorny brushwood.

Trusting James as a confidant, Kikthawenund, prodded by assurances from his daughter, had granted permission and builders for the new house. James hadn't lifted a finger to help.

The cornfield, always beneficial, would make the spot appear as though two families happened to pick a bad piece of land, mostly bedrock a few inches below the clay, and were stubborn enough to try to make it work.

As James and Sol were weeding the cornrows, twelve-year-old Jacob played with Lenape boys at the edge of the field, shooting each other with stick rifles.

Helping with the weeding were three Lenape women, about which Sol finally had to comment. "This is women's work, right?"

James didn't answer.

"Don't you have enough pull to get us into a men's group, like a hunting party or something?"

James glared. "You don't have to be here. Go to the post and be a blacksmith. Wasn't that your plan?"

"And this soil is pitiful. Too much clay." Sol bent to take a pinch and rubbed it between his fingers. "Did you know that of the three things it takes to live – animals, plants, and soil – soil is the least understood by the average person? Did you know that?"

No answer.

"So . . . why are we doing women's work?"

"We're farming, Sol. We're making the best of what we have. That's what farmers do. Brother Jesse's a farmer. Would you tell him he's doing women's work?"

"That's back in another world, Jim. I want to fit into this one."

"Well, you don't. You can't. Take your family away from here and this pitiful soil and go to where you can fit in . . . with whites.

"My family? We're your family. Why do you still fight shy of your boy? Don't you realize –"

"Shut up, Sol. Shut up, I'm warning you."

"Would he be your boy if Ruth hadn't died? If Ruth hadn't died, would you be his father?"

"That boy's father died the same day as his mother. He's an orphan with a crazy uncle."

Sol stared, trying to comprehend his brother's mulishness. It was exasperating. "I'm sorry but I just don't understand."

"When a man dies, he leaves his world. When he wakes in a new world there are no ties to the old. That's biblical, Sol. Isaiah 65:17."

"You're a Bible man now?"

"I'm a Lenape brave now."

"Weeding the corn?"

James stayed silent.

"How do you know that scripture?"

"And the Lenape," James said, "do not like meddlesome neighbors."

"Especially you squaws, right?"

James swung a fist into Sol's face. The blow knocked him to the ground.

Neither knew that Jacob had crept through the stalks and was watching and listening just twenty feet away.

Sol looked up, rubbing his chin. "He wants to live with you."

"He should live with his own kind. Everybody should live with their own kind. The mixing doesn't work. It can't work. It will never work."

Picking himself up, Sol said, "Oh Jim, he's so much like you. If you would just –"

"Why must we keep having this same conversation? He is not like me. He's not my kind. You're not my kind. It's only by the grace of my father-in-law that you get to be here."

"Not true, Brother. Whites are pouring into the Ozarks like ants to sugar. The Indians are going to have to go."

James was shocked. What did his brother just say? The Indians are going to have to go? Outraged by the audacity of such a cockamamie statement, James threw another fist.

Sol was ready this time and swayed out of the way.

"Go where, white man? Where are we to go?"

"I don't know, Jim. I'm sorry. I'm just telling you, the Government surveyors are coming."

Schoolcraft had spoken similar words, James recalled. "I heard that crap three years ago. Look, either shut up and get back to work or I swear . . ." He stopped and waved a dismissive hand. "Pfff. Just get back to work."

"You weren't going to threaten me, were you Brother?"

"You just threatened me."

Seven yards away, Jacob's eyes filled with tears as he crawled away trying to figure out the world. His world, so far, unfair and sorrowful.

CHAPTER 20

May 1826

Solomon Yoachum was sorry for the way he had spoken in the cornfield that day but he was not one to allow a squabble to fester – not for more than a year.

He spent the summer enlarging and refining his home.

That September, Sol spotted the floating black-market whiskey shop. He went down to introduce himself and to warn the men that they were easily viewable from the top of the hill.

The marketers were Clovis Pogue, a small dark complexioned man with a wispy black mustache, and Howard Jones who's most notable feature was a sixth finger on his left hand. He said he'd been born with a matching one on his right, but it got bit off in a fight with his brother, he couldn't remember at what age.

Sol thought it was interesting how they kept the jars of rotgut in the hollow of old bootlegs as though they were selling used boots for one-legged men.

From the top of the hill someone else spotted the three men.

John Polk Campbell conducted a surprise one-man raid. He knew their names and he would have to report them. They were caught red handed violating a most serious law, selling whiskey to Indians.

Sol protested. "First of all, I don't see any Indians. That point aside, I just met these fellows. Whatever it is they're doing here has nothing to do with me."

"You're selling whiskey to the Indians," Campbell said. "I'm no fool. If I catch any of you on Indian land ever again, I will arrest you on the spot and you will be jailed."

It hurt Sol to be accused along with the men who were actually guilty, but he knew that Campbell's authority was not taken seriously around Delaware Town. And, there was no jail. Still, to have his name recorded, to show up in a report somewhere vexed him grievously.

That same day, his wife, Mary, was behind their house to try her hand at setting up a procedure for distilling peach mash.

1827

The following spring Sol knocked on James's door to apologize. It was true, the things he had said, that field chores were women's work, and the surveyors were coming, everybody knew that, well almost everybody, but a fellow has to be careful with the truth, a thing not be dropped carelessly in a frontier cornfield.

Mekinges said that she would invite him in but it was not a good time. "Jimyocum is not here."

"Where'd he go?" asked Sol.

This was a question she could not and would not answer if her life depended on it. "He be back. You come for nìnaël." She nodded with a smile.

Sol's face was blank.

"Oh, uh . . . supper . . . is maybe word. End of day meal?"

"Supper? Really? You're inviting us to eat with you?"

"Yes."

"Oh, that would be wonderful, Mekinges. Thanks. Yes, we will." He started to turn.

"But I send husband to find you when he come back."

"All right. Yeah. Thanks."

When Mekinges heard James tap a stone against the underside of the floor, she loosened the pot bellied stove pipe from its flue and slid the bearskin upon which it sat from off the floor door, a laborious maneuver but one they had worked on many times. She unlocked the door and James popped up. She told him then, Sol had come to the house.

"What'd he want?" he asked as they pulled the bedroom back to normal.

"Your brother love you, Jimyocum. I ask him come for nìnël." She was ready to argue but James just shook his head.

"What time?" he asked. They had a Bavarian cuckoo clock now, on the wall in the front room, sent from Detroit in November, a Christmas gift from Schoolcraft.

Mekinges shrugged. "Supper time."

James gave her a musing glare then kissed her on the cheek. "I'd better go see him."

"I told him you would."

"Oh, you did? And how'd you know that?"

Mekinges pinched his arm. "I very smart woman."

"You're too smart," he said and headed for the door.

y

While cooking a kettle of beaver-tail stew in the fireplace, Mekinges heard a tentative rap on the door. She wiped her hands, then opened the door to see Mary on the porch by herself. She didn't let it show that she suspected something might be wrong, but smiled and said, "Mary! You come in here. Come in."

Mary stepped in. "Oh my God," she said. "It feels so good in here. How do you do that?"

Mekinges shrugged. "Good weather in this house. Sit down. I cooking stew."

Mary looked around. Her sister-in-law had, in comparison to her own house which was in a constant state of remodeling, a comfortable feeling front room. It had a large center table, four chairs and a lovely long cherry wood bench, which sat in front of the fireplace. "Do you mind if I take a tour?"

"If you see one, tell me. I maybe give."

"No, I mean, could I look around?

"Oh, yes. You see house. Look around. I cook."

Mary went into the bedroom. The Franklin pot bellied stove is what she noticed first. Two stoves in one house. Great for wintertime, she thought. The bed was no better than hers but the dresser was surprising. Not the craftsmanship so much, or the wood, or even the mirror – she had one of those – but the display of the articles on top; silver jewelry – earrings, bracelets, necklaces and armbands. She picked up some of the pieces, rolled them in her hands and studied them. She was about to try on a hair fixture when Mekinges startled her.

"You taste," Mekinges said, extending a ladle.

"What?" she asked guiltily, then turned. "Oh, I'm sorry. You surprised me." She sighed. "I don't know what's wrong with me. I can't seem to relax."

Mekinges held the large spoon to Mary's lips. "You still nervous with new change from old life," she said with sympathetic eyes.

Mary sipped and then struggled with a gag reflex. "Yug. What is it?"

"Beaver-tail soup. Too much sugar?"

"Oh, uh, no, Mekinges, it's probably very good. Just my first time, that's all. Did you say sugar?"

"Need more salt?" Mekinges asked as she motioned for Mary to sit on the edge of the bed with her.

"Well, I don't know. Maybe. Yes, more salt, maybe. What do I know about beaver-tail stew?" She thought for a minute and then unburdened. "I've been here almost two years and, well, Sol made it sound so romantic and exciting, coming down here and all, blazing a trail to the frontier, but it's nothing like he said. Nothing like I thought. How can he expect me to be happy in that ever-growing woodpile he calls our new home? He's trying to make it bigger and better all the time, I know, but I come from a wealthy minister's family and . . ." She stopped. How must her whining sound to this Indian woman?

"Nice house take time," Mekinges said.

Mary began to feel queasy.

"You marry Sol," Mekinges said.

"Yes," she said, her mind going back to the day. "We had a lovely wedding at my father's church. He's a Calvinist minister in Cahokia. Four years ago." She sighed. "Yes, I married him, but . . . should I have?" Tears surfaced in her eyes.

"He is good man," Mekinges said. "I feel." She patted her heart. "You married a good man like me. Brothers both good. Just have trouble feelings now."

Mary looked at Mekinges with wonder.

"When you marry," Mekinges lectured, "place no more your home. Husband is your home. Husbands is our home, ejaja."

Mary leaned forward, gagged, and then threw up.

Mekinges gasped. "Oh, no, you sick. Maybe have baby inside?"

Mary took a deep breath. "I can't," she rasped while wiping her mouth with her wrist. "I got pregnant twice, lost the baby after three months, both times." She winced at the remembered pain of the miscarriages.

"Here, you lay down."

As Mary eased back onto the mattress, Mekinges's silver necklace caught her eye. "You are a very kind person, Mekinges. Thank you."

Mekinges rose to open a drawer and pulled out a blue bottle.

With her skirt, she wiped the stew from the ladle's dip and filled it with the contents of the bottle. "Here, you swallow this. It saved my mother's life. Strong medicine. Help you. Here." She sat back down, raised Mary's head with one arm and tipped a dollop of laudanum down her sister-in-law's throat. "One more, maybe. Be safe."

After Mary swallowed the second dose she couldn't help but comment on the jewelry. "That is such a lovely necklace, Mekinges. And those pieces on your dresser . . . may I ask where you buy your jewelry? Not at James Fork Trading Post, I shouldn't imagine."

Mekinges immediately grabbed the necklace and pulled it off, over her head. "You like? You family. I make family gift." With Mary's head still in her left arm, she slipped the necklace over her sister-in-law's hair and tugged it down around her neck.

"No. Really? No. Oh, good heavens. Thank you."

"You lay. You feel better, then get up and look in mirror. See if you like it."

"Oh, I know I like it," Mary said, feeling nauseous again. "But . . . something else."

Mekinges waited.

"Mine and Sol's house . . . it's so hot. What's your secret? It's almost pleasant in this house."

Mekinges had thought about this because she noticed Mary sense the temperature difference when she first came in. "No secret. No secret." She pointed to the back wall. "Shadow of big hill."

"Oh," Mary said and closed her eyes, her mind beginning to swirl.

ℽ

An hour later, James and Solomon came through the door silhouetted by the late sun.

Mekinges, still working on the stew, sprang to James with a kiss. "Is all right? Everything?"

"Yeah," James said. "We were just walking."

"Supper ready."

"Whew, it feels great in here," Sol said. "How do you do that?"

"Shadow of hill," Mekinges said.

Sol furrowed his brow. "In the morning, maybe." He reopened the door to the glaring light. "Old Mister Sun is pounding on your front porch. Oh, and look who else is on the porch. Jacob! Hey buddy, where you been?"

"Nowhere," the boy said, fidgeting, peering in.

"Well, come in, come in. Get out of the heat."

"Really?"

"We have been invited into this fine Indian home to dine with them and I could not be happier. I'm starving and something smells delicious, doesn't it?"

"I can come in?" Jacob couldn't believe it.

"Yes. My brother and I have talked and . . . well, whatever disagreements we have, none of them are your fault. You are a Yoachum and the Yoachums are having supper together tonight." He looked to James.

James nodded.

"Oops," Sol said, "almost forgot my wife. Jake, run and tell Mary to come over, would you?"

Before Jake could turn Mekinges said, "She here. Mary is here."

"I'm here," Mary's voice called from the bedroom. "I'm here, Darling."

When she appeared in the door they stared open mouthed with shock.

"Look, Sol, I'm an Indian princess," Mary said, stepping out. She was completely naked except for every piece of silver from Mekinges's dresser top.

"Mary!" Sol howled.

"You like it? Am I beautiful?"

"You're drunk," Sol said, rushing to shove her back into the bedroom. "Good Lord! What in the world have you been doing?"

When the door closed, James asked Mekinges, "Is she drunk? Did she bring her brandy?"

Mekinges shook her head. "Medicine. Her stomach was sick."

Jacob had suspected that dinner with his father was too good to be true and now he was proved right. It was maddening. He began to whirl his hands around his head, his own stinging thoughts swarming his brain like hornets. He spun and ran out the door.

In the bedroom, Sol picked up the empty blue bottle from the floor. He sniffed it. "What is this?"

"That's my medicine." Mary burped. "I'm feeling better now." She burped again. "Hey, Sol, have you noticed all the Indians have silver jewelry?"

"So?"

"So where does it come from?"

"The Government pays the Indians to keep peace with each other, I think; the Delaware, the Kickapoo, I don't know, so they don't have to steal from each other, so they'll have money to buy things. My guess is they don't really need it. They trade with skins and pelts so . . . I guess they melt down their coins and make jewelry. What difference does it make? Look at you. You're naked. You just stepped out in front of my brother naked and . . . oh, good Lord, Jake! You just showed yourself naked in front of a fourteen-year-old boy. I don't understand this. You've obviously lost your mind. Where's your clothes?"

"On the bed. So wait. The Indians get free money and we don't? I don't think that's . . . I don't . . . I . . ." Mary's mind went dark. She crumbled to the floor.

"Dear Jesus, help me," Sol said, plucking the silver trinkets from her head and body. He swept her clothes from the bed and tugged them onto her body as best he could then lifted her in his arms and carried her back to the front room.

"Is she all right?" James asked.

"Well, I'd so no, James. She's not." He looked around. "Where's Jake?"

"He left," James said.

Sol thought for a moment. "Look," he said, "I'm sorry about this. It's embarrassing and all, but I think this dinner is too important to postpone. I'm going to take my wife back to our place, get Jake and we're going to come back, he and I, and eat with you. Would that be all right?"

"Yes," Mekinges said. "That is what to do. Let wife rest. You come back with boy. We eat and talk."

James rolled his eyes as Sol hefted Mary across his shoulder and departed from the house.

Mekinges went into the bedroom and picked up the bottle. James followed. "She drink rest of bottle," Mekinges said.

"Laudanum?" He scratched his head. "How much was in there?"

Mekinges spread her thumb and forefinger about an inch, then an inch and a half.

"Whew," James said. "She won't be right for days, I don't expect."

y

The beaver tail stew, two tails cut into chunks and soaked overnight in vinegar turned out good, Mekinges thought. Her secret was not cutting away the fat. That was what provided the delicious flavor in her opinion. She had added carrots, onions and celery, and at James's request, another half cup of salt.

If their guests, Sol and Jake, didn't like it they didn't say so and in fact, complimented her on how different it was from anything they'd ever eaten before.

Other than that there was not 'the talk' that Mekinges had hoped for.

Sol, his personality being what it was, kept the room filled with words, careful to keep his chatter light with stories of how he, Mary and Jake, had befriended some blacks back in Illinois. He said that although the French back there still treated the Africans like livestock and had called a convention to legalize slavery, a referendum just last year showed that sixty percent of the voters opposed slavery, so the efforts to make it legal had failed. "Illinois is a better place for that, I think."

"Then you should go back there," James said.

"No," Mekinges said. "You stay here. This is better place."

"Missouri's a slave state, you know," James said, "officially."

Sol did know but reckoned James was aiming to make a point of why nobody should come to Missouri. "They're trying to figure out now how to build a railroad bridge across the Mississippi at Rock Island," James informed. "Can you imagine that? Boggles the mind, don't it? And I guess you've heard about the Erie Canal."

They hadn't, but didn't answer.

"That plan is bringing in British, Germans, and Irish, thank God, to work on that thing, much to the consternation of the French, those bullies. They want Illinois for themselves for trapping and hunting only. They tromp onto private farms even when there are signs posted that say no hunting, and just trap away like they rule the world."

James harrumphed. "Nooo, really? Imagine that, people marching onto other people's land to do whatever they want. Have you ever heard of such a thing, Mekinges?"

Mekinges filled her mouth with a chunk of beaver tail.

"What makes the French so stuck in their ways, I wonder," Sol said. He took another bite. "Say, Jim," he talked through his chewing, "we're German, right?"

James looked up with a glare. "I'm not."

"Oh, yeah, right. Sorry. But things are changing. Things are changing. I guess that's life right? I mean everything changes. Look at little Jacob here. He's changing every day. I can hardly recognize him from one day to the next."

"We don't want change here," James said. "Change for the red people is always bad. Always."

Sol nodded. "Well, I guess that's true."

Mekinges spoke up. "Not all change bad. Look at your house. Maybe house is like life. You start and you build and make better and better. You fight bad change but . . . wetënnëmao . . ." She looked at James. "What is word?"

"Accept."

"You accept good change."

"That's right. That's right," Sol said. "I think that's in your Bible, Jim; a time to change for this, a time for that, etcetera."

"Ecclesiastes Three," James said.

"That's amazing," said Sol. "So you do have a Bible."

"About five years ago, one of the braves took it out of Schoolcraft's bag and gave it to me. He thought maybe it was plans for an invasion." He shrugged. "I read it to my wife sometimes in the evening on the porch. We don't understand hardly any of it, the Old Testament, but it's interesting. Mekinges says the creation story is very much like that of the Lenape version. And she loves the Psalms."

Was James opening up for a real conversation? Sol pressed hopefully on. "So anyway, here we are, and things are pretty good, right? I mean, I see no trouble on the horizon. And if there is, well, you're my brother and I will stand with you, no matter what. And Jesse'll be here soon, I'm pretty sure. He said he would."

"And Jesse's going to want land, won't he?"

"Well, he's a farmer. Farmer's need land. Everybody wants land."

"Indian land."

"Well . . ." Sol had tried to keep the conversation buoyant but James, it seemed, would take the slightest opening to sink it.

"You said the Indians were going to have to go. You said that," James said.

"I apologized for that."

"Yeah, but you said it. Do you believe it?"

"I think there's plenty of land for everybody."

"Indian land. Do you think Kikthawenund should have to walk around posting 'keep out' signs?"

"It's like Mekinges said . . ." Sol looked to her for support. "We must accept change."

"That's not what she said." He tipped his bowl to gulp the last of his stew, then wiped his mouth with his sleeve. "And I can tell you, Sol, if there is trouble, or when there is trouble, you are very likely to be killed. My father-in-law has drawn his last line. Hundreds will die."

"No," Sol said. "I don't believe it."

"You should go back," James said. "Go back to Illinois where you can raise this boy properly with his own kind."

Jacob threw his spoon to the floor and scowled at his father. "I'm not going back," he shouted, "and no one can make me!" He pushed away from the table, got up and stormed out the door.

They were quiet for a moment, staring at the open door, the last gray of the day in its frame.

James said, "That boy needs some discipline."

Sol, frustrated, maintained his composure. "Yeah," he said with a twinkle in his eye. "Yeah, you're right. Why don't you go give him some? Go after him and give that boy some discipline. Give it to him good."

James considered the challenge for a moment, then shrugged. "Not my concern."

Now, Sol lost his temper. "Really?" He thwacked his spoon on the table. "Really? Your son is not your concern? Well, tell me, Jim, what is your concern?" He glared. "Silver?"

The very walls of the room seemed to shudder as alarm flashed in James's eyes.

Sol saw it, and then he saw the same in Mekinges's eyes. He had struck a nerve, an apparently very touchy nerve.

"You should go now," Mekinges said "and take care of Jake."

"Not just yet," Sol said. "I've got more to say. Beat me up if you want to, brother, but you should know that people, Gilliss, Philibert, Wilson, and a lot of others, are talking about the silver they see the Delaware wearing and they don't think it's from melting down coins. You should know this."

They glowered.

Sol rolled his head. "For the sake of Pete, Jim, have I ever done a single thing to be unworthy of your trust? Anything? Ever?" He got up to leave but paused at the door. "Maybe this is Indian land, and I'm sorry about that but you deserve the truth. What I said that day about the Indians having to leave? Maybe not this year. I didn't say that. Maybe not for five years, but the truth is, and everybody but you knows it, is that the surveyors are coming and what the railroads don't own will go up for public auction." He stepped out and slammed door.

James and Mekinges rose to clear the table. "I think your brother is good man," she said. "I think he honest."

James was quiet for a long time, and then said, "I should tell The Captain what he said, I guess."

Mekinges nodded. "I talk to him too. I will tell him he can trust Sol Yoachum. We maybe need him to help us."

"You mean?" He pointed to the floor, through the floor, to what was below the floor.

Mekinges dipped her head. She peered up with a gleam that said, "You know I'm right."

CHAPTER 21

"The most incredible thing I've ever seen in my life," Sol said as James swung the lantern along the stacked silver ingots.

"Good heavens," Mary said, "we're rich."

"Now hold on, Mary," James said. "That's what I thought when I first saw it. We are not rich. The Lenape are rich. It belongs to them, but being the most sensible people in the world, they don't count this kind of thing as wealth."

"But they'll kill to protect it?" Sol asked.

"They will kill to protect themselves and their land."

"Then they don't need it," Mary said, thinking she was being perfectly logical. "We do. Think of what we could do with a treasure like this."

It was four days after the ill-fated Beavertail supper. Mekinges had once again persuaded her father to trust her instincts, this time regarding her yellow-haired brother-in-law and his wife.

The Captain had bristled when she included the wife, but Mekinges said, "You trust your wife, Father. When a person trusts a husband, you must trust the wife also."

The Captain nodded, relenting. "But not the boy," he said.

"Not the boy," she agreed.

"You can't trust fourteen-year-olds. They're too proud of their thoughts." He rubbed his chin. "At that age, the brain is too close to the tongue." He smiled. "Like yours was."

With a giggle she pinched her father's arm.

As they headed back for the ladder, Mekinges spoke to Mary's imaginings. "Yes, Mary," she said, "think of what we could do. We could get many peoples killed dead."

In the front room at the table, Mary still could not grasp the absurd notion of having a fortune and not putting it to use. "Who's going to get killed? I don't understand. Why would anyone get killed?"

James let out a frustrated sigh. "There are several other rooms in the cave," he said. "I should have showed you, I guess, but there are skeletons down there, lots of skeletons in one room, the bones of people who've already been killed because of that silver."

"No," Sol said, disbelieving. "Really? Who's down there?"

James looked to his wife.

Mekinges nodded. "Tell the story, Jimyocum."

"Well, I don't know it like Kikthawenund, but apparently some Spanish general, a few hundred years ago, in the 1500s, I guess, left a group of his men here to dig out the silver and . . ."

"DeSoto," Sol blurted. "Am I right? It had to be Hernando DeSoto."

James shrugged. "I don't know. Anyway, I guess they got the whole vein, all that was here – who knows? – and they melted it down into those bars, then got themselves executed by the Choctaw. Their bones are down there. Believe me. I've seen them." He looked into astonished eyes. "I guess the point is, well, not my point, my father-in-law's, who understands human nature better than anybody else in the world, I think, that people, white people, will stop at nothing to get rich if they see a chance, right or wrong."

The room was silent for a moment as each pondered that postulation, then Mary said, "Well, that's a theory, I guess, and I can understand being careful, but to have a fortune and not use it? I mean, to just let it sit underground, that doesn't make any sense."

James recounted the story of the bushwhackers on the trail from the trading post back to the village – when was that, two years ago? "There must have been eight or ten of them," he said, "with pistols. They were ready to murder us to get just the few pieces of silver we were wearing, and where are they now?"

"Where?" Mary asked.

"In hell," James said.

116

Sol nodded. "I think I understand."

"Well, you'd better," James said. "My wife convinced her father to trust you, and you should trust me when I tell you that he is not a man to double-cross."

"I do understand," Sol said. He turned to Mary. "Honey, you've got to understand this too. We've just been entrusted with the heaviest secret of our lives. It's an honor."

James and Mekinges nodded, pleased. Sol did understand.

"A secret so fearsome that it must never be mentioned to anybody, anywhere. Not even Jacob. Just us, in this room. Are you grasping this? Do you understand?"

Mary shrugged. "I'm trying."

Mekinges spoke up. "Now I have secret. Time to tell."

James looked at her, surprised.

"When I tell father that we trust you," she said, looking at Sol, then to Mary, "Father say white mens is trying to find our house."

"What?" James asked. "Who?"

Mekinges shrugged. "Safe for now but white mens is wèchia. What is word?"

James searched his mind. "Interested? Curious?"

"Curious," Mekinges affirmed. "They wonder about Lenape silver and try to find kanshilësu. What is word?"

"The source?" James asked. "They're looking for the source of the silver?"

"Father say he think yes, and is very dangerous mahtapama. What is word?"

"Uhh," James struggled, "situation, I think, or condition, or something like that." He looked up. "Dangerous situation; yeah, that makes sense." He thought for a moment. "Well, there you go, Mary. What you think is our treasure, people are already hunting for, and like I said, many have already been killed for it."

Mary nodded. She was getting it now. "Then we've got to make a plan," she said.

"What do you mean, Honey?" Sol asked.

"She's right," James said. "Good, Mary. Good. You are so right. If The Captain thinks this is a dangerous situation, even with all our protections, we need to make a plan to throw the fortune hunters off their game."

"I told you people were talking about it," Sol said.

"Yeah, I know," James said, "or I should have known. Gilliss told me the same thing last year." For some reason that James could not fathom, a tear came to his eye. He wiped it away.

Mekinges pinched his arm. "Husband is so glad to trust you, Sol, Mary. He need this from blood family. You good people. I knew. I knew." She smiled and took her husband's hand. "Jimyocum is like my father – always look for double-cross and worry."

Sol was so touched; he got up, walked around the table and bent to hug James's shoulders. "So what's your plan, big brother?"

James shrugged him off, wiping another tear away. "I don't know. I don't know yet. I'll come up with something. I need to think."

Sol straightened himself and said, "Well, on that note, I think Mary and I will leave while everything here is still neighborly." He smiled, winked at Mekinges and helped Mary from her chair.

Before they closed the door, Mary said, "Thanks, Jim. You've given me, like, some kind of purpose or something, which I haven't felt in a long time."

Mekinges nodded, wanting to do a personal victory dance, but that would have been prideful.

CHAPTER 22

Francis Moon had no idea that he and his six companions had been permitted to sneak through the woods to spy on the Yoachum cabins. His opinion was that the white Indians lived too far from Anderson village to make sense, considering that the chief's daughter was among them. Why would they not have a nice place somewhere along the river? He had searched for James Yoachum's house for miles along the James, never found it, and deduced that it had to have something to do with the silver that he had seen the Delaware tribe wearing, and that he had heard talked about.

Whitestone agreed. "By George, that makes bloody good sense."

In Delaware Town there were rumors that Moon, known as Moony, was a fugitive from Tennessee, some sort of false rainmaker who took farmers' money then absconded.

This was actually true of his friend, the Englishman.

For Moony, a huge gambling debt in Nashville had been his undoing, forcing him to hightail it from that city and from the sixteenth state altogether for that matter. He would have paid his debts in time, he told himself, but his time, and the patience of his dangerous debtors ran out. He took his wife, Olive, a professional saloon escort, and skedaddled.

Moony thought of himself as a man gifted enough to live by his wits but whom God had cursed with a streak of bad luck, possibly to teach him some kind of lesson, he wasn't sure. Then it struck him; the frontier!

That was the place to be, where a man like he could live unfettered by pigheaded judgments.

On the night of his departure he met the fraudulent rainmaker, Willie Whitestone, a former British soldier who volunteered to pay Moony's and his wife's passage across the Mississippi, if he could stick with them once in Missouri.

This was fine with the Moons and so they and Willie Whitestone had trudged westward.

y

It was the frontier, rumors or not, and so he hired a crew to build him a cabin at the edge of Delaware Town, a place where people left him alone. Wasn't everybody there escaping their past? Who amongst them was righteous enough to judge the arrival of another?

The answer to that question arose when Moony was unable to pay the men he hired to build his house. Three weeks in Delaware Town and he was eight hundred dollars in debt, some of it from gambling markers at The Cranky Crow where, as a smooth talker, he had been granted permission to exceed his line of credit.

But so what? he thought. Eight hundred dollars? They were going to squawk over a measly eight hundred dollars? He would take care of them. He would. Surely, as the sophisticated man that he was, he deserved the flexibility to be afforded a reasonable amount of time.

But how would he do it? He wasn't a hunter or a craftsman or a pig keeper, God forbid. The Lord just hadn't made him that way.

He could play the fiddle and sing, but unlike in Nashville where he had on occasion been paid a few dollars to entertain in some parlors, no one in the Cranky Crow, or anywhere else in the Ozarks for that matter, seemed to care.

He needed a lucky break. It would come; he knew it would, if people would just be patient. And then it did come. Rumors of a secret silver mine. The Delaware Indians wore lots of silver, too much silver some said, so much silver that they must have a secret silver mine.

Had anyone looked for it?

No.

Why not?

Because it would be suicide.

How so?

Because James Yoachum, "tough as bull's hide and keen as a rifle," had indicated as much to Gilliss.

"That's it?" Moony conversed with himself. "Well, isn't that enough?" No, he decided. It wasn't.

"Not for a smart man," he told Willie Whitestone.

"And that smart man would be you," Whitestone affirmed.

"Thank you, Willie. I'll get some men together, and we'll go find the Yoachum location. When I do, I'll send word back to you with directions."

Whitestone nodded.

"In the meantime, I need you to keep an eye on my place here."

"Jolly good," Whitestone agreed. He would keep an eye on his house and his wife.

Now, that smart man, bivouacked with six others whom he had talked into dreaming big, watched from the woods as Sol pulled up to James's house on one horse while leading another.

There had been seven men in his camp, but Moony had sent one, Howard 'Six-fingers' Jones, back to Whitestone with directions.

James came out of his house with a large saddlebag, placed it on the rump of the second horse, mounted and then led the way into the woods.

Moony kicked the rumps of his sleeping accomplices. "Get up," he said in an excited whisper. "Here we go. This is it, gentlemen. I can feel it. Come on, come on."

The men groaned but climbed onto their horses and followed Moony, who led them through the edge of the woods in the direction taken by James and Sol.

Moony's challenge was how to stay far enough back to follow undetected but could pass if he could just keep his band of idiots quiet. "Not a word, not a sneeze, or a cough or a burp," he said. "You gentlemen want to be rich, don't you?"

They nodded.

"Then keep sharp and mind your tongues. This is business."

For the Yoachum brothers it was not business. It was a lark. They chatted and laughed loudly as they rode East, then North, then west.

They rode for two hours, this way, and then that.

Sol, always the talker, told James about the Missouri Supreme Court ruling, that once a slave was freed he could not be re-enslaved. He read that in a newspaper from St. Louis, The Missouri Republican, he thought it was.

They decided to enter an open meadow and wait to see if they were still being followed. Sol didn't think so.

"Let's move back to the tree line and watch," James said.

As they stood waiting for something to happen Sol filled James in on other events his brother probably did not know. "Missouri's fourth governor, John Miller, is in office now."

James looked at Sol. "I don't care."

"I know you don't but you should. You need to keep an eye on these things because eventually, now don't get mad, eventually, you're going to need knowledge about what you're up against here."

James rolled his eyes.

"For instance, last year in St. Louis, the Shawnee signed a deal with William Clark for fourteen thousand dollars to leave Missouri and go to Kansas."

James's forehead furrowed. "Hah! Why would the Shawnee agree to that?"

"Twenty-five-hundred square miles of prime land, is what I read."

"And you think that's going to happen to us?"

Sol shrugged. "Well, the Osage too. They were paid seven thousand to move to Kansas. The Council Grove Treaty, it was called."

"But the Osage are still here," James chuckled, "so that's a load of crap."

"A lot of them didn't go. They're a quarrelsome bunch, aren't they?"

"They're horse thieves, is what they are," James said. "Slave thieves too, did you know that? The Osage keep black slaves."

Sol rubbed his chin. "Let's see, what else? Oh, yeah. Closer to home, Gilliss has built himself a big house and keeps three Indian mistresses there with him."

James thought about that and shook his head. "Disgraceful."

"Hah! You want to hear disgraceful? Your own niece, Jesse's girl, Perninia, has moved in with Joe Philibert."

"Whoa. Really? Jesse'll kill him."

"Maybe. If he ever gets here."

"Think he'll come?"

"I don't know. I wrote him a letter. Told him about everything we were doing, and said we could use his help."

James was taken aback. He glared. "You told him everything?"

"Oh, for Pete's sake, Jim, he's our big brother." He dipped his head. "What, you don't trust Jesse?"

They heard hoof beats. James pulled a pistol from his belt and listened. Some-thing was odd. It sounded like only one horse, and not from the expected direction.

"You think the braves stopped them?" Sol asked.

"Maybe."

There was a long silence.

"Something strange is going on here," James said. He curled a finger around the trigger.

"Ha!" A sudden voice startled them from behind. "Caught you!"

James swung around to fire.

A small man stood in the shadows.

James, less than a second from squeezing the trigger, saw that it was not a man. It was a boy with a big smile. He had come within a heartbeat of shooting his own son.

"Jake," Sol shouted. "What are you doing here?"

"You thought you could lose me?" His smile broadened. "That will never happen, Father."

"Jake," Sol said, "we're doing something here, like on a mission, that could have got you killed."

"By those numskulls that were following you?"

How did he know that? How could he know that?

"You made enough noise to wake the dead."

"We did that on purpose," James said defensively.

"Sounded like a traveling sewing circle with all the blabbering."

"We did that on purpose," Sol echoed as he walked toward his nephew. "But . . . what? You followed? What happened to those men? Do you know?"

"Aw, they were stopped an hour ago."

"But you were allowed to go through?" James asked.

"Of course. I'm sixteen now. I belong with the Yoachum men. My friends know that, even if you don't." He pulled out a cigar and lit it.

Sol smacked it out of his mouth. "No. Sixteen-year-olds can't be smoking. Where'd you get that?"

"Aunt Mary."

James huffed and then headed for a fallen tree. "That woman ain't right in the head."

"Don't start with that," Sol said. "Please."

"Were they killed – those men?" James asked.

"I don't think so," Jake said.

The three Yoachums sat on a Silver Maple that had fallen to the ground but was still healthy, its root ball clinging to an embankment on the other side of a creek in the woods behind them.

It was time for James to give the boy the scolding of a lifetime, and square him away on what was what, and how things worked on the frontier.

Sol noticed that Jacob seemed to enjoy the dressing down. The boy's father was at long last focused on him.

After the tongue-lashing, Jacob, his feelings only scratched, said, "Well, Father, just so you know, I can not only smoke cigars and track you as easy as pie, but I can use a rifle. I've trapped beaver and otter. I've killed bear, deer and buffalo. I can even dress the skins and make moccasins. What do you think of that?"

Sol crossed his fingers.

James stared, then spat and rose to remount his horse. "Good for you."

y

Jacob's guess of the time frame had been accurate.

Just as the brothers had decided to turn back West, Moony and his cohorts found themselves surrounded by a detail of Lenape braves who, being on foot, had grown tired of the game and decided to end it.

Moony would like to have kept things peaceful but his men drew their guns and fired wildly, one shooting off the tip of a brave's left ear.

For that, a penalty was in order. Pulled from their horses, their hands and feet were bound and they were left to squirm to whatever fate might befall them. Their prospects for surviving whatever carnivorous animals might happen upon them were not good. More than likely, it would be wolves or a panther.

But not Moony, the obvious headman. Conventional Lenape wisdom dictated that for the leader of such misdeeds, something special was warranted as a way to send a message.

y

After four days with Olive Moon in tears, Willie Whitestone figured that Moony's expedition to find the silver mine was either taking longer than expected, or Indians had killed him. Either way, he decided to get a few men together, including Howard Jones, the messenger Moony had sent back, and head off for the Yoachum place.

Maybe he would have better luck, which would mean all the more silver for him. How hard could it be? Jones knew the way and said the Moony crew hadn't seen a single redskin.

Within two hours they dismounted at Moony's cold campsite at the edge of the Yoachum property.

Whitestone studied the layout. Two cabins, one against the hill, one across the ground near a cornfield. No sign of Moony. No horses. No signs of life at all. He pointed to James's cabin. "That one. We need to go in there and take a look around."

"Is it safe?" asked one of the men.

"Is it safe, Jones?" Whitestone asked.

"Don't see why not," Jones answered. "Nobody around."

They walked across the cornfield, stepped onto the porch and then Whitestone opened the door.

Inside, Mekinges stood at the table chopping vegetables.

"Hello, Ma'am. Would you be Missus Yoachum?"

"Yes," she said, dropping her knife, staring at them.

"Your husband home?"

"No."

"Oh, that's too bad." He looked around. "Mind if we come in and look around your lovely home?"

"You will not like it here."

"Oh, I already like it" he said as he led his men inside. "It's nice and cool." He gave her an appraising glare. "Why do you think I won't like it here?"

Mekinges smiled. "Is dangerous for you." She picked up the knife and resumed cutting her vegetables.

"Dangerous, huh? You going to stab me with your knife?"

"No."

"Put it down then," he ordered. "Put the bloody knife down right now, squaw. I'm the dangerous one here."

Mekinges looked at the knife. "My knife not bloody. I cut carrots."

"He's British," Jones explained.

"Oh," Mekinges said, as if she understood. "I could hear by his funny speak, something wrong with him."

Whitestone was not amused. "We are going to search your house, Indian lady, and if you do anything that crosses me, I'll shoot you. Do you understand me?"

Mekinges nodded. "Yes. But . . . do you understand me?"

"What?"

She raised her head and shouted, "Yukwe."

As one of the men started to close the door, it was slammed back into his face. He yowled as he fell backwards to the floor.

Five braves swept in and knocked the others off their feet.

As what was becoming standard procedure for dealing with such whites, their wrists and ankles were tied with strips of hide. They pleaded for mercy as they were dragged out the cabin door.

Mekinges stepped onto the porch. "I told you was dangerous place."

"I'm sorry Ma'am. I'm sorry," Whitestone said. "Please don't let them kill us, please." He could see her sympathetic face over the toes of his boots as he was dragged to the woods.

Mekinges shrugged to indicate that it was out of her hands. She turned and went back inside where she chopped carrots and wondered what part of the plan, her husband's and her father's, was taking place at that moment.

y

James and Sol rode their horses slowly through what had become the square in Delaware town, with the end of one silver ingot protruding from James's saddlebag, gleaming in the sunlight. Draped over Sol's horse were two dead turkeys.

Gilliss and Philibert watched from the window disbelievingly as the brothers casually cantered past the store.

"You see that?" Gilliss said.

"Two turkeys," Philibert said.

"You didn't see that?"

Philibert wished he hadn't but a person would have to be blind not to have caught the flash. "The silver, you mean."

"Pretty careless, wouldn't you say?"

Philibert shook his head. "No, I wouldn't. Jim is not a careless man."

Gilliss furrowed his brow. "No. No, he's not."

They strained their necks to see where the Yoachums might be headed.

"So why is he riding through the square like that? I've never even seen him on a horse before."

"Everybody's going to know now," Philibert said.

"What everybody already knows," Gilliss said. He turned to think about it, then said, "Damn!"

"What?"

"Have you seen Moony?"

Philibert scratched his head. "About five days ago, I think. He and some other bums, they were packed up, headed out for a hunting trip, I guess. Why?"

"Five days," Gilliss mused, a worried look clouding his face.

"What?" Philibert asked.

"Nothing. I mean, well, the man owes me money. That's what." He untied his apron, dropped it to the floor and headed for the door. "Mind the store."

Y

Gilliss pounded on the door of the Moon cabin until it opened. "Missus Moon, hello."

A once-pretty woman of dubious repute, Olive Moon had matted brown hair with matching circles under her eyes. She wiped her nose with a wrist. "What?"

"I'm looking for Moony," Gilliss said. "Haven't seen him for a few days. I was wondering . . ."

"He owe you money?"

Gilliss considered the question. "A little, I guess. I'd have to check the books but that's not why . . ."

"He's not here."

"Do you have any idea where –" His question was interrupted by a yelp from the rear of the house.

The woman rolled her eyes, and turned her head. "Shut up, you moron." She looked back to Gilliss. "He doesn't have any money," she said. "He never has any money."

"Can I see him?"

She sighed and stepped back. "Why not?" She pointed the way. "You can see him, but you can't talk to him."

"I don't understand," Gilliss said as he headed to the back."

"He's got a fever or something. Yammering like a crazy man. I mean, you can talk to him but . . ." She shook her head and pulled open a door-drape. "You'll see."

Moony was there, rocking back and forth on the balls of his feet staring at nothing and muttering gibberish.

"Hello, Moony," Gilliss said, "Just stopped by to ask how your hunt went." He stared at a deranged man. "Did you find anything?"

Moony turned, his eyes darting as though watching a fly. "Piggy, piggy, piggy."

"Excuse me?" Gilliss said.

Moony held up a hand and started counting on his fingers. "You got piggy peas, number one, then you got your piggy pears, your piggy peaches, Piggy paw paws, and there's one more I can't remember." He pinched his little finger. "Plums, maybe." He tried to focus on Gilliss. "Is it plums?"

Gilliss shrugged. "What are you talking about?"

"He's talking about nothing," Olive said from behind. "Been babbling like that day and night, on and on. I think he ate a poisonous root or something."

Gilliss shook his head. "He say anything about silver?"

"Silver," Moony blurted and began to count again. "You got your silver moon, your silver tongue, silver spoon, silver lining, and your silver secret."

"That one," Gilliss said. "The silver secret. Tell me about the silver secret, Moony."

Moony thought for a moment. "Ah," he said, "yes, the secrets. You got your secret door, your secret lover, your secret hideout, your secret fishing hole and your secret hand of three aces." He flashed a wicked smile. "Yeah, that's right. I said three aces. What do you think about that?"

Olive Moon glared at Gilliss. "You know something about this, Mister Gilliss," she said suddenly incensed. "Why did you ask about that?"

Gilliss gave an innocent shrug. "I overheard him talking to some of his good-for-nothing friends about silver just before he left. I gave it no mind."

She stared into his eyes. "Tell me what you know."

"Nothing, Missus Moon. Folks around here talk about secret silver all the time. Surely you know that. Those tales get the blood flowing into people's imaginations, I guess, and there's some that get all fired up."

Her eyes narrowed to a piercing glint. "What happened to my husband?"

He shrugged again. "Like you said, something he ate, I guess. He seems physically well. Whatever it is will probably work its way through his bowels and . . . he'll be fine." He shrugged yet again.

He was shrugging too much as far as Olive was concerned. Suspiciously too much.

"That's my guess," he said as he turned for the door. "I hope so."

"Mister Gilliss?"

He paused. "Yes?"

"You're not being honest with me."

He flinched. "What do you mean?"

She wanted to tell him what she meant, that she was no fool and that he obviously knew something, but considering the consequences of offending the man in charge of the store, the man with the goods, the man to whom they already owed a considerable amount money, she checked herself. "Never mind," she said. "Tell me, Mister Gilliss, do you like my husband?"

He tilted his head. "Why else would I be here?"

She knew the answer but pretended not to. "Well then, we're going to need a little more credit at the trading post until he, you know, gets better, or," she said with a professional smile, "I'm going to starve to death." She rubbed a hand across her breasts. In a sultry tone she said, "Now, you wouldn't want that would you?"

Gilliss, at the door, smiled. "What do you need?"

"Food," she said. "And to be quite honest, there are ways I could show my appreciation that might amaze you."

He nodded. "Come on by. I'll see what we can work out."

She nodded. "Thank you."

y

Outside the long house, James and Sol dismounted. James grabbed the bar of silver from his saddlebag and led the way inside, surprised to see Mekinges there with Jacob. "Oh, good lord," he said as he tried to hide the silver behind his back, accidentally dropping it to the floor.

Kikthawenund rolled his eyes, seeming to have second thoughts about the plan. "How many whites know of silver because of today?"

"Nobody knows anything for sure, Captain. A few people saw it, I'm sure. That was the plan, right? And they'll be talking about it, but everyone will think it's five days away."

"What about your son? Young boy."

"He doesn't know anything, Captain, and he's not really my son." He glared at Jake. "Step outside, boy."

"No," Jake said.

James stepped over and smacked Jake across the face.

The slap stunned Jake for a moment and the sting of it burned his cheek. He glared and then bent and charged James with a head butt to the gut.

They went down in a fierce grapple, which everyone knew did not favor the boy.

The Captain rolled his eyes with disgust. "Son not honor his father," he said.

"He's not my son," James huffed, surprised by Jake's fierceness.

"I am too," Jake managed as he struggled in the big man's clutches.

"No, you are not."

"Yes he is," Sol said.

"Yes he is," Mekinges said.

Kikthawenund nodded and curled a finger. Two braves pulled the fighters apart and chuckled as they led Jake out the door.

James rose, embarrassed, then met with his father-in-law's hard gaze. "Captain, the boy knows nothing."

"Maybe you know nothing," Kikthawenund said.

James was muddled. "What do you mean, Captain?"

Mekinges stepped to James and pinched his arm. "Father know you guard silver with your life but you cannot guard your life with a lie."

James shook his head with frustration. He wanted to clarify his position, having thought about it since he first saw the boy in town, but in his ruminations, whether in the middle of the night or working in the gardens, he knew he had not come up with a satisfactory explanation. His resistance to accepting Jacob didn't make sense, even to him, so why was the spitefulness so ingrained, seemingly unyielding against even his own logic? How is it that a man's gut clings to an irrational conviction and won't let go, a feeling that he knows in his own brain is unjustifiable but remains resolute? He always came to this dead end and it was easier to shove it out of his head, or lock it up somewhere in a dark closet of his mind, than it was to deal with the irrationality. He was not going to accept this boy no matter what anybody thought, not even himself.

Now here he stood in front of his wife, his father-in-law and his brother, wanting to explain himself, but he couldn't. He wanted to talk but he had nothing to say. His face turned red with exasperation.

There was silence. Kikthawenund was not a man to waste words but this silent pause was long even by his standards. Finally he said, "Do you not know that a man who denies the truth about himself denies his own soul?"

James blinked. He had no answer.

The ice was broken by Winona. She poked her head in the door and said, "Mitsitàm."

"Yes," Kikthawenund said. "Let's eat." He looked at James. "Boy too. Son of you." He led the way out the longhouse door.

They ate a fine meal of smoked fish, but nobody talked except Mekinges and Sol. Those two could talk together about almost anything, any time. Today it was the size of the smallmouth on the table. Sol figured it had to be a six pounder. Mekinges assured him that she had seen bigger and they yammered about fishing techniques.

CHAPTER 23

March 1829

"You've got to go, Gilliss," Agent John Campbell said.

"Me?" Gilliss shrieked. "I'm not going anywhere."

"Yes, you are," said fifty-nine-year-old Pierre Menard. He had come to Delaware Town at last and was here to make some changes.

They were sitting at the table in the store.

"I built this place," Gilliss said.

"Under my authority and financial investment," Menard said.

"Six years," Gilliss protested. "I've kept this post running like a Swiss watch for six years, and you think I'm just going to up and move out?"

"The Government appreciates your accomplishments," Campbell said, "but with three Indian wives, well, this transition will just go a lot smoother if you go with them and let all this secret silver nonsense die down."

"I don't have three Indian wives," said Gilliss.

Menard looked at him appraisingly. "I know you've got the daughter of a Piankeshaw Chief living with you. Is that not true?"

"A lot of men around here have Indian housekeepers."

"Her name is Kaketoquah. She's got two little half-breeds by you. Have you named them or do you just call them little bastards?"

Gilliss glared, wondering how the Colonel knew.

"I could go on."

Gilliss raised a halting hand. If the Colonel knew more, he didn't want to hear it. He made an effort to make it seem logical. "Single white women just plain do not exist around here."

The Colonel spread his hands in a gesture of sympathy. "I guess not. Life on the frontier, eh?" He drew a long breath. "Well, the Indians are going, Gilliss, and you're going with them. So is the blacksmith, James Pool, and his – what did you call them – housekeepers."

"Come on, Colonel. This is buzzardguts. John Campbell, here, he knows it too, don't you, John? But will you say so? No. Because you've been an Indian lover since you got your big promotion to agent, whatever that is."

"So have I," Menard said.

Gilliss huffed. "When I first got here, I told them what you told me to tell them, Colonel, that other tribes call you a great white father. Guess what? They didn't believe it." He smacked his forehead with sudden new insight. "Think about it, Colonel. With the Delaware cleared out, good old Indian Agent Campbell here will have access to the silver all for himself." He put his elbows on the table and steepled his fingers for the sake of profundity. "Do you realize," he said softly, "what a boon that silver would be for the state treasury? Missouri could become one of the wealthiest states in the nation."

Campbell rolled his eyes. "Henry Rowe Schoolcraft sent a letter to the treasury department stating that there is no silver in Missouri, at least none to speak of." He reached into his jacket pocket. "I have only this one quote," he said unfolding the paper. Then he read: "'It is to be regretted that the elements of speculation concerning a silver reserve in the Delaware sphere have fallen into the minds of civic men who spoil historical studies with their lack of scientific enlightenment.'" He looked up while refolding the parchment.

Gilliss was not impressed. He had a piece of paper of his own. He scurried around behind the counter and opened a drawer. "Listen to this," he said, a yellowed newspaper clipping in his fingers. "In Missouri, silver is more abundant than in any other part of the union; the demand for money less pressing; and the whole community animated with consciousness, that all the comforts of life lay within the reach of every industrious man." He looked up with a smirk. "The St. Louis Enquirer, June 25th, 1819."

"That paper went out of business five years ago," Menard said, "for printing flapdoodle like that. Schoolcraft is the authority. Wrote two books on the subject. Nothing but lead, galena and zinc here."

"He's wrong."

"Those trinkets you see on the Delaware?" Campbell said, "You think I haven't studied on that? Schoolcraft thinks it came through an Indian trading network that reaches clear to Mexico."

Menard said, "You want to pursue your fantasies of a secret silver mine, Gilliss? Move to Mexico. There's plenty down there. Hell, they make America's money. He slapped an eight-real down on the table. "Go to Mexico. That'd be fine."

Gilliss threw his head back and stared at the ceiling. "Hogcrap. Hogcrap, and buzzardguts."

"In exchange for your cooperation you will be gifted five hundred acres of prime riverside land," Campbell said.

Gilliss snapped back. "Where?"

y

Ten days later, at six in the morning, Captains Beaver, Pipe, Ketchum and Anderson, representing their respective tribes, met in the store with Menard, Campbell and Gilliss to confer on a new deal, one that it would be crazy not to accept, at least in the minds of the whites.

Also present were James, Mekinges, Philibert and Perninia, who stood back by the counter watching nervously.

Campbell spread a large map on the table and pointed as the chiefs bent to look. "This, right here," he said, "is the Kaw River Valley. Can everybody see?"

No answer.

"Well, it's an amazing world of its own, where you can live in peace with absolutely no interference from whites anywhere, and the Government will pay you a handsome allotment regularly to make sure you can sustain your people with anything, everything, they may want or need for a new and happy life."

"They've heard it all before," James spouted from behind. "The land we're on right now was promised to them forever."

"Forever is over," Menard said, "and you're not part of this meeting, Sir, so please . . ." He raised a hushing hand.

George Ketchum interpreted for The Captains who did not speak English.

"I'm sorry," Campbell continued. "New problems call for new solutions."

"Ha!" James said. "You think this is a new problem for them?"

Campbell turned to James. "Mister Yoachum, this is the best idea for everybody and I am counting on you, most of all, to help our red brothers' departure be a smooth one."

James cleared his throat and spat on the floor. "You're no brother, Mister Campbell. Brothers don't drive their brothers off their own land."

The chiefs nodded along with Ketchum who agreed.

"Mister Yoachum, please," Menard said. "Try to be helpful here. Do you have a better idea?"

"Yes," James said as he stepped to the table. "Yes I do. My idea, for your so-called red brothers is for them to take a stand and say . . . no more. Not again. We won't do it."

"But why?" Campbell asked. "This is truly a great plan."

"Because if we go along with this, like my father-in-law has done so many times, where does it end? We know from history, you will drive the Native Americans to another location again and again until they end up at the bottom of the western sea."

Kikthawenund could not have been prouder.

Once George Ketchum had interpreted for the other chiefs, they exchanged glances, lowered their heads, and walked out.

Menard looked furious.

Gilliss looked pleased.

Campbell looked despairing. "I fear that when I tell Governor Miller that the proposition was rejected . . ." He shook his head.

"If they want war –" Menard started.

"No," Philibert said, "they don't. Can't you give them some time to think? They don't make fast decisions, but I'm sure they don't want war."

"If they do –" Menard said.

Campbell interrupted, "If they do, I'm not sure I wouldn't fight on their side."

"You know who you need to talk to?" a soft female voice asked from behind.

All eyes turned to Perninia.

"Mekinges," she said.

Campbell rubbed his chin. "Well, forever more," he said. "Yes, you're exactly right, Miss." He looked at Menard. "James Yoachum's wife."

"She's got a lot of push," said Philibert. "Good idea, Perninia." He gave her a proud squeeze.

Campbell nodded. "I'll ride out there right now."

As they stepped out the door discussing who should go along with Campbell they were stabbed in the eyes by the realization that no one would be riding out to anywhere.

The stable doors were open. The horses were gone. Not one horse could be seen anywhere on the grounds.

"The chiefs stole our horses," Menard said.

Campbell squatted to study the dirt. He looked around batting a finger against his lips. "I don't think so."

Philibert agreed. "The chiefs wouldn't do this."

"They left, what, fifteen minutes ago? And now every horse in town is gone? How did they do that?"

Gilliss stepped to the alarm bell and started clanging.

Within minutes men were running to the store in their long johns, guns and rifles in hand, jabbering questions, "What is it? What's going on? What's wrong?"

"Men," Gilliss said, "go get your horses. Everybody, go get your horses and bring them here."

They stood and stared.

"Why?" a bald lanky man in the rear asked. It was fifty-year-old Lum Booth, speaking from under a huge brushy mustache.

"Horse thieves are afoot," Gilliss said, not realizing his pun.

The crowd laughed.

"I mean they're at work, as we speak. Bring your horses here so we can guard them."

Booth looked at the post stable. "Where're your horses?"

"Stolen," Gilliss snapped. "That's what I'm trying to tell you."

"And you want to guard our horses?" another asked. There was murmuring and chuckling.

"I am Colonel Pierre Menard," Menard said, stepping forward to take charge. "I need to requisition four horses right now. Please, four of you, go get your horses and volunteer them into service for the state of Missouri and your country."

The men in their underwear nodded and scuffled away as though they intended to comply.

When after twenty minutes none had returned and were in fact leading their own horses into hiding, Menard was furious. "Who do these people think they are?"

"They're frontiersmen," Campbell said. "Our horses were stolen from under our noses and you expect they should trust us with theirs?" He shook his head. "Looks like we walk."

"To the Yoachum place?" Gilliss wailed. "It's seven damned miles!"

"Then let's get started," Campbell said. "You know the way, don't you, Gilliss?"

"We know the way," Philibert, said. "Perninia and I don't mind walking out with you."

"Good," said Campbell. "The more the merrier, but we need Gilliss to come along as a show of his cooperation."

Gilliss sensed a veiled threat. The offer of five hundred acres could be rescinded.

"Well, I'm certainly not walking seven miles for a pig in a poke," Menard chortled.

Campbell shrugged. "The word is out as to why you've come, Colonel, to drive the natives off their land . . . again. But if you feel safe alone here at the store . . ."

They locked the store and walked the seven miles, Campbell, Gilliss, Philibert, Perninia, and Menard.

Y

When James answered the door he was astonished. "Good lord," he said. "I didn't hear you ride up. Come in. Come in. This is truly a surprise." He turned. "Mekinges, come in here. We have guests." He peered out the door. "Where are your horses?"

Menard huffed, "As if you didn't know."

Campbell rolled his eyes apologetically. "They were stolen."

"Ah," James said. "The Osage, I bet. They love doing that. Come in. Sit down." He gestured to the bench in front of the fireplace. He studied Menard. "You mean you walked out here, the great Pierre Menard, himself? How funny."

Menard stared. "Why is that funny?"

"You probably don't remember when you threw me out of your place in St. Louis, do you?"

Menard shook his head.

"Well, I'll try to be a better host." He looked at Gilliss. "And William Gilliss walked seven miles for a visit to our humble abode? Must be serious."

"It is," Menard said.

Mekinges appeared with a smile. "Tea, anyone? Fresh mint tea? Just made it."

"Yes, please," they each answered.

"And my beautiful niece? Perninia, what are you doing with these queer fellows?"

Perninia smiled. "Hello, Uncle Jim."

"May we use your table?" Campbell asked.

"I've already seen your map of the new land of milk and honey," James said. "I don't think –"

"Give me another chance," Campbell said. "I know you have influence with your father-in-law, and I know we did not present this offer very well to the chiefs, but –"

"Offer?" James chortled. "It's an offer now?"

"No, it is not," Menard said. "It's a directive from the Federal Government."

"Colonel, please," Campbell said. It was too late.

James ignited. "A directive," he bellowed, "as in a command?"

Mekinges pinched his arm.

"How about I open this door, snap my fingers and make you disappear like a magic trick? You want to see a directive?"

"You want a war?" Menard countered.

James scratched behind his ear as though mulling the question. "If that's what it takes to be left alone by the likes of you, I guess I do."

Mekinges pinched his arm again. "No," she said. "We do not want a war."

"Thank you, Missus Yoachum," Campbell said as he spread the map across the table. "Look," he said, "the Kaw River Valley. Bigger river, bigger land, better farmland, more room, and many, many more buffalo. Thousands of Buffalo, as far as the eye can see."

"No," James said. "And I speak for Kikthawenund."

Campbell sighed. "The thing is, James, that if I report this to the governor, and I will have to, there will be a fully armed militia here within a month who will probably make sport of this situation, if you know what I mean?"

"I think I do."

"Well, then . . ."

"Comply or die. You're threatening a massacre."

"Why would you say that?"

"What if I came to you and said, Agent Campbell, the Chiefs have a new directive. All whites in this area must move back east of the Mississippi or our braves will make sport of you."

"You're being ridiculous, Yoachum," Menard said.

"Am I? Say soldiers come here to enforce your plan and we resist. They'll use guns, won't they? Cannons, maybe?"

Campbell shrugged. "Let's don't let it come to that."

James nodded. "No, let's not. You said if you report this."

"I'll have to."

James wagged his head. "Wouldn't I be the fool to allow you to make that report?"

"What do you mean?"

"I mean, when I open this door and yell 'palitun' . . . " James turned up his palms, a gesture indicating it would be out of his hands. "You will never again report anything to anybody."

Menard said, "Yoachum, are you threatening our lives?"

"You're threatening ours."

"Stop," Mekinges barked.

All eyes turned to hers.

"This is silly talk. Kikthawenund is not here. He make decision, not Jimyocum."

"But Honey," James started to protest.

"Chitwesi," she said. "Quiet." She studied the eyes of the whites. "You should know," she said, "my father prepare for this. Our Lenape braves play war games." She shook her head with discouragement. "Many peoples will die, red and white. Maybe will happen, I don't know. But I wonder first, if you could show The Captain this Kaw River Valley. Yes? No?"

"Yes," chirped Campbell. "Yes. An excellent idea Missus Yoachum." He turned to the Colonel. "Again, a woman makes the most sense." He looked back to Mekinges. "Would he? Would The Captain ride up for a look?"

"But Honey," James said, "you as much as anybody should realize this is just a ploy to shove your people into another box."

"Maybe Father want to look in box," she answered. "I don't know, but is his kishitèhe, not yours."

Campbell smacked his forehead. "We handled this all wrong. I'm sorry." He wasn't sure whose eyes to look into, James's or Mekinges's, so he lowered them to the floor. "It would be my honor to escort Captain Anderson and any of the other chiefs up to the new land, so they can see it for themselves." He looked at Mekinges. "Could you arrange this, Missus Yoachum?"

"No," James said.

"Maybe," said Mekinges. "Come back tomorrow, high sun."

They looked at each other. Campbell considered it a breakthrough.

"Can you loan us some horses?" Gilliss asked.

Mekinges shook her head with a sympathetic smile. "Horse loan you must get from Osage."

Campbell nodded with a long sigh and looked at Menard. "We'd better get started back."

"Oh, good lord," Menard said.

Perninia said, "Joe and I will just stay here then, if it's all right with you, Uncle Jim."

James looked at his niece. "Of course. Good idea. Avoid that long, dangerous walk back."

At the door Campbell and Menard looked back, trepidation in their eyes.

Mekinges chuckled. "You can believe me for safe walk."

"Thank you, Missus Yoachum," Campbell said. "We'll be back, noon tomorrow."

CHAPTER 24

June 1829

"The Great Spirit raised both the white man and the Indian. I think he raised the Indian first. He raised me in this land. It belongs to me. The white man was raised over the great waters and his land is over there. Since they crossed the sea I have given them room. There are now white people all around me. I have but a small spot of land left. The Great Spirit has told me to keep it."

– Mahpiuah Luta "Red Cloud," Ogalala Lakota

The border, which in all practicality meant the westernmost edge of white settlement, beyond which lay raw nature and savagery, was being moved again. This time, it was thought, for permanency. The western edge of civilization would stop at the Missouri border, and that would be that.

Of the Kaw River Valley, Captain William Clark, in 1804 wrote, "The country about the mouth of this river is very fine, teeming with elk, deer, buffalo and bear, plus a number of parrotqueets."

The Chiefs were Kikthawenund, George Ketchum, Suwanock, Killbuck, Black Beaver, John Quick and Captain Pike. They sat on horseback along with John Campbell and William Gilliss looking down on what was known as Kaw Point, the confluence of the Missouri river to the north and the Kaw (Kansas) to the south.

The Kaw tribe, having moved by their own volition to the land of Toh-pi-kah, had left the area fairly unoccupied.

Kikthawenund had known for some time that the Ozarks were over-hunted. Animals were scarce now, a problem for which he mostly blamed the likes of Pierre Menard, whose pelt and fur industry had become a subsidiary to The American Fur Company owned by John Jacob Astor, America's first millionaire. Everybody knew this. But The Captain also blamed the other whites that had swarmed into the Ozarks like locusts, and killed any bear, boar or buffalo they happened to come across, often just for the amusement of it.

After a two-day tour of the valley, they concluded, like Lewis and Clark twenty-five years earlier, that this was a good place. There were many springs, plentiful buffalo, fertile soil, and easy wooded hills.

Kikthawenund had no illusions that the border would actually stop at the Missouri line but agreed with his co-chiefs that for now, to avoid an Indian slaughter, this would be an excellent area to make a home for their people.

It was a well-judged decision.

In 1830 Congress passed the Indian Removal Act, which created "Indian Territory" and called for all tribes to be removed to the west of the Missouri border.

By this time, The Delaware Indian Reserve had officially been created.

Still, because of the Santa Fe Trail, they saw white people passing through their new land at least once a week. They considered demanding compensation for passage, like they heard the Comanche were doing, but concluded it might be more trouble than it was worth.

By the mid 1830s all the emigrant tribes had signed treaties relinquishing their Ozarks lands in exchange for lands in Kansas.

George Ketchum, born 1787, lived to be 100. He married Lucy and had five children – Lewis, Elizabeth, Charles, Mary and Jacob.

Kikthawenund, Captain William Anderson, Chief and protector of the Turkey Clan of the Delaware Indians, born in 1749, died of chicken pox in 1838.

Two years before his death, he did make one return trip to the Ozarks along with his wife and four sons. They went back for two affairs, a party and a funeral.

CHAPTER 25

Because they agreed to move peacefully the Delaware were allowed one month to leave the Ozarks at their own pace. Upon completion of the relocation they would be granted a deed to the Kaw River Valley making it theirs forever, not counting the piece of land promised to William Gilliss.

Kikthawenund appreciated this but with his usual circumspection, divided his braves into three groups; an advance group to deal with whatever unseen threat might lurk in the new land; a journey group, adaptable to the needs of the migrants along the chosen route; and a rear guard to protect the village, since many would choose to make two or three trips.

Gilliss was the only one with wagons. He had two. The Lenape had five community mules, which could carry a lot but not enough. There were those who had accumulated some things, which they did not wish to leave behind, including cages of white chickens and some very fine domesticated hogs. Metal tools and glass mirrors were now also highly treasured, and then there were the elderly who required painstaking special assistance.

Although most of the tribe made the trip on foot and departed only once, it took weeks to get everything and everybody moved with satisfaction to Kansas.

When the rear guard broke camp late afternoon, Friday, July 17th, Mekin-ges wept softly, recalling her coming-of-age years in the now ceded village.

It was a hot evening as she sat with James in the first cabin he built for her, which her father had turned into an office for confidential conversations and for smoking, and she wondered aloud if they shouldn't be moving to Kansas along with everybody else.

"We can't, Mekinges," James said. "You know that."

She sighed. "The silver is a curse."

"Of course it is. Those skeletons down there could tell you that."

She started to ask about talking bones but was stopped by the sound of hoof beats. Four, maybe five horses were galloping their way.

"White men," Mekinges said.

"Yeah. Let's hide, see what they're doing."

"Why hide?"

"Do you know who they are? What if they're coming to shoot stray Indians?"

"Stray Indians?" she thought. She started to squawk at this ridiculous notion but James covered her mouth and pulled her down, below the cabin's window.

They watched as five horsemen entered the village from the East. Two of the riders they did not recognize. The third was Francis Moon, the fourth was Joe Philibert and the fifth was, much to the dismay of both James and Mekinges, Jacob.

Mekinges drew a sharp breath. "Your son."

James rolled his eyes. "Don't start. Please."

"What are they doing?"

"Scavenging, I guess," James whispered as the riders strode by.

It was a new word for Mekinges. "I do not know –"

"Looking for stuff, anything of value left behind, like vultures."

She wanted to ask why they would be looking for vultures but realized it was no time for humor. "That is not bad. Nature need vultures to clean up."

"But they're not looking inside the wigwams and they rode right on by this cabin, didn't they?" He rose to watch, to assess the course of the riders. It was obvious. The clay kilns, where he and Mekinges had first discussed the possibility of their marriage, where the Lenape silversmiths pursued their craft and made things, beautiful silver things, for their people.

Mekinges knew too. "No silver there," she said.

"But, Honey," James lamented, "it's proof that there is silver somewhere near here. They see those kilns, you think they're going to stop looking?"

"Everybody already know," she said. "People already looking. I don't think father care no more."

"Well, I do."

"Why?"

"Because he trusted me with the secret."

"But he's gone. Everybody is gone to new land where no silver danger is. We should go too."

"No," James said. "I'm going to guard that silver with my life."

"Why?" Mekinges asked.

"Because it's all ours now. It's all ours."

Mekinges turned to study her husband's face, a shadow of worry casting across on her own.

CHAPTER 26

Prior to the War of 1812 the Ozarks Hills were generally called Osage Country by the whites in Ste. Genevieve who had little interest in the area.

The first whites to visit the area were French voyageurs in 1785, who had heard tales of De Soto finding gold and silver in the territory.

Returning, they reported plenty of lead indications but none of the precious metals. "It is a land very rough, mountainous, and hard to travel through," they said, which incited little interest for anyone else to bother with it.

That same year, back east, Thomas Jefferson proposed that the United States begin minting a silver dollar coin. The struggling young country had no U.S. mint and was using Spanish eight-reale coins for currency.

After the Secretary of the Treasury, Alexander Hamilton, presented Congress with a report on a Mint and a monetary system, a dollar coin with the approximate weight and purity of the Spanish coin, the statute of the Mint Act authorized the striking of silver dollar denomination coins.

The first U.S. Silver Dollars were struck in 1794. Although everyone recognized the U.S. coins as inferior to the Spanish coins, the dies for striking them, and the quality controls, kept improving through 1803. Then, for a jumble of confusing reasons none were minted in 1804, or for many years following.

The Osage were in southwest Missouri, the Kickapoo, and then the

Delaware, and life was good for the Native Americans with plenty of game, fresh water springs, and caves.

Eventually the white men did come and now the Indians were displaced once again.

Not James Yoachum though, or his wife Mekinges, who stayed and lived above their secret mine-cave.

In the meantime the Spanish, in Mexico, wealthy with silver, coined their silver dollars, some illicit, and many of those made their way north through long distance traders like William Becknell, or came to Missouri by way of the Santa Fe Trail.

Missouri, having no official bank, thanks to Senator Thomas Hart Benton who for political purposes used his power to prevent re-chartering of the St. Louis bank, was flooded with wildcat paper money from other states.

Missourians learned the hard way that many of the paper notes floating around as currency were issued by banks that did not have the gold or silver capitol to back them up. When too many of the notes came back to be redeemed, the banks simply locked their doors and went out of business.

July 1831

James and Solomon Yoachum were doing their "squaw" work, weeding their field of corn, beans, and squash – what the Lenape called "the three sisters" – while they were discussing a new religion which was rumored to be causing problems to the north.

"Mormons, I think they're called," Sol said.

"A new religion?" James asked. "How could there be a new religion?"

"What I heard was, and I know this sounds crazy, but they think Missouri is their promised land."

"Well, that's what the Lenape thought," James said with a flip of his hand.

"Well, yeah, but that was from the Government. These people think their claim comes directly from the Almighty Lord."

"A new religion," James mused. "How does something like that get started?"

"I have no idea, but people don't like it."

James started to reply but stopped at the sound of hoof beats, pounding through the peach orchard hard and fast.

"It's Jake," Sol said.

James nodded. "Yeah.

"Wonder what's got him all worked up."

A moment later on a sweat-lathered horse, eighteen-year-old Jake stopped in a flurry of hooves and turf. "Something bad at the trading post. I could have handled it, but Aunt Mary told me to come and get you."

"What is it?" Sol asked.

"Lum Booth says he's going to hang Philibert. Aunt Mary says hurry."

"Let's go, Jim."

James bent back to the soil. "Lum Booth wouldn't hurt a fly. You go. I got work to do."

Sol, disappointed, shook his head then swung up behind Jake. "To my horse."

CHAPTER 27

Riding into the compound, Sol saw a rabble of men gathered around the porch of the store shouting and cursing. He dismounted and shoved his way through the mob to the porch, then stepped up and turned to face them. "Whoa, whoa, whoa," he said, raising his palms. "What is going on here?" He looked into the face of the man Jake mentioned. "Mister Booth, my wife is inside this building and you fellows are scaring her."

"Read them signs," Booth said, pointing past Sol.

Sol turned. Two parchments were tacked to the door, the top one with one word, CLOSED. Beneath that, a scribbled notice too lengthy to read at the moment. He knocked on the door. "Mary? Mary, it's Sol. Let me in."

"We're scared," she shouted through the wood.

Sol turned back. "Lum?"

Lum Booth nodded.

"It's all right. Let me in." The door cracked open. Sol slid through.

Mary grabbed him with an embrace. "Thank God, you're here."

"What's going on?"

Philibert rushed in from the back room. "Sol, you got to help me. They want to string me up, and this isn't my fault. This is not my fault."

"You can't just, out of the blue, close the only trading post, Joe. What are you thinking?"

"It's not my trading post, is it? I don't follow orders from myself."

Sol squinted. "That's a queer thing to say, Joe, but . . . you're talking about Menard?"

Philibert nodded. "My orders came by carrier yesterday. He's got a new agreement with the French Union for all the fur business. I'm supposed to close the post immediately for reorganization."

"Reorganization?"

"He wants to go back to pelts, skins and furs only. That's what he said. No more money."

"He doesn't want money?" Sol scratched his head. "Who doesn't want money?"

"He says it's no good, the paper money."

Sol walked behind the counter, grabbed a bottle of his wife's peach brandy and poured a glass. "The paper money," he repeated, thinking out loud. He took a sip. "I'll tell you what's no good . . . the situation the Colonel has put you in, here. Those people outside, they need things, and they think you're in charge now, since Gilliss left."

"But I'm not."

"Yeah, you are, Joe. Right now, you are in charge. You'd better open the door."

"But Menard . . . "

". . . will be just fine. What's he going to do, fire you? I'd rather be fired than hanged."

Philibert nodded. "You're right."

Sol took another sip then set the glass on the counter. "Let me go out and explain the situation, that it's not your doing, that as a good man, you're going to overrule the Colonel, because, by God, that is no way to treat a fellow's neighbors. I'll tell them to stock up because the post is going to be closed for awhile for reorganizing and it's not your fault."

Philibert fingered his forehead. "Yeah. Yeah. Thanks."

"While I'm doing that, you unlock this door, get behind the counter and act like . . . I don't know . . . act like a friend, who's on their side. You are, aren't you?

"Yes, I am."

"Mary, you come out with me. I don't want you in here. Where's Perninia?"

"Here, Uncle Sol," she said, stepping out of the back room.

"You come with me and Mary."

She looked at Philibert. "I guess I should stay with my husband. Looks like it's going to be a busy day here."

"I'll stay too," Jake said. Perninia had let him in through the rear entrance.

Sol didn't like it but resisted insisting. He nodded. "I know what it is," he said. "It's that gol-gummed American Fur Company. John Jacob Astor is making all the rules now."

y

When the mob of men charged in, they looted the store. If their money wasn't good enough for Menard, why bother checking out with it? Grab all you can and skedaddle was the credo of the hour.

CHAPTER 28

In the hill house, around a bottle of peach brandy, James, Mekinges, Sol, and Mary sat to discuss the situation.

"An exclusive arrangement with the French Union," Sol said. He splayed his palms. "What is that?"

"Damned dirty French," Mary said putting a cup to her mouth.

"Well," James said, "There are so many different bank notes floating around Missouri, Menard doesn't trust any of it. Why should he? He's a bastard, but he's a business bastard. A shrewd one."

"Filthy French," Mary said to no one.

"It's the American Fur Company, I'm sure of it," Sol said, "but that millionaire, Astor, wants to keep his dealings in the shadows."

"Maybe this'll make the whites move back east," James said.

Sol shook his head. "Nobody moves East, Jim." He pinched the bridge of his nose. "Those people worked hard for that money. All their pigs and corn and ..."

"Paper money," James said. "It doesn't work. I've known that for years." He snickered. "People are so stupid."

This irked Sol. "Jim, when I stepped out to face that crowd, I promised them that I would come up with a solution."

James's eyes widened. "Hmm, interesting." He leaned forward, amused. "Tell me, little brother, what are you going to do?"

"I don't know but you should have seen them, the look in their eyes. They weren't the people I thought I knew. They were getting ready to burn that store down and punish Philibert, I really think so."

"But they didn't."

"No, they just rammed their way in and stole everything. It was bad, Jim. Shameful really. I don't know what's going to happen now."

"Let me tell you about the French," Mary said, her head beginning to wobble.

"We know about the French, Honey," Sol said.

She took another gulp of Brandy. "Their buckskin shirts and breeches are black from smoke, greasy from suet, they smell terrible, their language is obscene, they can't read or write and they stink. They're filthy."

"Don't drink up all our product, Honey," Sol said. "Save some for the store."

"Why? So the French can get it all?" Mary said, her words slurred.

"You just said you were going to find a solution," James said to Sol.

"Yeah, well, I think you and I need to talk about that tomorrow."

"Sol, I got to tell you, I really don't give a fart about what happens to that store." He leaned back. "Sorry."

"Really?" Sol nailed his brother with a hard stare. "I hear tell, you needed that store one night to save Winona's life and I hear tell it was Philibert who rode into harm's way with you to bring medicine."

James wanted to say, "People talk too much," but he was suddenly tongue-tied by the memory of that night, and how good it felt the next morning when he was considered a hero by the whole village, especially Kikthawenund.

Mekinges nodded. "True," she said.

James supposed that he did owe the trading post some concern for that life-changing occurrence. His shoulders shifted into a conceding shrug. "What's your solution, Sol?"

"Tomorrow, outside. I'd rather you and I be the only two people on earth to discuss what I'm thinking."

James's eyebrows went up. "I trust my wife. Don't you trust yours?"

Sol shook his head with dismay. "Why do you say things like that? Why are you always so anxious to stir up a storm? Of course, I trust my wife, but tomorrow, just for tomorrow, we need a brother-to-brother heart-to-heart. All right?"

"Yes," Mekinges said, nodding. "That is good plan. Brothers together alone is always good plan."

Why did she always take Sol's side? James wondered.

y

When James stepped out on the porch the next morning he could see Sol at the edge of their field turning over the bobcat scat they had placed around the crops to discourage rabbits and squirrels.

Stirring it from time to time would refresh the threatening scent, but they would need more soon.

Sol looked up as his brother approached. "Morning, Jim."

"Pretty dry, isn't it?" James said.

"Good for another week I reckon. I'm almost done."

James picked up a stick and started to help. "I can hardly wait to hear your plan."

Sol, scratched his head, looked at his brother. "You're trying to sound sarcastic but I think you already know, don't you?"

James looked to the peach orchard and took a contemplative breath. "I guess I do." He twisted his lips. "The question is, how?"

Sol smiled, reached into his pocket and pulled out an eight-real, a Spanish silver dollar. "Don't forget, Brother, I'm a smithy." He handed the coin to James.

James studied it, then looked up. "We could do this?"

"You'll see in your Bible that coins have been made for thousands of years, so, I reckon we can."

"Hmm."

"The trick is to make them uniform in size and weight. It's called lost wax casting."

"Lost wax?"

"Never mind. I'll show you. I can make the castings with my tools."

"I'll need to get Kikthawenund's permission."

"There's no time, Jim. Get his daughter's permission. Should we go ask her now?"

James knew how that would go. She would say yes. If the evil silver could be turned into a good thing for everybody, of course she would say yes. "And in the meantime?" James asked.

Sol had thought about this all night. "We chip up a bar tonight, take it to Philibert in the morning. We take it in bits, little pieces about an eighth of the size of one of these Mexican coins. We say, 'Here Joe, here's real silver. Eight of these bits add up to a dollar. Weigh them and see. Menard will love you for this. When the store is restocked and people come in to beg for supplies, you give them what they need and tell them the Yoachum brothers have already paid the cost.'"

"The Yoachum Brothers have already paid the cost," James repeated, imagining the scene.

"Yes."

"Good Lord! This will make me the king of commerce in the Ozarks."

Sol rolled his eyes. "Don't get carried away, King James. God only knows how this will work out."

James slapped Sol on the back. "It's a grand idea, Brother. Grand."

"The first thing we need to do is clean the silver, get the guano and dirt off those bars."

"The women can do that," James said.

Sol shook his head. "I'm going to move Mary and Jake to town for a while. They can give Joe and Perninia a break. It could get dangerous around here."

James spread his hands to indicate an unspoken problem. "Your wife is a little too overly fond of the bottle," he said. "You do know that."

Sol glared. "I would slug you if you weren't so ignorant." He shook his head, turned and walk away.

James followed.

They stopped at the giant white oak at the Southeast tip of the property.

Sol told James about Mary's two miscarriages.

James hadn't known.

"Twice, James. You know what that does to a woman? It grieved her into doubting God, and her father's a preacher! It grieved her into trying alcohol for the first time. It still grieves her something terrible. I shouldn't have to explain to you how grief can drive a person over the edge."

James recoiled.

"We would both love to have a child and we both think you're an ungodly fool for not wanting yours."

James went vacant.

"So, I'll thank you to mind your own wife. I'll mind mine."

CHAPTER 29

Three weeks after their decision in the field, the brothers were in the smoky cave standing beside a clay crucible that Sol had made to melt the silver. He had also made, from the same clay, casting trays.

James, after adding a dozen new oil lamps to the walls, had built three long wooden tables as instructed by his brother. Sand was spread evenly across the top of each surface.

They raised the crucible of molten silver by two wooden handles and grunted as they carried it to the casting table, their faces shining with sweat. They poured the molten silver into the casting tray, then took a breather as they watched the castings congeal.

"Now we run it through the roller," Sol said, "to make sure the thickness is just right." Sol had no idea that just right meant 27.07 grams of weight for each coin with a diameter of 39.5 Millimeters. He had only the one Spanish coin to judge by.

The roller was another contrivance he had fashioned from two lead pipes, their original purpose being to drain water from the black smith's shop in Delaware Town.

A turning crank was attached to roll a sheet of the soft silver into a uniform flatness.

Their first try was disappointing, way too thick. Over the course of another week, Sol worked every night to tweak the mechanics of the operation to near perfection.

Another thing they needed to work on was ventilation. There was a chimney, the flue of which James had fashioned to enter the bedroom stove from the bottom so it couldn't be seen, but he never imagined he'd actually use it. "There was a time," he explained to Sol, "when we had nothing to do here at all. Nothing, except guard the place, so I built a few things."

Sol coughed, "It's not going to be enough."

James coughed and spat black phlegm to the floor. "I thought most of the smoke would breeze on up and out the other end of the cave."

During the day, Mekinges worked in the field.

Mary had moved into town with Jake to tend to their little peach brandy business, some bottles labeled for social purposes, some labeled as medicinal. The remaining Indians in the area knew to always purchase the medicine.

Sol worked on the design of the molding, using bee's wax. He thought James would fight him on the idea of shortening their name to the simpler spelling of YOCUM – it would make the minting cleaner and easier – but James liked the idea. He wondered if maybe the letter K would make the name even clearer but they decided to keep the simpler C.

The wax molding was then dipped into a soup of a watery clay mixture, left to dry, then dipped again and again until the clay dies were about a half inch thick, then kilned into a rock-hard die to be a negative copy of the wax design.

They knew their coins would not be as sophisticated as the Pesos, which had four or five words and a profile of some king or another along with the year, but they didn't care. They correctly reckoned that folks wouldn't care how fancy the coins looked as long as they were acceptable as money.

At the end of the line the brothers would inspect the forged blanks for inconsistencies. The heavy ones were filed down, the light or misshapen ones were tossed back into the crucible.

Once they figured out how to press the soft silver into uniformly circular planchets, they gently stamped each coin with the negative clay dies. Both sides would look the same, "YOCUM" on top, a "1" in the center, and "SILVER DOLLAR" on the bottom.

They rolled each coin to make the edges slightly higher than its surface, which was painstaking but worth it, James decided, because it made them feel more "official."

"They don't have to be perfect," Sol said, coughing.

James thought for a moment. "Yes, they do," he said, holding up the Spanish coin. "As close as possible, anyway."

"Well, we've done that, big brother," Sol said. "Come morning we can check them in sunlight."

𝑦

With skin and garb blackened from head to toe and their lungs aching from the long night's work in the smoky cave, the brothers were exhausted and yet boyishly giddy as they sat at the main table, each holding a coin.

Mekinges served a breakfast of chicken eggs with a mash of boiled tomatoes and potatoes. "You happy, Jimyocum?" she asked.

He looked up. "Why do you ask, Honey?"

"You seem happy."

"Look at this, Mekinges." He handed her a Yocum Silver Dollar. "What do you think?"

Mekinges studied it, then nodded and smiled. "Look like real money," she said.

"Then yes, I'm happy. We just made money. Made it, our own money from right out of the ground."

"What you buy with your made money? We don't need anything."

Sol picked a tomato seed from his teeth. "Here's the plan, Mekinges," he said wiping his chin with a black sleeve. "We buy whatever anyone wants to sell."

James had had this conversation with her one night in bed but she didn't seem to grasp it. Maybe he'd been too tired to explain it clearly. Now was the time. "You're right, Mekinges. We don't need anything but the people around here do."

"But you don't like the peoples around here."

"I don't, true enough, but if they've got nothing to barter with, hides and such, they'll start turning on each other, robbing, looting, maybe shooting each other."

This agitated Mekinges. "Shooting each other? For what?"

James shrugged. "A pig, a bushel of apples . . ."

"Silver," Sol said.

James nodded. "So we make these trade coins to keep the peace. He who controls the money controls the people."

"They're going to be looking for our little foundry, though," Sol said.

James nodded. "I've got an idea about that. You know how the French trick the birds out of the skies?"

"Decoys."

James nodded. "We dig a couple false tunnels that look like entryways to something, then connect a tripwire to a scatter gun. After two or three nosey neighbors go back to town with a foot blown off, well, that should put an end to the snooping."

"That's evil," Sol said.

James shrugged. "Takes evil to purge evil."

"Says who?"

"Deuteronomy, I think."

"What you do with things you buy from people?" Mekinges wanted to know.

It was a question for which the brothers were unprepared. They looked at each other and laughed. "Well," James said, "I guess we're going to have to build ourselves a depot."

Sol nodded. "We can hire workers and pay them with our first coins. We can hire Jake as the manager."

James shook his head. "I don't trust him."

Sol rolled his eyes. "You know you're going to lose him, Jim, and that would be a heartbreaking thing for me. Jake's as smart as a whip and he's family and we could use him now."

"Lose him?"

"John Campbell loves the kid. Wants to take him to Springfield."

"Illinois?"

"No. Half a day north. Didn't you catch Winona's horse up there? New settlement. Wilson wants to name it Springfield after his hometown in Massachusetts. He and Campbell are building up there."

"What's he want Jake for?"

"I told you. He loves the boy. Everybody does. Jake's going to have opportunities everywhere he turns, but you know what? He would trade away his ears if he could use them just once to hear you call him son, just to hear you call him your son one time."

James gave a needled sigh. "I'm going to the river." He got up from the table and headed for the door. "I feel like a lump of coal."

Sol shrugged. "Yeah, wait, I'll go with you. Thanks for the breakfast, Mekinges. It was real good."

She was staring at her husband. "You are hard man, Jimyocum," she said. "Someday, when too late, you will hurt big."

"Yeah, yeah," James mumbled as he left the house.

PART FIVE

They counted not their own lives dear;
They challenged death and pain;
They gathered wives and little ones
and sailed across the main,
That they might rear an altar to Freedom's God, and then
They builded in the wilderness, a home for God's free men

–Anonymous

CHAPTER 30

November 1831

The depot, or storehouse, as most folks called it, was built near the abandoned village, beside the river, and it was a success, or even a miracle in the minds of some, who traveled miles by land and water to bring personal belongings to trade for Yocum Silver Dollars.

Kikthawenund had not only approved of the plan, but sent two of his sons back to help. Sarcoxie and Shawnanuk watched over their homes, gardens and the peach orchard, while their sister and the Yoachums were away.

By the second month of business the brothers had furniture, art, glassware, wooden barrels, lumber, sacks of grain and piles of pelts, making them, by material standards, the wealthiest men in the Ozarks.

You never knew what would come in from one day to the next and they had no idea what to do with all their new worldly goods.

They considered allowing the people to keep their things after the transactions were made – they never really wanted all these things, but Mekinges advised that, somehow, this idea would lead to a bad outcome. She reckoned, like her father had, that the prospect of something for nothing would bring out the worst in people. The brothers trusted her instincts.

While constantly stacking and rearranging their new possessions, James and Sol were mindful of the position Mekinges was in, stationed as the head clerk at the front of the store, negotiating with the hopeful sellers.

When a monger wanted five dollars, she would offer three and invariably the seller would leave happy with four. But it was a dangerous occupation for a woman, sitting beside a sack of silver. Anything could happen. For this reason, the brothers hired four Osage men as watchmen and if necessary, enforcers.

The braves' simple instructions were to stay invisible, protect Mekinges and prevent robberies. Anyone caught committing a crime was to be dealt with in the Osage way, which would be best that the Yoachums not be made aware of. The Indians understood.

On a warm day, by November standards, Friday the 27th, a man named Alf Bolin, Sr., arrived at the depot to sell a Negro slave.

Mekinges rejected him outright with a lecture about human beings not being chattel. She told him that he should be ashamed of himself, to get off the property and never come back.

Bolin cursed her, and turned to walk away. When the African hesitated, Bolin picked up a stick and whacked his property across the side of his head.

Although the black man barely flinched, Mekinges caught the pleading in his eyes. "How much you want for this man?" she asked.

"He's not a man. He's a nigger. A good one too, who could easily bring five hundred dollars at the courthouse auction in Springfield, but I'll take two hundred, cash on the barrel head."

"One hundred," Mekinges said.

"One-fifty," Bolin said. "Not a dollar less."

Mekinges would have given all she had for the African man's release but what kind of door would that be opening? "What is his name?"

"August."

"One hundred, twenty-five is top offer for August. You don't take it, you go away."

Bolin bristled. He looked around. "How about I keep young Augie here, and take my fair price anyway, Squaw?" He made another quick scan of the area for possible witnesses, and missed the faint smile that crossed the squaw's face. Bolin tugged open his coat to reveal a pistol lodged under his belt.

Mekinges was not impressed. "Back down to one hundred now, Top price. No more."

He put a hand to the pistol. "You are one irksome bitch, you know that?"

Mekinges scrunched her face to consider that.

"Two hundred was more than fair," Bolin snarled, "but you've made me mad. I'll take three hundred now, and I shall have it." He pulled the gun. "Or else."

Mekinges could whistle a fair imitation of a Goldfinch, which she did.

Bolin was puzzled.

"Then you get 'or-else'," she said, hoping the guards heard the whistle and were alert for their first confrontation.

They were.

She saw one, three, then four. It was a déjà vu moment as she remembered the day Willie Whitestone had forced his way into her home. She knew the Lenape braves wouldn't have permanently harmed the men, not without her father's orders, but these Osage were different, and James paid them well to do whatever it was they did to their enemies. Now, Mekinges began to feel sorry for Mister Alf Bolin Senior, as foul a man as he was.

Mekinges considered not mentioning the incident to James and Sol, but even in the back of the building, they could hear the man's cries for mercy. They rushed to the front.

Sol decided Mekinges had handled herself righteously.

"What do we do with this fellow?" James asked, bending to release the Negro from his shackles.

"You can go now," Mekinges said to the man.

"Yeah," James said. "You are free now, Sir. Go do whatever you want."

August looked doubtful. "Where could I go? Somebody will catch me and knife out my giblets?" He rubbed his wrists. "Could I work for you?"

Sol turned to James. "Your decoy trap idea? We ain't done nothing on that, and I sure think we should."

James nodded toward to the black man. "Can you dig, August?"

"Like a mole, Sir. I hope you'll call me Augie."

"All right, Augie," James said, "but you will not be a slave. You are free, and we will pay you." He extended his hand. "Augie, call me Jim. This is my wife, Mekinges, and this ugly fellow here is my brother, Sol."

Augie couldn't believe it. "I don't understand."

165

"Well, you'll catch on," Sol said. "You hungry?"

Augie smiled. "I is always hungry, Sir."

"Honey," James said to Mekinges, "when the braves come back from their, uh, chores, take a couple with you, take Augie home, and . . ."

"Yes," Mekinges shrieked. "I fix Augie food and make nice bed in barn. I can tell, he good person. My brothers always want to meet black man." She giggled, grabbed Augie by the hand and pulled him out of the depot.

As he was led away, Augie raised his eyes to heaven. "Thank you, Jesus."

CHAPTER 31

March 1832

Delaware Town was bustling. Thanks to the Yoachum brothers, the settlers were happy, well-to-do homesteaders, unaware of the outside world's money problems.

When James and Sol came to town on Monday, the 12th, they were greeted by a throng and heralded like heroes. The brothers were now household names whose preeminence in the community was celebrated like royalty.

Sol whispered to James, "This is not right." To his dismay, he saw that James was enjoying the adulation, nodding and bowing.

Philibert came out of the store. Sol thought he made things worse. "Ladies and gentlemen, make way for the first white man in the Ozarks."

Sol stepped onto the porch. "Don't be doing that, Joe. The man's self-importance is a getting out of hand."

"Aw, he deserves it. Colonel Menard is as happy as a French clam, the homesteaders are happy as otters, and . . ."

"So everything's all right?"

"Everything's good."

"Where's Mary?"

Philibert lowered his eyes. "Oh, she went out for lunch."

Sol pulled his watch from his trousers. "Ten after four." He shook his head. "The Crow?"

Philibert nodded.

Sol walked around James's admirers.

Y

In the doorway of the Cranky Crow, he stood for a moment to study the room. Noisy fools, he thought. Blasphemers, lovers of mockery and gambling. Don't these people have responsibilities? He shook his head with disgust, and then spotted his wife. She sat at a table playing cards with three strangers. Approaching from behind, he put his hand on her shoulder.

She turned. "Honeycake, hi. What are you doing in town?"

"Let's go."

"Wait. I was just telling these fellows about you." She turned her head. "Gentlemen this is my husband. Scoot over. Make room."

Sol looked into their scowls and gave each man a polite nod. "Mary, aren't you supposed to be watching the stand?"

"Perninia's got it. It's a slow day and I've got a good hand here, Sol, I think." She raised her cards for him to see.

"The richest man in Missouri," the biggest one said, "and you won't play one hand? Come on."

"Sol, meet Dave Titsworth. He thinks I'm pretty."

"Mary, let's go."

"She's in the middle of a game of euchre, rich man," another player said with a challenging glare.

Sol sighed. "Boys, this is embarrassing enough already. Please don't do this."

"Don't do what?" James asked, suddenly behind the men.

The strangers turned to see a surprisingly large man.

"You must be the Indian brother-in-law," Titsworth said. "Got the same features as your brother here, who's trying to interrupt our game." He stroked his beard. "I don't appreciate that."

"Mary, what have you been telling these men," James demanded.

"Yeah, that's my Indian brother," Sol said. "Careful. He hates white folks."

"Well, what do you know?" Titsworth said. He laid down his cards. "I hate Indians."

His companions chortled.

"Mary, I asked you a question," James said. "What have you been telling these . . . bums?"

"Private conversation, Chief," said Titsworth.

Sol grabbed Mary by the arm and pulled her from her chair.

One of the men rose to throw a punch but was easily stopped by James who snapped the man's wrist with a cracking sound. He fell to the floor and wailed with pain.

A hush fell over the room. Chair legs scraped against the floor as some strained for a better view. Others stood to watch. A few dared to gather around.

Titsworth stood, pulled open his vest and put a hand on his pistol.

"I'll tell you what, Mister Titsworth," Sol said, pushing Mary behind him. "How would you like to make an easy hundred dollars?"

James rolled his eyes. "Now what?"

"You know, Brother, your favorite game."

Titsworth dipped his head with a suspicious glare. "A hundred dollars? For what?"

Sol turned toward the bar. With one arm he shoved a drunk off his perch, grabbed the stool and pulled it to the game table. "See what I did there? I knocked that fellow off his stool. If you can do that to my brother, I'll give you a hundred dollars."

"I don't get it," Titsworth said.

"I'm going to sit my Indian brother – by the way, his name is Jim – on this stool. If you can knock him off this stool, I'll give you a hundred dollars. You don't get that?"

"What's the catch?" Titsworth asked.

"No catch," James said, recalling how he and Sol had seen their father pull this trick when they were boys.

"Oh, wait, we need a stool for you," said Sol. "Wouldn't be fair if you were standing."

Another stool appeared immediately.

"Here you go Mister Titsworth. You adjust your stool however you want it, next to this ugly blond Indian here. You take a swing, knock him off, and take your money."

Titsworth smiled as he positioned himself on the stool. "You people must be crazy."

"We are," James said, as he seated himself on the first stool. He sighed as though he were bored. "All right, your turn first."

Titsworth's brow furrowed. "What do you mean?"

"Well," Sol said, "you get the first punch."

"Wait," said Titsworth, trying to imagine how James might avoid his swing.

"I won't duck," James said, "if that's what you're thinking. You punch me as hard as you can. If I manage to stay on the stool," he shrugged, "well, then it'll be my turn."

"Right," said Sol. "The first person to knock the other one off, wins. If you get killed, Titsworth, you will lose the easiest hundred bucks ever, but don't even think about the last fellow."

"The last fellow?"

"I knocked his nose bone up into his stupid brain," James said, folding his arms. "Gave him first swing too. You going to play or not?"

Sweat began to bead on Titsworth's brow. "Yeah, I'm going to play. Stand back, everybody. I need some swinging room." He balled his right hand into a fist, rubbed it, then blew on it as if for luck. Then he looked into the face of James Yoachum.

What he saw was a calm man with a sly smile, daring him with eyes like blue ice. His heart started to thump.

The crowd began to chant. "Swing, swing, swing."

"I'm waiting," James taunted.

Titsworth took a deep breath then looked around into the faces of the goading gawkers. He thought about his nose bone being shoved into his brain. Every skull he'd ever seen never had a nose bone, just a hole, but he put a finger to the bridge of his nose and it did feel hard like a bone. Who were these people? Why should he risk his life to impress these drunken idiots? Maybe he was drunk. He could do this for sure if he were completely sober like his opponent apparently was, which suddenly seemed unfair. Too unfair.

"A hundred dollars," James said, teasingly.

"Oh, what the hell?" Titsworth said. "What are we fighting over? Who started this? That woman?" He pointed to Mary. "She's just a drunken floozy anyway."

James nodded. "I agree."

It was Sol who threw the first punch – a right hook into James's jaw, which did knock his brother off the stool.

CHAPTER 32

September 1832

The brothers worked the farm that summer without speaking to each other unless necessary for business. The subject of Mary, who mostly stayed in town with Perninia and Joe Philibert was avoided.

They had to make more silver dollars because those which were spent at the James River Trading Post, most of them, made their way east to Colonel Menard, who melted them down for his own purposes, but it was surprising, Philibert reported, how well the local system worked with homesteaders buying from, and bartering with, each other.

The new arrivals brought merchandise to the depot and Mekinges, judging their need by appearance and mannerisms, was generous to a fault.

She and Augie worked the warehouse under the watchful eyes of the Osage guards whom she had grown to like and respect. They in turn felt the same about their employers, although it was obvious the two brothers were not on good terms.

Things were so peaceful, it was decided that Sarcoxie and Shawnanuk could return to the Kaw River Valley, and Augie would manage the farm.

One late September afternoon, a fog settled on the land and shrouded the gold and red of the trees in a beautiful net of mist, enveloping the farm in what looked to James like a painting he'd seen as a boy in the Cahokia courthouse, entitled, Landscape with Saint Francis in Ecstasy. He sat on the porch recalling how he had wondered how anyone could paint such a thing – haze, you could see through, with all its shimmering facets of light. He wondered again now, how can bristles on the end of a stick create such gossamer beauty?

Through the mist, across the field he saw the form of his brother sitting on his own porch, and then someone else stepped out to sit beside him. Mary.

His wife's voice startled him. "She is not enemy, Jimyocum."

James turned and sighed. "I never said she was."

"You act like it."

"I think she drinks more brandy than she sells. I know she's got an excuse for it, but darn it, if brandy gets into a fight with a secret, which one do you think wins?"

"No," Mekinges said. "We would know by now. Six full moons go by, everything still good. Everything but pride of brothers that lead to poison spirit." She squeezed his shoulders with loving hands. "I don't want my husband's spirit more sick. Already too sick from son who go away. Your heart is sick."

"My heart is fine."

Mekinges shook her head. "You still hide from your own feelings."

James scratched his jaw, then finally said, "Go tell them they can come over if they want to."

"No," she said, with a hard pinch to his arm. "You go there. I go with you. Night is beautiful. We go share with family." She stepped in front of him, grabbed his arm and tugged him from the chair. "Now is time, Jimyocum."

The surrounding trees were now filled with the screeching of birds. James felt sure they were mockingbirds.

CHAPTER 33

October 1834

When in 1834 the United States began minting silver dollars again, they used the same die they made for 1804. The new coins were actually stamped with a date thirty years past.

y

James and Sol were unaware of this as they worked strenuously in the mine minting their own silver dollars.

If their records were correct they had, in the last five years, stamped nearly ten thousand coins. Beneath the black film of carbon-coating on their hair, the golden curls were now, fittingly, touched with silver.

Finishing a night of thirty-seven more coins, Sol nonchalantly said, "Oh, by the way, did I mention that Jake is coming down on Wednesday?"

James headed for the ladder. "Is he still in Springfield?"

"Yeah, doing real good up there."

"What's he coming back for?"

"His birthday, Brother," Sol said. He saw James stiffen. "Twenty-three. Can you believe it?"

James climbed the ladder.

"You know, Jim," Sol continued, "aside from how you've treated her son, Ruth must be very proud of you. Look at the life you've made for . . .

not just yourself, but everybody in these hills."

James pushed the floor door up and open. "Everybody but the Indians."

"They're doing fine. Mekinges says they love the Kaw River Valley."

The brothers emerged topside, blackened from head to toe. Mekinges handed them rags and closed the lid to the cave.

"Some of Jake's friends are coming down for the party."

"Party?" James said. He turned to Sol.

"The birthday party. Jake's been to Kansas a couple times to visit his old pals. Some of them are coming down for his party, which Mary and I will be hosting at our house."

"And we will be there," Mekinges said.

"We will?" James said.

Sol put a hand on his brother's shoulder. "Aren't you tired, at long last, of being spiteful to the boy you really love?"

James lowered his eyes. An uncomfortable tingle rose in his spine. His impulse was to curse and walk out, or wave a hand to dismiss the meddling blather. But he didn't. Suddenly he couldn't help but ask, "What does Jake do?"

"He's an apprentice at the Surveyor's Office." Sol turned to his sister-in-law with a wink. "Mekinges, don't you tell this man anything?"

"I tell, but he not listen. Only person he ever listened to was my father, The Captain, and he is gone."

"I figure it's a good thing," Sol said, "to have a family member on the inside of what the Government is thinking."

"The Government," James huffed.

CHAPTER 34

While Augie and Mekinges spent the next few days walking the woods, gathering hickory nuts, walnuts, paw paws, hazelnuts and persimmons, Sol and Mary worked to prepare their home for the party.

It was a big house now, as fine as any in the Ozarks, with a second-story addition in back. Sol was a modest man but smart, and so had modeled his home to be fitting of his neighbor's expectations. Pioneers held big houses in high esteem as a sign of what was possible on the frontier.

There was no way to know how many guests would show, but Sarcoxie and Shawnanuk had returned a day before and carried tables and chairs from the storehouse along with other accoutrements to ornament the yard, a wooden Indian, a pair of elephant tusks and a stuffed monkey.

Augie slaughtered and gutted two hogs, filled their hollowed areas with vegetables, wrapped them in corn-fiber bags and slow roasted them underground for two days.

Around noon, as Mekinges and Mary watched a flock of wild geese flying high overhead, a horse carrying two people came prancing from the woods.

It was Jake, and he had a girl.

His cousin, Perninia, was the first to reach him as he dismounted, then Sol, Mary and Mekinges. Each hugged him and held him out for a look.

"And who is this lovely creature?" Sol asked as he reached to help the girl from the horse.

Jake blushed. "Please meet my very good friend, Alice Patterson." He introduced her to what family members were there, as his eyes scanned the yard for someone else.

"He'll be here," Sol said. "He promised. I think maybe he's gone to buy you a present."

Jake nodded. "Aw, I didn't expect –"

"He'll be here," Mekinges assured.

"It doesn't matter," Jake said. He forced a smile. "I just wanted to see how you folks were doing without me underfoot."

Augie approached, clearing his throat for attention. He pointed.

Indians were coming out of the woods. Sol counted nine.

Jake ran to greet them. "Hey, you made it," he yelled, calling each one by name. He walked them back to the house.

Mekinges was also thrilled to see old acquaintances, boys who were now men. How many years had it been? Six, she thought and then wondered about James. He had promised.

y

There were games all afternoon, archery competition the most popular.

Around five o'clock, Mekinges walked to her house to see if James was there. He wasn't. She performed the arduous task of moving the stove to open the floor door, and went down into the cave for the first time alone. He wasn't there.

Sorely disappointed, she returned to the party to discover that John Polk Campbell and James Wilson had arrived and were already participating in dice board games with some of her nephews.

Sol was irked by this. Who invited the man that had accused him falsely of breaking the law and put his name in a report? That wasn't right. And what if he were here to arrest Mary for the medicinal peach brandy she sold to the Indians?

He learned later that the former Indian agent was a tavern keeper now, going by J.P. Campbell, and considering running for political office.

As Augie, Sarcoxie and Shawnanuk raised the cooked hogs from the ground, the musicians Sol hired began to fill the field with music. There were two fiddles, a banjo, a clavichord from the storehouse, played by the man who sold it, and several drums.

Mixed with the aroma of the succulent pork, it was a sunset charged with merriment for almost everybody.

Not Mekinges. She was sad. Sol was too. If Jake was, he didn't show it as he helped build a bonfire to light the settling night.

Everyone stuffed themselves, drank peach brandy, danced around the fire and sang:

Turkey in the straw, turkey in the hay,
Turkey in the straw, what do you say
The funniest thing I ever saw
Roll 'em up, twist 'em up, a tuck-a-caw-haw.

As Mekinges sat off to the side alone, worrying about her husband, she felt a pair of hands caress her shoulders and heard a precious voice.

"Nichan," the voice said. "My daughter."

She sprang up, turned and threw herself into the arms of her father, so happy she began to sob. "Kichi hàch ne le?"

"Yes, my child, I am really here."

She pulled back, firelight gleaming in her tears of emotion. "And speaking very good English," she giggled.

He smiled with a shrug. "Conquer his tongue, conquer the man."

"You came down for Jake's birthday?"

"I came to see my little girl." He pulled her back against the loving heart in his chest. "And for the mending."

"The mending?"

"You will see." As he took her hand to lead her toward the fire, he said, "Winona is here too."

Mekinges froze. "Mother is here? Where?"

"I take you to her soon," he said, nudging her closer to the flames.

Mekinges noticed then that the music had stopped. All eyes were on them, her and The Captain. They paused at the edge of the ring of fire.

Kikthawenund turned and shouted, "Jimyocum."

Mekinges lowered her head with embarrassment. "He's not here, Father. I'm sorry."

Kikthawenund smiled. "He is here. I talk with him today at far end of cave. He was hiding, like a rabbit. We have long talk."

Then he was there, James, her husband, with two braves walking him from the woods.

On the other side of the fire standing on the sprawling front porch of Sol's house, Jake appeared dressed in full Lenape garb, from moccasins to feathered headband. His skull was freshly shaved, evident by a few trickles of blood.

Alice, his 'very dear friend,' was shocked.

Accompanied by two braves, Jake walked toward the fire. When he got close he faltered nervously.

His cousin, Perninia, stepped forward, took his hand and walked him around the fire circle to within six feet of James.

Kikthawenund spoke softly to James. "It is a night for repentance, to break down the wall that locks you in spirit-war. Your secret hurt will make tracks when you open your heart door. Let dark trouble run out of you and let son come in." He patted James's chest. "Love is already here. Wait no more."

James began to tremble with a sour churning in his belly. A tear escaped his eye and slid down his cheek, leaving a fire-glazed trail. What was there to fear?

Kikthawenund knew. James, in the moment of facing his son would be forced to face himself, a fearsome encounter for any proud man who had lived twenty-three years in denial.

"I don't know what to do," he whispered to Kikthawenund.

"Just wait," The Captain said and then nodded to Jake.

Jake lowered himself to his knees, then raised his eyes to James. After a nervous breath, he entreated James in perfect Lenape: "Father of my flesh, I cross the divide between us for that which is to me above all things, the joining of my spirit with yours that we may fellowship together." He let out a quivering sigh, his heart pounding.

Although the whites didn't know what he said, a pregnant pause filled the air as though even the creatures of the forest were holding their breath.

James stepped forward and stretched down his hand. "I have been the king of fools," he said for everyone to hear. Then to Jake: "My son, my son, please take my hand and rise to forgive your father if you ever can."

Jake looked up, dazed. Tears made their way into the eyes of many witnesses as he leapt from the ground into his father's arms. There was a sudden burst of applause.

"It's all right now," Jake said. "Everything is all right now. Thank you, Father. I love you."

"Happy birthday, son."

"Truth is Pa, I don't know if it's really my birthday or not. I think Uncle Sol and Mekinges came up with this idea."

"No, this is it. Sometimes Sol gave you two or three birthday parties a year. You know how he is, but you came into this wicked world on this date, October the twelfth 1813. I was there."

Jake felt as though he were in a dream, at a loss for words.

James pulled from the embrace, wrapped an arm around his boy and nudged him to walk.

Another cheer went up with more applause as the musicians broke into their rendition of Joy to the World, and the dancing resumed.

"You didn't have to shave your head," James said.

"I wanted to look like a brave for you."

James laughed and tightened his arm around Jake's shoulder. "Let's go talk."

Alice started to follow Jake but Mekinges grabbed her hand. "They need together alone," she said. "You come to porch with me."

Alice hesitated, then nodded. "He's bald," she said.

Mekinges laughed. "Yoachums are funny men. Make me laugh all the time. You will laugh too."

As they turned toward the house, Mekinges saw her father and four brothers standing off to the side.

Her father nodded to her.

Sol was suddenly beside her. "Mekinges," he said, "let me take this pretty girl and give her a tour of my house. Do you mind? Come on, Alice," he said, taking her by the arm.

Mekinges ran to her Lenape family.

CHAPTER 35

They were a quarter of a mile into the woods when Mekinges saw firelight flickering through the trees. She broke from her father and brothers and ran into a campsite, jolted by the sight of some fifty Lenape, who rose from the ground to greet her.

Her father had explained that Winona was dying and wanted to come back to have her whole family together one last time. "She is only half as big as when you saw her last."

Mekinges ran to her, squatted beside the only mother she'd ever known and was shocked by the smallness of the woman's frame, even under the blankets. Still she protested, in Lenape: "Mother, if you are sick, there are white doctors here who can make you well."

Winona smiled up from her pallet. "No, Daughter. Great Spirit let me know it is my time, and all is well. It's so good to see you."

Mekinges began to cry, then looked up to Kikthawenund. "Can we take her to my house?"

Winona chuckled. "Why you ask him? I am the one to be considered."

The Captain shrugged.

"If all family can come, I would love to see your home. Make me happy. If your house is dirty, I will punish you."

Mekinges chuckled through her tears and nodded, "Yo." (All right.)

y

James and Jake spent the night talking on a bank of the James River.

James, trying not to sound defensive of his abhorrent fatherhood, tried to explain how the loss of Ruth had been like a lightning bolt that splits an oak into two parts, neither of which could ever be whole again. He wanted to tell his son how the devastation of that loss made him crazy, that his very soul had been wrenched from his being, but he realized as they conversed that it was even more of a loss for Jake who on that morning had lost both parents, innocently.

It wasn't Jake who had failed to send for the doctor in time.

Now James saw that his son was stout of heart and possessed a natural courage. As much as the boy looked like his gentle mother, he was made on the inside like a Yoachum, to fight for his beliefs, no matter what the odds. This made James both proud and ashamed.

Jake wanted to know everything about his mother – how they met, what she liked, what she thought was funny, did she have any special talents, how tall she was, what things would make her mad, who were her friends?

James found it gratifying to respond to the questions and was surprised by the stories he could attach to each answer, stories he did not realize had been locked inside him.

They were silent for a while, then James asked about the morning that he and Mekinges watched Jake ride into the village with Philibert, Moony and some other fellows.

Jake's head angled up. "I was in the store that morning. Moony came in with Willie Whitestone and . . . oh, the man with six fingers. They were going to ride out to look around." He shrugged. "Joe and I thought it would be fun to go along."

James nodded.

"I knew you were there though."

James looked skeptical.

"You were in that cabin you built."

"You saw us?"

"The top of Mekinges head," Jake said with a chuckle. "I could tell it was her, and I knew if she were there, you were there. I didn't say anything."

Now, James thought, Jake would ask about the silver, and he would tell him, he'd already decided. The boy was trustworthy.

But Jake did not ask. The subject of silver never came up.

Y

The robins are always first, as if to play reveille for the other birds. When the Carolina parrot keets began to chatter, James said, "Good Lord, it's dawn already. We'd better get back to your birthday party, see how it's doing."

Stepping out of the woods James was shocked to see some sixty Delaware Indians, men, women and adolescents, bivouacked around his house, not playing games, but doing something, each sitting on the ground, somberly attentive to a personal project. "What's going on, Jake? Do you know?"

"No Sir, I don't."

As they ran across the field they saw that the Indians had slender poles stretched across their laps and were busy carving designs into the wood. James had never seen this before.

They scuttled into the house.

A group was gathered around the table upon which Winona lay on her back talking softly to those near her.

Mekinges turned to James and whimpered into his chest. "Mother come home to die, and won't change mind."

James pulled away and bent over Winona.

When she recognized him she smiled. "Mëshatàm këmili Lehëlexeokàn."

Mekinges: "Mother say she remember when you save her life."

"And we'll do it again by God." He looked around. "Philibert? Where's Philibert?"

"He go back to town with Perninia," Mekinges said. "No matter. Mother wants no medicine. She don't want wèlathakèt for bleeding, or shaman smoke. She say she come to James River to trade."

James tilted his head, befuddled. "To trade?"

"This world for next world."

"No," he protested. "We have to try."

"And she want ashes here."

"Ashes? What?"

Winona motioned for Mekinges.

Mekinges put an ear to her mother's lips and then smiled and looked up to James. "Mother say, she very happy now. You take your son into your heart, and she feel like she is home, and everything is good for everybody. You not worry."

James stared as Winona whispered more to her daughter and they both chuckled.

"Mother say to thank you, Jimyocum, for the worse horse she ever did see."

James's face reddened with shame.

Mekinges listened for more, then relayed it to James. "That horse died on the journey from here. But now is time to go find that bad horse because she loved it very much."

"No," James pleaded. "Winona, I'll get you another horse, a really good horse this time."

Winona rolled her eyes.

Kikthawenund put a hand on James's shoulder. "My wife stubborn like yours."

All day, visitors came into the house to wish her well. Where they all came from, James had no idea, but Winona, although obviously weakening, had something to say to each one.

CHAPTER 36

She died of smallness. That's what the shaman said when Winona passed peacefully around three the next morning.

In Germany, progress was being made in the understanding of cancer but it was an unknown thing on the American frontier.

The woman who died looked frail but otherwise fine on the outside. All that could be conjectured was that something had gone wrong on the inside to bring on the condition of smallness. Who but the Great Spirit could ever understand such a thing?

As the wife of the head chief of the Lenape nation, her funeral was to be a momentous event.

Wrapped by her sons in colorfully dyed flax linen blankets, her body was carried a quarter mile to the James River where James was surprised to see that a pit, four feet deep, had already been excavated and filled with dead wood.

At each end of the pit were poles of birch forked at the tips. With strips of leather, the body was suspended three feet above the hollow.

James figured it couldn't have weighed more than seventy pounds. He watched in wonder as one by one, each Lenape who had carved a pole approached the grave and carefully placed it to form a teepee-style structure around the corpse.

He and Mekinges stood off to the side. In a whisper he asked if she had ever seen such a thing.

Mekinges shook her head slowly. "I hear about it long ago for great chiefs but not never for a woman."

James nodded. "She was your father's great chief."

Mekinges fingered tears from her eyes.

Never before had James seen her cry. He remembered her father's tears the morning Winona had come out of her fever.

When all the poles had been towered, Kikthawenund appeared from the woods in full regal Lenape dress; a feathered headdress, a robe of splendor, and a painted face. He held a burning torch, as did each of his sons who were adorned likewise.

Amazingly to James, a hundred more Indians from various tribes emerged from the forest to join the circle. By law, they were not supposed to be here. Truly this was an overriding occasion.

Kikthawenund waited for the first Robin's song, which came only moments later, then put the torch to the templed staffs of wood. His sons followed, placing their torches around at even intervals.

James felt as though he were in a dream.

Mekinges squeezed his hand to lead him and Jake into the circle. Behind, Sol and Mary joined, and then Philibert and Perninia who had returned from town with a bottle of Doctor Sappington's anti-fever pills.

The congregation began to move slowly in a circle with soft chants, each, his own. Each, her own.

It was a powerfully spiritual euphony, emotional and poignant, the likes of which James perceived must be a song for the heavens.

Some stepped forward and cast a gift of respect into the flames; necklaces, feathers, woodcarvings and silver jewelry.

The cacophony of voices grew louder and then crescendoed as the pyre culminated with a roar of orange spears spiraling up into the breaking dawn.

Seared through, the leather strips gave way, releasing Winona's mortal remains into the pit.

A great sobbing howl went up as the embers flared, sending a million new sparks flurrying up into the genesis of the new day.

The mournful beauty of it all was dazzling.

James stood frozen in awe.

y

By the time the sun had cleared the treetops, only Kikthawenund, James, Mekinges, and her brothers remained.

The smoking ashes in the pit were above ground level but The Captain explained that they would settle once he covered the grave with a layer of soil and a topping of rocks. There would be no enticement for scavengers. Mother was gone, completely.

Suddenly a voice from the woods called out. "Father, you'd better come quick."

They turned to see Jake at the tree line.

"I think Uncle Sol is going to kill Moony."

"What?"

"Hurry."

Kikthawenund motioned with a raised hand. "You go."

James rose and broke into a run to follow his son.

y

In the barn Sol was being pulped by what looked to be half a dozen men.

"Blazes, Pa, I only saw Moony. I shouldn't have left."

"You did the right thing. You always do."

Jake leapt onto the back of one of the mob and put a strangle hold around the man's neck.

"Damn it, kid, get off me or I'll shoot you," the man rasped through his compressed larynx. "I swear I'll shoot you."

James saw then that there was indeed at least one gun and this was unac-ceptable. He stepped in, grabbed two off his brother, knocked their heads together, and then grabbed two more.

From behind, a shovel struck his head. James again saw orange sparks in the air, and then lost his vision along with the ability to stay on his feet.

The barn-breakers, realizing things were not going as promised, turned to make a run for it but then froze.

Evenly spaced across the barn door stood four Lenape braves in full regalia and paint. Sarcoxie, Shawnanuk, Pushkies and Secomdyan. Tomahawks in hand, they had grins on their faces.

One of the prowlers raised a pistol. Sol grabbed it just in time to save the idiot's life. "Mister, another second and you'd have had a 'hawk blade in your chest."

"That would just break his heart, Uncle Sol," Jake chuckled.

"How's your Pa, Jake?"

"I'm fine," James said trying to rise to his feet. "You get everybody?"

"One or two may have slipped out, I don't know. We going to hang them, Jim?"

James shrugged. "Just desserts for horse thieves."

"We ain't horse thieves," a man named Pogue said.

James sidled down the line. "Let me see who we got here. I don't think I know any of these fellows except for Mister Moon. Moony what are you doing in my barn beating up on my poor little brother?"

"Ha!" Sol huffed. "I could have handled them by myself."

James nodded. "And I was fixing to let you do that, Sol, you and Jake, but I saw this one here had a gun." He stopped at the one who had drawn the pistol. "He's a bad man." He stared into the culprit's eyes. "What's your name, bad man?"

"Clovis Pogue, Mister Yoachum, and I ain't a bad man. I just got scared. I . . . I got scared of them Indians."

Sol said, "I know this birdbrain. And that one," he pointed. "Howard Six-fingers Jones. They're the ones got me reported as a bootlegger." He looked at Moony. "Where's Whitestone? Did he slink out on you?"

Moony glared.

James shook his head. "I would have thought you'd learned your lesson, Moony, but I guess not." He turned to look at his brothers-in law. "Those fellows? You were afraid of them, Pogue?"

Pogue nodded.

"They're family. You were going to shoot my family?"

Pogue trembled. "I didn't know. I'm sorry."

"Oh, you're sorry."

"Yes Sir, I am. Moony said there wouldn't be no trouble."

"Shut up, Clovis," Moony said.

"He said you was at a funeral and we could come get hunks of silver and be gone by the time you got back."

James stared at Moony. "What hunks of silver?"

The men turned to where they had brushed straw away from a metal covering, level with the dirt floor.

Moony finally spoke. "It ain't right, Yoachum. You set yourself up like a king, blessing the people who praise you. The Delaware are gone. That silver ain't no more yours now than anybody else's."

"What silver?"

"The silver under that floor door there."

James shook his head and sighed. "Sol, should we let Moony go down there and get a few bars of silver?"

Jake was shocked. Why would his father allow this?

"It's dangerous," Sol said, "but all right. Go ahead, Mister Francis Moon." He motioned for the others to step back.

"You're just going to let me?" asked Moony.

"There's no silver down there, Moony," James said.

"I'd like to see for myself."

James rolled his eyes, and then extended a go-ahead hand. "Root hog or die."

Sol wagged his head. "Don't do it, Moony. It's dangerous."

Moony lifted the lid and peered down a man-sized borehole twenty feet in depth, then making a hard turn. A ladder was already there, the top rung just two feet below the surface. He looked up and smiled. "Dangerous, huh?"

"Yes," Sol said.

"No silver, huh?"

"None," James said.

Something wasn't right, Moony knew, but decided that the brothers were bluffing. He would call that bluff, go down and follow the tunnel. "It's dark," he said.

"I'd give you a torch but you'd set the barn on fire," James said.

"So that's it," thought Moony. "He thinks I won't find it in the dark."

When Moony settled his weight on the third rung, a twine tripped the trigger of the scattergun. With a deafening blast, it blew flesh, muscle and toes from his right foot. He fell into a V position; his body folded between the ladder and the shaft walls.

He would have screamed but his diaphragm was too compressed for any passage of air.

His cohorts froze in horror as they squinted into the hole.

James tied a rope around a barn post. "Better get him up out of there," he said, "and get him to a doctor, or he's going to die and it will be on your hands." He looked each one in the eyes. "All of you."

They were too stunned to move.

"Clovis Pogue," James shouted, "get down there and bring Moony up. Do it now or it's a trip into the woods with my red brothers."

"The ladder's broke," Clovis said.

James handed him the rope.

As Pogue wriggled his way down, James made a pronouncement. "Yes, I am King James. It's my silver. It's my river. This is my world. Pass that along to all your thieving friends."

"Yes, Sir," Howard Jones said.

After Moony's crew managed to pull him from the hole, James let them go.

They carried his body for six miles before they realized he was dead. Francis "Moony" Moon died of blood loss one mile from his house.

One of the lead pellets from the scattergun had flown high, into a femoral artery.

CHAPTER 37

April 1837

While the deterioration of the Second Bank of the United States was producing runaway inflation in the rest of the country, the people of the hills around Delaware Town were blissfully unaware of the financial crisis, which became known as The Panic of '37.

Things were good in this neck of the woods, thanks to the Yoachum brothers, the eldest of which some folks did refer to as King James.

James thought that was funny, but it did give him a sense of power that he enjoyed.

Sol thought it was blasphemous.

y

James took Jake to the bluff to show him where, while contemplating suicide, he had slipped and fallen over the edge to a sure death. "Nothing is certain in life," he said. "I know that now. You just never know what God has in mind."

"But you read the Bible," Jake said.

"I do, and you should too. It helps you to know that no matter what you're going through, Jesus already went through it and paid the price."

"For white people, you mean."

James scratched his beard. "Whites do think they're the special ones, don't they?"

"Pa, the Indians are as smart as white people, aren't they?"

"Absolutely. In many ways, I think, smarter."

"So how is it that they allowed the European invaders to come here, to America I mean, and take control over them?"

James rubbed his brow. It was a good question. "The whites brought guns and steel when the Indians were still using stone." He shrugged. "That's my guess. And disease. Mekinges swears they brought diseases that killed thousands of Indians. I'll have to ask my father-in-law."

He wouldn't. They both knew that.

They sat quietly for a while admiring the valley beyond the river below.

"It's a beautiful spot, Pa."

James sighed. "Last time I was here there were no cabins down there. Now you can count, what, a dozen?" He shrugged. "And they're feuding all the time." He looked at Jake. "I guess that's what I brought you here to talk about."

Jake flinched with a sudden tickle in his heart. His father was going to ask for his opinion on something.

"Tell me how it works, Son, what you're doing."

"Oh," Jake said, thrilled that James would take an interest in his work. "Well, with the Indians gone and more whites moving here every day, who knows where one man's property ends and another's begins?"

"Is that important?"

"It will be. There are some, like Thomas Hart Benton, who are fighting for squatter's rights."

"Squatter's rights?"

"That means if you're already here and settled, you should have the right to call that land yours. Jefferson believed that's what would keep America secure."

"Of course," James said. "My land is my land."

Jake winced. "Well, yeah, but the Government wants a payment for that land so they can keep a record of all the borders and boundaries and county lines and such."

James dipped his head with suspicion. "Why?"

"So they can tax it."

"Wait. I'm going to have to buy my own land and then pay taxes on it?"

"You're going to have to have a title to it, a deed, to prove it's legally yours. This is the way they do it."

"And you're in on this?"

Jake knew to tread cautiously. After the miracle of his father's request for forgiveness, it would be a terrible thing to alienate him now. "Oh, it's simply a way to keep things organized, you know, so there's no confusion over the fact that your land is your land, in case some lawyer comes along and says that it isn't." He smiled. "You'll be able to prove it."

James pondered this.

"It's like you said about those people down there in the valley. What is it they feud about? I'll bet its boundaries. What is whose and whose is what?"

James gazed at the cabins below.

"It's still a few months off, maybe a year or two, but I'll be able to let you know when the surveyors are coming and help you out with the process."

"The process?"

"We use a new invention called a theodolite. It's got a string and . . . well, it's called a plumbline and –"

"Whoa," James interrupted, confused. "Just do like you said. Come help me out when you think it's right."

"Absolutely, Pa."

James was proud of his son. He grabbed him by the scruff of his neck and kissed the top of his head. "You're an amazing kid."

"Of course I am," Jake said with his famous grin. "I'm the son of King James."

CHAPTER 38

June 1840

A crowd was gathered at the post store in Delaware Town.

James stood with Philibert on the porch to address the gathering, while holding an official document. "Gentlemen, this notice is from the Government and what it says is, 'section lines having been established, we are ordered to abide by homestead laws.'"

He looked down to read the hard part: ". . . relative to securing title to property on which you live . . ." He looked up, then back down and skipped a few lines. "And that part of this requirement is to pay a filing fee at the Government Office in Springfield."

The crowd erupted with boos.

James nodded his agreement. "Some of you know my son, Jake. He is a fine man and he believes in this, but to be honest with you, I do not. The Government has always been corrupt. Just ask the Lenape. In my opinion, this is an assault on our freedom and I will stand against it if you men choose to fight."

Sol was shocked as the crowd cheered. He stepped onto the porch. "Gentle-men, gentlemen, as usual, I do not agree with my big brother. If paying a filing fee is all that is necessary to get official deeds to our land . . . why not?"

"Because it's a sneaky step towards controlling our lives," James said.

Philibert stepped forward. "I agree with Sol. Why would the Government want to control us? Their only job is to defend our freedom to make good lives for ourselves."

James rolled his eyes as Jake stepped up again. He smiled. "I have learned the hard way that my pa is a stubborn man and never gives in easily. Maybe he won't today." He shrugged and winked at James. "But I can see his point of view. He loves the Indians who have been cheated many times by the Government. There is no doubt about that."

James nodded.

"The question today is, do we want freedom by battle or freedom by good order? I ask you all . . ." he turned to James, "and I ask you, Father, what would be lost by paying a few dollars to own titles to our land?"

James had no answer for this and the crowd saw it. Bested by his sharp-witted son, he stepped off the porch frustrated, but proud. "Fine," he said gruffly, "you all do what you want."

CHAPTER 39

With a population of three hundred, Springfield, Missouri was incorporated as a city in 1838 and became the county seat for Greene County, named after Revolutionary War hero, Nathaniel Greene.

The following year the town witnessed firsthand the horror of the Trail of Tears, as the Cherokee Nation was forced through town in heart-rending condition, thousands already having died of exposure, disease and starvation since departing Red Clay, Tennessee.

The sight of the tragic parade sickened Jake to the marrow of his bones. He asked Campbell if there wasn't something that Springfieldians could do to offer some relief, some food and rest, maybe some clothes and blankets.

Commanding General Scott would have none of it. His focus was his mission, to drive the tribe mercilessly onward to reach the Oklahoma territory as expediently as possible, no matter what.

One of his soldiers, Private John G. Burnett, wrote in his diary; 'Future generations will condemn this act and I do hope posterity will remember that privates like myself, and like the four Cherokees who General Scott forced to shoot their chief and his children, had to execute the orders of our superiors. We had no choice in the matter. I have seen many men shot but the Cherokee removal was the cruelest work I ever knew.'

CHAPTER 40

June 1842

Without James's knowledge, Jake had paid the filing fee for the land on which his father and uncle lived. Gradually nearly half the other settlers had done the same for themselves.

One day a final notice arrived at the post for those who had not paid yet and it listed names.

On the porch of the James River Fork Trading Post Jake had to do some fast-talking to another angry mob. "Of course, they have names," he said. "After my colleagues and I surveyed your properties we turned in your names with petitions for deeds to the plots of land that you claimed as rightfully yours. The Government, being the awkward behemoth that it is, knows that nothing ever gets settled without a deadline. We knew this day was coming, didn't we?"

Lum Booth, in front, said, "So, what do we do?"

"Just go up to Springfield and pay your filing fee, ten dollars, and do it within ten days or, I have to tell you, somebody else will, and that wouldn't be fair, would it?"

"Would you go with us?"

"I'll be there in the Surveyor's Office. You gentlemen pick a day, make the trip together, come by my office and I'll go with you to the treasurer's office and help you get everything settled. How about that? Then we can have a picnic on the square."

He got some nods, some smiles and a few chuckles.

"Why can't they just leave us alone?" a voice called from the rear.

Jake smiled. "It's the Government, Pa. They can't leave anything alone."

This got a few more chuckles mixed with some good-humored cursing. The dagblasted Government – who did they think they were?

Thursday, June 16th

Twenty-four men from the hills around Delaware Town paced their horses cautiously into Springfield, a flat city that smelled funny and where the people dressed oddly and rode around in carriages.

The aroma was a mixture of dust from various mills, fresh bricks, mortar, baked goods, sweet sorghum and horse waste.

They walked their mounts past the services of a saddler, a wagon maker, a grocer, a fortuneteller and a newspaper printer, The Springfield Advertiser. Stacks of lumber and pallets of bricks were nearly everywhere. They gawked at a sign in one window that was advertising The Druid Horn Blowers, June 18th, one show only.

They were relieved to find the Surveyor's Office without having to interact with any of the strange townsfolk. By Lum Booth's watch it was eleven thirty.

Jacob Yoachum, excited to see them, was good to his word. He hung a closed sign on his door, told the men they could corral their horses behind the building, and then walked them across the square.

The land office, built in 1834, was on a side street just off the square.

Jake did not recognize the young man behind the counter when he entered, and asked, "Where's Alfred Rountree?"

"He quit to help his brother with the school."

"How about Mister Scroggins?"

"Sick. Pretty bad too, from what I hear. I'm Nathan Massey." The young clerk rose and extended his hand.

Jake shook it. "Jacob Yoachum, with the Surveyor's Office."

"Guess I'm in charge for now," Massey said as he studied the group of obvious out-of-towners streaming through the door.

They had to pack themselves closer to each other than was comfortable for hill folk.

"How can I help you gentlemen today?"

"Paperwork, I'm afraid," Jake said. "These fellows have ridden all morning from south Greene County to pay their filing fees. Their petitions are already on file so I guess if you just get their names and take their money, we can let them be on their way and I'll help you with the books."

"What about the picnic?" Lum Booth asked.

"This'll take about an hour, Mister Booth. You men go look around town, maybe buy something nice, some perfume maybe, for your sweethearts."

The men guffawed and started to turn.

"Whoa," Jake said. "Business first. Get out your money."

The second he saw the silver dollars, Nate Massey balked. "Nope, sorry," he said. "Can't take those."

Jake smiled. "What do you mean?"

"New regulation as of last year. We just got it a few weeks ago." He rolled his eyes in a way that said you know how it is. "All official land dealings require Federally-issued coins."

"That's not true," said Jake. "Half the land owners down there have already paid with the Yocum coins. I paid my Father's and my Uncle's claim fees last year with them. There wasn't a problem."

"Like I said, we just got the notice a few weeks ago. Maybe it's because of your coins. Mister Rountree sent some of those to Washington." He shrugged. "I don't know."

There was silence for a moment, which was then shattered by an eerie click, and then another.

Lum Booth had drawn his double-barrel Derringer. "Mister Massey, we came here to do the right thing. Since when has silver been unacceptable as payment for anything? Missouri don't even have an official bank. We ain't got no Federally-issued coins. Now either you accept our payment or we'll just burn down your useless office, and all them stacks of paper I see back there will turn to ashes. How'd you like that?"

Jake knew he should intervene but he himself was so enraged and embarrassed, he decided to just stand by, at least for the moment.

"And then we'll go back," Booth continued, "and tell King James he was right all along."

"K-k-king James?" Massey stammered.

"My father," Jake said. He turned to the men. "Put your shooters away, gentlemen. This fellow is just a puppet. I am sure our silver is good." He turned back to Massey. "When you get the go-ahead from Washington in a few years," he said sarcastically, "come over to the Surveyor's Office and let me know. We'll work something out from that point." Jake emphasized his next words with a pointed finger. "But you let whoever needs to know, there will be hell to pay if they put one square inch of these men's land up for public auction before then." He stared at Massey.

The land office manager nodded. "I'll do as you ask. Good luck, men. I really do mean that."

The men nodded, cursed, spat on the floor and shuffled out, in no mood now for a picnic.

CHAPTER 41

In Washington, the Whigs terminated the independent treasury when Martin Van Buren left office.

The next president, William Henry Harrison, was in office for less than a month when he caught pneumonia and died. One of the few appointments he was able to make was Thomas Ewing as Secretary of the Treasury.

Ewing did not get along with Harrison's successor, John Tyler, and resigned in protest along with all the other cabinet members with one exception, Daniel Webster.

Tyler then appointed Walter Forward as the next Secretary of the Treasury, but he too disagreed with Tyler on almost everything, especially his devotion to state's rights, which he held to be above nationalism.

However it was Forward who had the job when the Yocum silver dollars first landed on the desk of the Secretary of the Treasury.

He met with his advisors; four of them, in the splendid, new Greek styled Treasury Building on the corner of 15th Street and Pennsylvania Avenue.

Each twiddled a Yocum coin while studying its configurement.

"Crude," said the red haired Michael Falk.

Harold Bridges, a handsome black haired man with a neatly trimmed matching mustache disagreed. "Simple, you mean. Hardly crude. They are uniform in size and weight, the weight being superior to the Spanish Coins used by most of western civilization."

"So they are in fact, real silver?" Forward said.

Bridges nodded. "Purer than I've ever seen."

Forward cleared his throat. "And they're legal?"

"Why wouldn't they be? They did this in Denver too, didn't they? We didn't say anything. These coins are American, at least, as opposed to South American." He shrugged. "Should we ask the president?"

Forward huffed. "I wouldn't ask that idiot for the time of day. The problem, gentlemen, as I see it, is that Missouri is a Southern State." He paused to let the implication sink in. "Can the Government allow some bumpkin with a secret silver mine to make his own currency? What if he's sympathetic to the abolitionists and decides one day to fund an uprising against slave owners? Something like that could lead to a war."

"There is no silver in Missouri according to Henry Rowe Schoolcraft," Bridges said. He tilted his head with a dubious expression. "A secret silver mine?"

"So I'm told," Forward said. "And with the stress of our own silver supply, being so limited, I propose we confront this Yocum fellow and require that he sell his mine to the Government for the sake of our unified democracy."

Bridges bristled. "The president won't like that."

"Of course he won't. He's a moron. He's against annexation, for Pete's sake."

"An act like this would at least require congressional approval, wouldn't it?"

"That could take years. Who's the governor out there?"

John Henderson answered, "Thomas Reynolds. He's a Democrat."

"Thank God for that," Forward said.

There were murmurs around the table.

"By thunder, Gentlemen, it is imperative for the Government of the United States of America to be continental of mind in order to become properly one nation. Tyler just doesn't seem to grasp that."

"One Government-authorized currency for all," said Michael Falk.

"It's inevitable."

Falk nodded. "Makes sense."

"And the eight-reales?" asked Bridges.

"They're not a threat. We cut them off, at some point of course, but that will take twenty years, when our monetary system will be in better shape with the Gobrecht dollars."

His advisors scratched their heads. "So . . . what's the move?" Falk asked.

Forward templed his fingers and put his elbows on the table. "We execute an order of eminent domain, gentlemen, for the sake of the country." He waited a moment. "Why should this one man own a stockpile of silver for a ten-dollar land-filing fee?"

"It's his land," Bridges said.

"But he's manufacturing money in a southern state."

Bridges rubbed his eyes. "Is there any precedent for this?"

"It doesn't matter. It's the right thing to do." He thought about that for a moment. "There may be some judicial ambiguity here, but we'll be fair with the man, with an honest appraisal. We'll pay him equitably. Well, to a point."

"And . . . if he resists?"

Forward thought for a moment. "He's a backwoods farmer. When he sees Federal troops on his land, as sophisticated as he may be with his little money factory there, what kind of resistance could he even consider?"

CHAPTER 42

Wednesday April 12th, 1843

Jacob Yoachum rode hard from Springfield down into the hills, across the Finley River, and into what was once Lenape Land. He loved his horse, Becky, so he stopped for breath and water three times, but made it to his father's house in a fast three hours.

Augie told him that James was at the storehouse.

Jake smacked his forehead. He should have known. He remounted. "Come on, Becky, just a little more and you can take the night off."

y

"They're coming, Pa, Federal agents," Jake said. They're coming for the silver."

His father and uncle were seated at a newly acquired round oak table in the back of the building.

"What Federal agents?" James asked.

It was a worthless question, Jake thought. "I don't know. There're two of them with black jackets and badges and they've got a half dozen soldiers with them. They're going to head out in the morning, probably be here around one or two o'clock. What are you going to do?"

James and Sol exchanged glances.

"Where do they think they're going to find this silver?" James asked.

Jake shook his head. "I'm sorry, Pa, but everybody knows it's under your barn. You got away with those three-day trips for a while, riding through town with silver sticking out of your saddlebag. I even followed you on one of those trips, remember?"

"Nearly got yourself shot as I recall," said Sol.

"That was a grand day," Jake said, smiling. "And I was there when Moony found the tunnel in the barn. I'm sure those other bums blabbed about it."

James lit a newly-purchased pearl-inlaid pipe and leaned back to think. "Can you still ride, Son?"

"Not on my horse, no."

"With a fresh horse?"

"Sure. I'm fine. What do you want me to do?"

James puffed and then coughed. "Go to everybody you can think of and tell them the Government is coming to destroy our way of life."

Sol scratched his head. "Well, that's a little overblown, don't you think?"

James snapped, "Do you think it isn't true?"

Sol considered the question, then finally shook his head. "No. Come to think of it, you're probably right."

James looked to Jake. "Tell as many people as you think you can trust to be on the main road by ten tomorrow. And tell them to stay out of sight."

Jake shook his head. "That's not the way, Pa."

"Sol and I will do the same."

"Pa, please. You don't want to want fight them. It won't solve anything. It will make things much worse."

"We're just going to give them a little scare, son. If they're coming with just eight people, they're not looking for a fight either. We're going to show our resolve, you know, that we are not a people to be trifled with and hopefully make them change their minds."

Jake's emotions, as always, showed on his face. He was worried.

"Jake," James said, "should we allow eight men from who knows where to come on our land and steal from us just because they have badges? That can't be legal, can it, Son?"

Jake mulled the question, then shook his head. "No, it can't be." With an uneasy shrug, he said, "Your plan might be good, I guess, as long as no one gets hurt . . . or killed, God forbid."

"Well, King James," said Sol, "we'd better get moving."

As they mounted their horses, James said to Sol, "That boy of mine is really something, isn't he? I've never met a more virtuous fellow, have you?"

Sol rolled his eyes and bit his tongue.

Thursday, April 13th

Because of the wagon, the Federal contingent of dispatched soldiers didn't make it into the Delaware Town area until nearly five pm the next day.

Two Federal agents denoted by black tunics with brass badges were accompanied by Captain Alexander Doniphan, Jr., and a platoon of eight Missouri militia men wearing no particular garb other than a blue scarf tied around the right arm of each, swords swinging by their sides.

Having to lead a four-horse battery wagon over uncharted, rugged terrain made the expedition slow and arduous.

The ambush took place a quarter of a mile from Delaware town. Gunfire erupted from the trees on both sides. Horses reared. Soldiers cursed.

A shout from the woods commanded them to "halt."

They held up and looked around.

Federal Agent Cockrell, a slender man with dark hair and small ears fitted close to his head, turned to the young army officer. "Captain Doniphan, what do you make of this?"

"Hard to tell, Sir," Doniphan answered, his rifle already against his shoulder, fanning for a target. With sharp green eyes, he had red hair and sideburns escaping from under his uniform cap.

The voice from the woods – it was Lum Booth – shouted again. "Throw down your weapons now, trespassers, and you won't be harmed."

"Not trespassers," Cockrell called toward the direction of the voice. "We are special agents on a mission for the United States Government." He squinted, trying to catch a glimpse of who or what he was dealing with. "Are you men patriots or bandits?"

A volley of gunfire erupted again. The shots were from close range but the feds could see nothing but a few traces of gun smoke, not enough to get a fix.

"Now, see here," the second agent, shouted.

"Shut up, Teter," Cockrell said. "You want to get us killed?"

"They wouldn't dare." Affirmed by his girth and puffy red face, Teter was a man of obvious appetites.

"Captain Doniphan?" Cockrell said.

"It goes against my nature, Sir," the Captain said, "but their advantage cannot be gauged. I say, cooperate till we can change the situation and maybe negotiate some sense into them."

Agent Cockrell agreed. He nodded and ordered his unit to raise their weapons high to make a show of dropping them.

"Swords too," the voice commanded.

Cockrell shook his head and shifted in his saddle. As a former army officer, the first thing he was taught was never to surrender your last weapon, considered in the military to be an act of fatal cowardice.

"If you wish to test us," the voice said, "your mothers will forever wonder what became of you."

Cockrell imagined his men being shot from their saddles. Wouldn't it be better to stay alive for time to make a strategy? Live for tomorrow? "All right," he shouted. He drew his sword and dropped it. His squad followed his example.

"Now get off your horses and walk away."

This was too much. "I cannot abandon Government property," Cockrell said.

A lone gunshot sparked a rock in front of his horse.

"Your wagon and whatever its load will be safe. Get off your horses and start walking."

"No," Cockrell shouted. "I can not do that."

There was a lull till the voice finally said, "There will be no return of your bodies for funerals. Five, four, three . . .

"I will not have my men killed this way," Cockrell muttered to himself. He scanned the woods but could still see nothing. "All right," he called, raising a halting hand. "Hold your fire." He looked at his squad. "Gentlemen," he said, "we walk now into the unknown. I want twenty feet between each man. Walk with authority, tall and proud, but stay sharp-eyed for quick cover."

The un-uniformed regulars had not volunteered for hazardous duty.

Now they weren't so sure of their leader's wisdom, or lack of it.

Captain Doniphan barked, "You heard the man, twenty feet between each swinging clapper. Right now. Dismount and spread out. Move!"

y

The defenseless platoon paused at the edge of Delaware town to assess the layout. Everything looked normal for a frontier post village.

Cockrell pointed to the main store. "There," he said and led them across the square, twenty feet between each man.

When the two agents and the captain entered the store Philibert greeted them with a smile. "Good afternoon, gentlemen. Welcome."

"I'm afraid I can't appreciate the welcome," Cockrell said, pointing to his badge. "We were fired upon just twenty minutes ago and forced to relinquish Government property including our wagon and horses."

Philibert came from around the counter and gestured for the men to sit at the table. "Well, we do have our bad apples," he said, "like any other town, I guess. Anyone get hurt?"

"No, but our lives were threatened."

"Sit down, sit down." Philibert showed them how. "What brings you to Delaware Town?"

As the men sat they noticed the room suddenly filling with late-afternoon shoppers.

The Widow Moon was among them but didn't bother to pretend being a customer. She stood near the table to listen.

Cockrell removed his hat. "As I understand it, folks here have been unable to pay their land filing fees because of fraudulent silver dollars."

Philibert rubbed his chin. "I did hear a rumor to that effect," he said, "but I don't understand it." He placed a Yocum on the table. "Does that look fraudulent to you?"

"It doesn't matter what it looks like to us," Teter said.

"Shut up, Teter," Cockrell said.

"I assure you, Sir," said Philibert, "Colonel Pierre Menard himself has approved these coins to be as legitimate as any in the world."

Cockrell gave a sympathetic frown. "Unfortunately, he is not my commanding officer. My orders come from Washington."

"Well, I'm sure we can rectify this situation. Would you gentlemen like some nice peach brandy?"

Agent Teter was about to raise his hand but caught Cockrell's glare.

"That's why we're here, Mister . . ."

"Philibert. Joe Philibert."

"I'm Federal Agent Cockrell. This is Federal Agent Teter. We're here to rectify the situation, Mister Philibert."

"Situation?"

"I have come with the authority to grant amnesty for everyone who turns in their illegal silver dollars."

The gathering eavesdroppers snickered and hooted. "Oh, sure," a voice said. "Let's give our money to the Government."

"The idea," Cockrell said, "is . . . or was . . . that we would trade a genuine official U.S. silver dollar for each unlawful one turned in."

The crowd simmered somewhat.

"Why are they unlawful?" a female voice asked. It was Perninia.

Cockrell ignored her. "That way you can pay your land filing fees with bona fide money and rest easy that all is well." He cleared his throat and looked around. "Unfortunately, we were ambushed and lost our wagon."

Philibert tilted his head with an expression of puzzlement. "You didn't lose your wagon."

Cockrell glared.

"It's right outside."

"What?"

Philibert gestured toward the window.

The agents rose to take a look. They saw their wagon and then rushed out.

The wagon, along with their horses, was there. The six soldiers were relaxed on the porch enjoying mugs of libation.

Captain Doniphan ordered his men to drop their drinks.

After long final gulps they obeyed.

Cockrell and Teter pulled back the tarps covering the wagon. To their surprise and relief, the cargo looked untouched.

"You see there?" Philibert said, Perninia by his side, "Nobody's violated you or your mission. It's just that, well, with our unique situation here, we have to take precautions. You understand."

"I understand nothing more than my orders, Mister Philibert, and you had better understand mine." He looked around. "Where are our arms?"

"Your guns?" He shrugged apologetically. "I'm sure they'll show up."

He opened his arms. "You fellows must be tuckered out. We have some traveler's rooms behind the store. They're not much but why don't you take a load off and rest up for the night?"

"We can guard the wagon, Agent Cockrell," Captain Doniphan said.

"With what?" bellowed Agent Teter. "Sticks and stones?"

"Shut up, Teter," Cockrell said. If they were to be robbed of more than their weapons, it would already have been so, he thought. He softened. "On behalf of the United States Government, thank you for your offer of lodging. We accept."

As Philibert and Perninia led the contingent around the back of the store and down to the old shantytown, Cockrell asked, "Who is King James?"

Philibert looked confused. "I'm just a simple shopkeeper, Sir – pretty much uneducated."

"Right," Cockrell said with obvious skepticism.

"Honey, do you know?"

Perninia thought for a moment. "I think he's the fellow who wrote the Bible. My Uncle Jim would know."

The sight of the rotting shacks reeking of urine and decay appalled the agents, but they had no other option than the outdoors, which would afford no protection, and besides, although the days had been unseasonably warm, the April nights were still iffy and their original plan was in shambles.

"This will do nicely, Philibert," Cockrell said. Thank you."

"Always glad to help the Government."

"Could you make sure that the word goes out about the coin exchange?"

"It's going out, right now, Sir, I assure you."

ɣ

Nearly a hundred Ozarks citizens were gathered the next morning around the wagon, which had been turned into a currency exchange center.

The two agents, Cockrell and Teter, stood aboard, while the captain and his men tried to organize the hill-folks into a line.

Earlier, Captain Doniphan had tried to talk Cockrell into canceling the idea until they regained possession of their weapons. "These people are loaded for bear and we have nothing. How do we keep control?"

"With our authority," was the answer.

At eight o'clock he addressed the crowd. "Good people," he announced, studying their faces, "you are doing the right thing, but you must be patient.

As you turn in your unlawful currency, we will record your name and the dollar amount, then trade one official coin for each local coin."

"Why do you need our names?" a voice called out, a voice they had heard threaten their lives just the day before.

"Just simple common business accounting," Cockrell said, scanning for the head from which the voice had blurted. "Who said that?"

Everyone looked around as though clueless.

As the sun reached its crest, the line was down to fifteen people, then ten, then five, then one – Lum Booth, who decided to speak in a soft, raspy tone. "Thirty, please," he said.

"We have only ten left," said Teter. "It worked out nearly perfect."

"All right," Booth said. "Ten, then." He laid ten Yocums on the wagon floor. "But I can see another bag in the corner there, says five hundred."

"That's for something else," Teter said. "Now don't give us any trouble. I'm going to have to confiscate your other twenty coins and the Government will owe you that amount. What's your name?"

Booth would have snatched the agent by his blubbery throat and forced him to the dirt, but he remembered his promise to Jake that no one would be hurt. "Well, sir, I can't do that. It's a matter of, you know, like the man said, 'simple common business accounting." He spat on the wagon and walked away.

"Forevermore," Philibert said as he stepped close. "Thirty-three hundred dollars? I had no idea. And it went off without a hitch, didn't it?"

Cockrell looked down. "We'll see."

"If you fellows come back next month, we can do it again. I'm sure there'll be more takers next time."

"There will be no next time," Cockrell said. "Where are our weapons?"

"Fair enough," Philibert said. "They're neatly stacked right behind the row of bunk houses where you fellows slept. Everything's fine, just fine."

Cockrell nodded to the captain who was already on his way.

"Don't anyone go anywhere," the agent said to the picnic-like crowd, studying their new silver coins. They liked the artwork on them, a seated Lady Liberty. "We have five hundred dollars left for one lucky person, just as soon as all Government property is returned."

This was a crowd pleaser. What would it be? A game of chance? What an interesting day this was for Delaware Town.

When Cockrell saw the soldiers toting rifles and swords back up the hill he called to the army officer. "Captain Doniphan?"

The Captain nodded. "All accounted for."

Cockrell scratched his neck and looked at Philibert. "You've been good to your word, Mister Philibert."

Philibert shrugged. "What is a man without his good word?"

"Exactly," Cockrell agreed. "Now someone deserves a reward."

The crowd pushed in.

"The last five hundred dollars will go, with no questions asked, to the person or persons who will lead me to the Yocum silver."

The sunny mood of the gathering was turned by a sudden chill. Most shuffled away as though they heard their babies crying and had to get back home.

Olive Moon stepped up smartly, a few of her husband's old cohorts behind her. "Hand that money over, mister. I know where that silver is. My husband was murdered for having stumbled upon it and these men will testify to it."

"Oh, Missus Moon, don't," a female voice implored. It was Perninia. "My uncle would never murder anybody."

"Yes he did," said Clovis Pogue. "I was there."

"It's high time somebody put a stop to Mister King James," said Missus Moon, "so yeah, we'll show you, won't we boys?"

"Yeah, we'll show you," Pogue said. "You want to go now?"

Cockrell and Teter hopped off the wagon.

"The horses are good," Captain Doniphan said.

Cockrell looked around for potential hazards. The crowd had scattered. The town looked peaceful. He turned to the young officer. "There will be no repeat of yesterday, Captain. This time we take cover and fight. Are your men ready?"

"Absolutely, Sir." He turned. "Ready for some action, men?"

The men stared back bleakly. Action? After yesterday?

"There'll be no trouble," Philibert said. "I'm sure of it. Please don't shoot anybody."

"We will if we have to," Teter said.

"Shut up, Teter," Cockrell said. "Troops, mount up." He swung up into his saddle and looked down. "You've been straight up so far, Mister Philibert. Thank you."

Philibert felt a tingle of patriotism.

y

Clovis Pogue let Olive Moon ride with him as they headed out for the Yoachum land.

They stopped at the edge of the farm and cantered in cautiously. Seeing no signs of danger they dismounted at Sol's big house and then heard some shouts from the field.

It was James, Sol and Augie, looking for all the world like they were planting crops. They were.

"Hello," James called, waving his hat. "Over here."

The lawmen remounted and rode toward the three in the field.

"Afternoon, Gentlemen," Sol, said. "You fellows lost?"

"Which one of you is Yoachum?" Cockrell asked.

"They're both Yoachums," Missus Moon said. "The two white ones."

"Why Missus Moon," James said. "I see you've joined the army. I hadn't heard." James stretched up a welcoming hand. "I'm James Yoachum, this is my brother Sol, and our farm hand, August Winter."

Augie nodded with a smile.

Instead of taking James's hand, Cockrell handed him a silver coin. "Is this a bit of your work?"

James took the coin. "One of ours," he affirmed. "My brother and I used to make silver coins for folks around here so they could feed their families. Thanks to the American Fur Company, this area got so over-hunted, nobody had any way to buy supplies for their families. Trade coins seemed to be the answer. Why, is there a problem?"

Cockrell dismounted. "Where's the silver?"

James scratched his head. "Oh, the silver that we used to make the coins? Long gone, I'm afraid. We only had the one buckboard. Stumbled across it in Arkansas next to some dead Mexicans."

"That's a lie," said Clovis Pogue. "It's under the barn."

James studied Pogue's face. "I know you?" he asked.

"I was here the night you shot Moony."

"I never shot anybody in my life."

"Liar," squawked the widow Moon.

Cockrell drew a folded document from his Jacket pocket and extended it to James.

"What's that?"

"It's a warrant to search your property for a silver mine and to secure it as national property for the U.S. Government."

James laughed. "Is this a joke?"

"The U.S. Government doesn't joke."

James gave an 'excuse me' grimace. "I'm sorry you rode all the way out here for nothing. Besides this land is legally ours. I got my registration papers in the house. My son – oh, say, he's a Government man too – he says no one has the right to steal chattel from a landowner."

"Are you going to give us trouble, Mister Yoachum?"

James rubbed his chin. "Well, I'm thinking about pounding Clovis Pogue there into a bloody stump, but I don't know. Does he work for you?"

"No."

"Good." James looked at Sol. "What do you think, Brother?"

"What's your name again?" Sol asked.

"Federal Agent Cockrell."

"Seems like an honorable fellow to me," James said. He looked up. "How can we help you, Cockrell?"

"We're going to search your barn."

James looked bewildered. "Why?"

"You know why."

"Do I have the right to refuse this?"

"Why would you want to?"

"I don't know. Just seems kind of un-American."

"I'm just following orders."

"Oh. Well, we all have to follow orders I guess." James gestured with a hand that said, be my guest.

Cockrell remounted and headed for the barn. His men followed. James and Sol moseyed over on foot.

Inside, the troops saw what looked to be remnants of the coin making operation, in parts, piled in a heap.

James pointed. "That's the equipment we used to make the coins. My brother made all that. He's quite a smithy."

"Over here," Pogue said, falling to his knees to claw the straw away.

Cockrell went to look. Under the straw was dirt.

"They've covered it up," Pogue, sniveled. "Kick the dirt away. You'll see."

The Captain ordered his men to scrape the dirt away, which did seem suspiciously loose. Within a minute they uncovered a lead plate, an obvious lid.

Cockrell looked at Sol.

Sol shrugged. "That's where we kept the silver hidden."

The door was secured in concrete by twelve steel locks.

"Unlock that hatch, Mister Yoachum."

James looked at Sol. "Where are those keys, Sol?"

"We threw those keys away a long time ago. It's a sinkhole, just too dangerous, you know, what with kids playing around here and all."

Cockrell glared.

"Well, listen," James said, "We've got field work to do, women's work according to my brother, so if you don't mind . . ."

"I do mind," Cockrell said. "You're staying right here until we get that lid up to see what's what."

James huffed a sigh, and then pulled three ready chairs from behind a bale of hay. "Fine, he said. "Root hog, or die." He, Sol, and Augie made themselves comfortable to watch the show.

The soldiers took turns chipping at the locks with whatever metal implements they could find around the barn and they tried shooting them.

Three hours later the final lock broke loose. There were smiles all around.

Teter and Doniphan lifted the metal hatch from its rest and dragged it aside.

Cockrell bent over to peer down the hole. It was fifteen feet deep with boulders resting on the bottom. He looked up with a desultory gaze.

"I got a ladder," James said, "if you want to climb down." He pointed.

When Teter went for the ladder his eyes caught a flash of the unmistakable gleam of silver. Two bars sat on a shelf against the wall. "Ah-ha," he woofed, and grabbed them both. He held them high. "Here we go," he said with victorious glee.

Cockrell looked back to James and then raised his eyebrows in a way that said, Now what?

"We were lucky to pull out those last two bars before the shaft caved in."

"Last two, huh?"

"Yeah. Probably foolish to let them set out in the open like that. You're not going to take them, are you?"

Cockrell sighed with frustration. "I'm afraid so. They're Government property now."

James exploded. "How are our personal possessions Government property?"

The ladder was lowered into the hole. Doniphan climbed down. He stomped around, then looked up. "It's solid."

Coming out of the barn, Olive Moon was livid. "No, no, no. It's down there, you morons. It's a trick. Clovis, tell them. You saw the silver down there. Tell them."

"Well, I didn't actually see it but . . ."

"Mister Government man," James said, "your mission was folly, and as I see it, a waste of taxpayer's money. What is the cost for this kind of fool's errand?"

"I just follow orders, Mister Yoachum." He started to mount his horse but was stopped by a big hand on his shoulder.

"I'm sorry," James said, "I'm going to need a receipt for the silver that you're confiscating. You understand. Just simple common business accounting."

Cockrell recognized his own quote. The Yoachums had been forewarned.

Some of the soldiers snickered.

"Not that we don't trust you to keep the records accurate for the Government, but . . ."

"You're right," Cockrell said. He reached into his saddlebag and withdrew a sheet of journal parchment with a lead pencil. He wrote out a receipt and signed it.

James read it and nodded approval. "Thank you, Sir. Have a safe journey."

As the representatives of the U.S. Government galloped away, James, Sol and Augie waved goodbye, and then laughed till they rolled on the ground.

y

Cockrell decided that he and his men would spend the night in the same putrid quarters as the night before and then head back to Springfield in the morning.

CHAPTER 43

Friday, April 14th, 1843

Just before dawn Cockrell heard a rustling outside his room. He grabbed his handgun and sprang for the door. He opened it slowly, stepping back behind the wall.

No one was there. He looked down. On the floor was a small folded sheet of paper. He picked it up and read, "It's in the house." The shape of a spade like on a playing card signed the note. He pondered, and then dressed.

Cockrell pounded on the doors of the other shacks. "Get up, get up. Move, move, move. We're going back."

Ten minutes later the platoon was hard-riding back to the Yoachum property.

Cockrell hammered on James's door.

It opened. James yawned. "Now what?"

"We're going to search your house. Step aside."

James did not step aside. He considered killing Cockrell with one blow from his right arm but checked himself. What would that lead to?

"What is this?" Mekinges asked appearing from the bedroom.

"They want to search our house."

"For what?" she asked.

"Yeah," James said. "For what?"

"I think you know what."

James rolled his eyes, then stepped aside extending a welcoming arm.

The men burst through the door.

"Check everything," Cockrell commanded. "Turn over everything. Search every nook and cranny."

"You think I've got a silver mine in my house?"

Sol and Mary had come running. Breathing hard they entered and watched with horror as the soldiers dug into the fireplace and then crawled around inspecting the floor, tugging rugs and moving cabinets and bureaus.

In the bedroom they pulled the dresser from the wall. They dragged the bearskin rug aside.

Then Cockrell eyed the bedroom stove. He pointed. "Move it," he commanded.

When the stove was disconnected from its pipe and shoved aside there was still nothing but flooring. He lowered himself to knock on the boards. There was no hollow sound.

He rose frustrated and embarrassed. "I was obliged to look."

"How's that?" James demanded. "Obliged to who?"

"Damn," Teter said.

"Yeah, damn you," James said. "I've got a claims deed for this property and I've got your receipt stating that you took possession of what silver there was from this place. Get out of my house."

"Check around back," Teter said to Doniphan.

"Check anywhere you like," James said. "Then go back to Springfield and get ready for your trial."

"Sorry, Mister Yoachum," Cockrell said. "We got a bad tip."

"What?" James said with disbelief. "You got a tip that I have a silver mine in my house?"

"Do you?"

"Sure, I do. It's under the porch. You didn't even think to look there, did you?"

Two soldiers ran out to check.

"Who told you that? I have a right to know. Who gave you this so-called tip?"

"Again, I apologize," said Cockrell. "We'll be on our way."

When the Government men were gone, James glared at Mary.

Sol said, "It wasn't Mary, Jim. Don't be silly."

"It wasn't me, Jim," Mary said. "Why would I?"

"Maybe you were drunk and don't remember."

Sol shook his head with disappointment and led his wife out the door to walk back home.

"It wasn't her," Mekinges said.

James stared. "It had to be. Who else knows? Jake doesn't even know."

y

The military plan had been to leave Captain Doniphan and his men to guard the Silver mine, but the agents had found nothing to guard.

As they rode back, Teter said, "We didn't look in the brother's house."

"It wouldn't be there."

"How do you know?"

Cockrell thought Sol's house looked too conspicuously inviting, and the rumor was about King James, not King Solomon. "Shut up, Teter."

His men were hungry when they arrived back in Delaware Town. He would buy some salted meat and they would be on their way. Upon his return to Springfield, Cockrell would send a message to Jefferson City, the new State Capitol, that the hypothesis of a silver mine was a frontier myth, romanticized into the imaginary character of King James.

There had been a wagon-load of silver at one time, from Arkansas Territory, but it was gone, the last of it to accompany the communiqué. His gut knew there was more to the story, but what else could he say? He had followed his orders.

Entering the store, Cockrell saw Philibert arranging shelves behind the counter and Perninia sweeping the floor.

"Good day to you sir," Philibert said. "We thought you left. Did you find the silver mine?"

"I need meat for eight hungry men," Cockrell said. "Can you help?"

"Got some fresh deer jerky in the back. You'll want about, what, five pounds?"

"Fine."

"I'll go wrap it for you."

Philibert returned with the jerky wrapped in pages of newspaper. "Fresh jerky wrapped in fresh news, the latest edition of the Boonslick Times, only six months old." He chuckled. "How many newspapers in Missouri now?"

"I don't know. Twenty-five, or so. How much?"

"It's on the house." Philibert hoped this would prompt more conversation but it didn't. "So, what happened out there, Agent Cockrell? Tell me."

"Nothing to tell. We came to do a job. We did it. We're leaving."

Philibert pushed the package across the counter to the agent and motioned for him to come closer.

Cockrell obliged, leaned in.

In a whisper, so Perninia could not hear, Philibert said, "I slipped a little something extra in the wrapping."

"What?"

"Just a small reminder that I tried to help."

y

James, Mekinges, Jake and Augie had dinner that night in Sol and Mary's house, discussing the events of the last two days. The mood was serious.

James was still unnerved by the fact that somebody told the Government that the silver was in his house. Why hadn't they searched Sol and Mary's house? Recalling Mary's drunken card game with a fool named Titsworth, he rationalized that the loose lips had to be hers. Alcohol trumps secret skeletons.

Tears brimmed in Mary's eyes. "If it was me Jim, why wouldn't I have told them how to get down there?"

"Get down where?" Jake asked.

"Who else knows?" James said

"Knows what?" Jake asked.

Sol looked to Mekinges. "Your brothers maybe? Sarcoxie and Shawnanuk? They know."

Mekinges mouth fell open, offended by the very notion.

"We're just talking here, Mekinges. I'm sorry. Of course it wasn't your brothers. The question was, who else knows?"

Jake couldn't believe his ears. "Whoa. Wait." He looked at James. "The silver was under the barn, right? And the shaft caved in, right?"

Nobody spoke.

"You mean the silver really is in your house?" He looked for clues on his Father's face. "How can that be?"

"Under the house," Mekinges said. "Silver down there. Long time Indian secret."

"We built the house on top of the entrance," James said.

Sol explained. "After you told us the agents were coming we put a lead covering over the hole and nailed old boards on top." He shrugged. "It worked, thank God."

"But somebody knows," James said.

"No, somebody suspects," Sol said. "But we've dealt with that. It's over."

James looked to his wife whose intuitions were usually on the mark.

"I think not over," Mekinges said. "Something bad is in the air."

"This is unbelievable," Jake said. "In fact, I don't believe it."

James nodded. "Good. You're safer that way."

Jake wanted to ask a hundred questions but realized that his father was still glaring at his Aunt Mary. He decided to change the subject and tell them what a wonderful person Alice Patterson was.

Saturday, April 15th

As Jake rode back to Springfield the next morning he thought about what his Father had asked him to do – get hold of Agent Cockrell if he was still there and, Government worker to Government worker, see what he could find out. James thought the agent had been somewhat well-mannered and had a gut feeling that the man was basically honest.

CHAPTER 44

Monday, April 17th

Jake did not have to look for the agent. Monday morning Cockrell came into the Surveyor's Office to introduce himself.

"I hear you're the son of James Yoachum."

"I am," said Jake, extending his hand. "Jake Yoachum. You must be Agent Cockrell."

Alice appeared from the back room.

Cockrell removed his hat. "Ma'am."

"My secretary," Jake said, "Alice Patterson." He smiled. "I'm glad you came in, Agent Cockrell. My father wanted me to ask you about your raid on his land. What was that all about?"

Cockrell tilted his head. "Your father is a very clever man. I know he tricked me down there, had me scratching gravel, as they say, but I did all that I was legally allowed to do."

"Tricked you, how?"

"Don't play me for a fool, son," Cockrell said, reaching into his vest pocket. "The thing is, I liked your pa." He laid a scrap of paper on the counter. "This note was dropped at my door, one of those god awful shacks down behind the store, in Delaware town."

Jake read it. 'It's in the house.' He looked up. "What does that mean?"

"Look at the bottom."

Jake squinted. "What is that? An apple?"

Cockrell laid something else on the table, a playing card.

"Ace of spades," Jake said.

Cockrell nodded. "That was wrapped in with the deer jerky I bought at the store."

Jake's brow furrowed. "I don't understand."

Cockrell shrugged. "You don't, huh?" He shook his head and turned to leave. "No cause for concern then." He went to the door and gave Jake a 'last chance' look. "All right then, wish your pa luck for me. I got a feeling he's going to need it." As he stepped out the door, a rumble of thunder sounded in the distance.

y

"Don't ride down in the rain," Alice pleaded.

"I have to, Alice." He wrapped his arms around her and kissed her passionately. "I'll be all right."

One second later, with a ferocious thunderclap, a bolt of lightning struck the big oak tree across the square.

y

The rain was torrential as William Gillis rode into town that afternoon for his first visit back since he had departed as part of the Lenape removal plan.

What he wanted to visit first was a bottle. He left his horse in the rain and entered the Cranky Crow, dripping wet. Others were also wet so it didn't matter.

Clovis Pogue recognized the man immediately. His hair was white now and he was fuller around the middle, but it was definitely him, the famed first citizen of the town he started. "Mister Gillis?" he ventured.

"Yes."

"I'll be hanged. I knew it was you. Welcome back, Sir. Can I get you anything?"

Gillis looked around. "A table in the corner and a bottle of your finest whiskey would be nice."

"Well, I don't work here, but I'm sure I can handle that for you. Who all knows you're here?"

"I just rode in."

y

"Philibert?" James said as he looked up, his face twisting into a scowl of incredulity.

Jake shrugged. He had changed into dry clothes and was telling his father about Cockrell's visit. "I left the office then and rode down through the storm because he told me to give these to you, like it was important."

"And that's all he said?"

"Yes Sir."

As James sat at his table, he studied the note and the playing card, straining to bring some forgotten incident to mind that would provide an axiomatic realization.

Sol and Mary came in with Augie, whom James had sent to get them.

"Why in blazes would you have us slosh over here in the biggest downpour since Noah?" Sol wanted to know.

James handed the note to Mary. "You told Philibert?"

Mary understood the accusing question but reacted simply, "No, Jim. I did not."

As Mekinges led her to the fireplace, Sol took the note and read it. He looked up with confusion. "This was the tip the agent told you he got?" He shook his head with disbelief. "Joe Philibert? He wouldn't . . ."

"That's his writing," Mary said from over her shoulder.

"What about Perninia?" James asked.

Mary turned from the fire with a hand over her heart. "Jim, for the hundredth time, I never told a single soul."

"Are you worried the Government will come back?" Sol asked.

"Who knows? We've got to figure this out."

Mekinges agreed. "Somebody dreaming of silver now and will not rest till he make trouble. Father says, 'people hate those who have what they wish for.'"

James nodded. "I reckon that's true."

"We should make . . . make . . . uh . . ." She couldn't think of the word. She looked to James. "Nemikwiha?"

"A trick?"

"Yes, trick." She smacked her forehead. "Need to make trick for rabbit to come out of hole."

"So there really is a silver mine under this house?" Jake asked.

James laughed. "Yes, Son, there is. Want to see it?"

y

"Best move I ever made, fellows," Gillis said. "I own several prospering businesses, including a quite lucrative slaughterhouse. Kansas City is quite the cow town." He was playing poker with Philibert, Clovis Pogue, Willie White-stone and Olive Moon. A bottle of Kentucky bourbon sat at his right hand.

Missus Moon shuffled and dealt.

"I hear the Feds came down and found the legendary silver mine," Gillis said as he arranged his cards.

"No, I don't think they did," said Philibert. "We haven't been out there, but the way that Agent acted before he left – well, that's the thing right there. He left. Took all his men with him."

"Hmph," Gillis puffed, twiddling some chips. "Government employees are lazy and thick. They're paid to be that way."

"So there is no silver mine?" Clovis Pogue asked.

Philibert put a cigar in his mouth and pretended to consider his hand of cards but he could feel the eyes of the others on him. It was a moment he did not know how to handle.

"Well?" said Gillis.

Philibert took a deep breath. "All right," he said, leaning in. "I have it on good authority that there is a silver mine."

"Where is it?" demanded Missus Moon.

Philibert looked around. "Please, not now. Not here."

"My husband was murdered over that silver and I have a right to know."

"Joe's right, Olive," said Gillis. "This is not the place."

"Let's go outside then," she demanded.

"No, thank you. I nearly got struck by lightning twice on my way down."

"The store," Clovis Pogue suggested.

Philibert shook his head. "Perninia's there." He thought for a moment, and then looked at Missus Moon. "Your house in the morning, say ten?"

The widow put a palm to her forehead. "Oh, it's such a mess."

The men rolled their eyes. "Let's do that," said Gillis.

Interest in the game went flat. They tossed their cards to the center of the table.

"Let's drink," said Gillis, and picked up the bottle to refill their glasses.

Philibert raised a declining hand. "Too much to think about," he said, pushed back and then got up.

He needed a walk in the rain. What was he doing? To help the Government was one thing, but who or what would he be helping with the idea that was now battering around like a beetle trapped in his brain? He was forty-two years old now. He had heard about the silver mine since he arrived here at age twenty. Wasn't it time people knew?

Walking slowly through the downpour across the squishy square he thought about the post that Perninia had received from her father in Illinois, Jesse Yoachum, who, at the bottom of the letter, had written a post script. 'Is there really a silver mine under Jim's cabin or is that one of Sol's jokes just to get me to move down there?'

That had been two years ago and Philibert never mentioned to his wife that he had read that letter because she never offered to show it to him. In fact, the day after, he saw her throw it into the flames of their fireplace.

y

Even though it was raining and dark, Augie kept guard on the porch while the family went below to enjoy Jake's first look at the silver and the underground coin-making factory. By the light of each flash of lightning Augie scanned the tree line as he thought about Mekinges's recommendation of a trick.

In the cave, the wives were surprised by some of the homey touches the boys had added over the years – table and chairs, some napping cots and a well-stocked wine stand with a fancy lantern on top. Best of all, to Mary's mind, the bats now avoided this end of the cavern.

Thirty minutes later as Augie was resealing the entrance, he told James that while sitting on the porch, a notion for the trick they needed had come to him in a flash of lightning.

James thought about it, decided that it was just the right idea and complimented Augie on his cleverness. "Like setting a mousetrap," he said as they sat again at the table.

"And we should do it immediately," Sol said.

They all agreed. In the morning Augie would make a routine trip into town for supplies and nonchalantly mention to as many as he encountered that the brothers and their wives would be making a trip to Springfield to file a complaint against the Government. He was to make a mental note of anyone who asked when.

CHAPTER 45

Tuesday, April 18th

At ten thirty, Perninia was uncrating a new shipment of Doctor Sappington's Anti Fever Pills and thinking about the recent outbreak of malaria. The sound of the door startled her. She looked up and then smiled. "Augie," she said, "nice to see you. Everything all right at the farm?"

"Yes Ma'am, Missus Philibert. Just need some stuff." It occurred to him then that what particulars he should buy had been overlooked in the plan. "Just the usual things," he said looking around. "The brothers are going to Springfield tomorrow. I'll be out there by myself."

Perninia was taken aback. "My uncles are going to Springfield? That'll be a first. Why?"

"Government business. Is your husband here?"

"No. Probably out trying to collect on some bills. Said he'd be back in an hour. Would you like some coffee?"

"No, thank you, Ma'am. Just put some . . . uh . . . normal supplies together. I'm going to walk around a bit and see what's new." He opened the door. "Be back in a short while."

As he left he heard Perninia chuckle. "Normal supplies?"

Augie surprised people with his unusual chattiness at the livery stable, the candle shop, the blacksmith's and the doctor's office, but failed to spot any of the usual suspects.

Probably in the Cranky Crow, he reckoned, an establishment that he, being a Negro, was forbidden to enter. He was a free Negro though and so within his rights to dawdle out front. This would be dangerous by late afternoon but he saw no risk in giving a cheerful "good morning" to customers going in at this time of the day. "How about that storm last night? Say, did you hear, the Yoachum brothers is going to make their first trip up to Springfield?" Several thought it was interesting, he could tell, but only mildly.

When he heard a voice half singing, half groaning from around the side of the building he went to see what it was.

A man sat leaning against the wall chanting a rhyme: "Quinine, quinine is our cry – give us quinine or we die." The front of his ragged shirt was crusted with vomit and blood.

Augie figured the man was dying of fever from malaria. There was nothing he could do but petition the Lord with a quick prayer.

Besides, he determined, lingering any longer at this place would be over the line peculiar. "Reach out to Jesus, Sir," he said to the man. "He'll be there." He left then to return to the store.

Perninia told him that he had just missed Joe. "He was here only five minutes ago," she said, "and then he ran back out. Said he forgot something."

"You got my stuff ready?"

"Augie," she laughed, "You never told me what you wanted."

"That's all right," he said. "I forgot my money anyhow."

"Forevermore," Perninia chided, "You don't need money. You're like family."

Augie was touched. "Thank you, Ma'am. That's as kindly as Jesus, but Mister Jim said nobody should ever buy nothing on credit." This was a lie. James had never told him any such thing, but he figured James would have, had they had such a conversation. He felt guilty about telling this lie because he knew in his heart then, that Perninia Philibert was as honest as sunshine.

CHAPTER 46

Wednesday, April 19th

It was an early spring that year, about two, maybe three weeks early by the brothers' reckoning. The trees were about ninety percent leafed out, the meadows were soft and green.

Those few days of rain seemed to have magically caused wildflowers to appear along with songbirds and butterflies. The redbuds were fading and the dogwoods were in full bloom.

Mekinges had already done the first cutting of new spinach from the garden.

It was a beautiful day as James, Sol and Augie made a strategy for what they hoped would not happen but somehow knew would.

This was the day that the brothers and their wives were rumored to be heading to Springfield to find an attorney to sue the Federal Government.

They discussed bringing at least one of the four Osage braves as a backup for Augie but he insisted he could handle things by himself. Besides, if folks thought the Yoachums were out of town, some might also think it was a good day to rob the warehouse which was now so large it needed all four guards if not more. And he would not really be by himself. Sol and Mary would be there, watching from just across the field.

They figured that if anyone was going to try anything it would be by cover of darkness, but decided for equanimity to make the grounds look empty by the time the sun touched the treetops, around six pm. It would be fully dark by eight with the moon a little more than three quarters full.

James and Mekinges descended into the cave at five. Augie replaced the lead door, locked it down and replaced the floorboards.

If anyone should happen to make it that far – "over my dead body," Augie said – they would see the same configuration of security that had frustrated the Federal troops in the barn just a few days earlier – a metal door secured by twelve locks set in concrete.

Just before six Sol and Mary carried chairs, blankets and a picnic basket into a young but dense stand of hazelnut trees at the northwest corner of their land. The probable intruders, if they came at all, would most likely try to creep in from the Southwest.

They were right about the direction, but off on their timing, if only by minutes.

Clovis Pogue watched from behind a large white oak where he had arrived at five forty-five. As Gillis had instructed, he had come on foot to the Southeast corner of the farm just as Sol and Mary were carrying their chairs into the grove of Hazelnuts. "A trap," he said to himself. "Gillis was right."

Philibert had been glad to report to the group that the brothers and their wives would be out of town on this night. It meant that no one would be hurt. He couldn't go, of course. Perninia would be sure to wonder and perhaps find out. He felt bad enough already by what he knew James would perceive as treachery.

Gillis explained that he too needed to stay in the public eye, in town, because it would be too coincidental, this deed being done, upon his first return in years. But he was more than happy to be the brains of the operation.

"Cowards," Clovis said.

"What?"

He turned, startled. It was Whitestone.

Gillis had instructed them on how to do the reconnoitering. "Get off your horses a quarter mile from the Yoachums' and go one by one on foot, every fifteen minutes. If there are Indian guards, just a couple of you will get caught and sent back to town as simpletons, no worse for worry. Get there early enough for plenty of time."

Clovis Pogue, Willie Whitestone, Howard Jones, and seven others whom Gillis neither knew nor trusted – what difference did it make – were all at the white oak by seven thirty.

"Sol didn't go," Clovis told them. He pointed. "Him and his woman are hiding in those little trees, yonder. They got guns."

"They bloody well knew we were coming," Whitestone said.

Clovis considered this. "If they did, wouldn't they have some reds guarding the place?" He thought for a second. "The great King James probably ordered his brother to stand guard all night. I don't think the poor fellow can take a shit unless the King tells him to." He pointed again, this time to James's cabin.

Whitestone squinted through the fading light. "Is that an Indian on the porch? Because if it is . . ."

"That's their nigger friend, August Winter. He's got a gun too, I'm sure." He turned and smiled. "Who wants him?"

"I do," said Howard Jones, raising his rifle.

Clovis slapped the rifle barrel down. "Not now, moron."

"Free niggers," Jones huffed. He wagged his head with bewilderment. "Think about that!" He blew a spiteful puff of air. "What is the world coming to?"

Whitestone said, "If we take him alive, you know, we could get five hundred dollars for him in Arkansas."

Pogue turned with a smirk. "We ain't here for no measly five hundred dollars."

"What's the plan?"

"I'm thinking." He was quiet for a moment. "Did you bring the dynamite?"

Whitestone patted his bag. "I did, but why?"

"Just in case."

"Right." A worried look. "In case of what? I couldn't get any of the regular stuff. This is the most powerful shite they make."

Explosives had not been mentioned during the two meetings at Olive Moon's house, the second being after Philibert had run back out of the store to re-gather the group.

The first meeting, the one at ten o'clock, had been a waste of time. Whitestone explained that he had stepped into Jim's house once before and felt lucky to be alive. He wasn't going to do that again. Fear had decreed the end result of that meeting, much to the exasperation of William Gilliss.

The news that James and Sol would be away on business brightened the impromptu second meeting considerably.

Now as they waited for darkness, Clovis decided that the high-born William Gillis had been too long gone to know what was what around here, and had no business telling him what to take or not to take, or anything else for that matter, and Philibert had been wrong about Sol, and both men, Gilliss and Philibert, were apparently too lily-livered to be here, and did they think they would be entitled to a share of the booty? He didn't think so. No risk, no reward. "Piss on them," he said aloud.

"What's that, mate?" asked Whitestone.

"What?" Clovis said, coming out of his thoughts.

"You said something."

As he looked around he judged the noise of the night bugs to be unusually raucous for April. "I said, early spring."

"Yeah," Whitestone said, as he smacked a biter on the back of his neck. "Early mosquitoes too."

y

Mekinges was surprised to see the table in the mine set for dinner, with a silk tablecloth, fine china and crystal goblets. She chuckled with delight. "When you do this?"

James, coming from behind the smelting stove with a basket of smoked fish, bread, and field greens said, "Augie thought we should have a nice dinner tonight. He did this. Sit down, Honey. I've got another surprise."

He went to the wine case and returned with a bottle of Moët et Chandon champagne. "Napoleon's favorite," he said, "or so I was told."

"Who?"

"Napoleon, some big chief across the great water." He popped the cork.

"Ah," she yelped with delighted surprise. "A funny noise."

"No other sound like it," James said as he decanted some of the bubbly liquid into her glass. "It's called champagne. Now wait, and we'll have a toast."

"We have toast?"

He laughed and then gently poured some into his own glass. "No. Before we drink we will bump our glasses together and agree on something that we both love." He raised his glass. "You ready?"

"Yes."

"All right. You can make the toast."

Her face scrunched with confusion. "How can I make toast down here?"

"Never mind. I'll make the toast." He thought for a moment. "Got it." He cleared his throat. "Ah-hmmm." He looked into her eyes. "Here's to the wind that blows, and our love that grows, and all the things God only knows."

Mekinges stared at him mystified.

"Now we touch our glasses together."

"I understand," she said. "Glasses like our hearts?"

James thought about that. "Well, yeah, Honey." He nodded. "That's beautiful."

They clinked their goblets then pulled them back for the first sip.

"Ah-yee," Mekinges squealed. "It jumps out and makes tickles."

James laughed again. "You like it?"

She grimaced. "Maybe take time, but I like toast. I never hear you say words like that before."

"Oh, one more thing," he said, reaching down under the table. "This is for you." He pulled out a bouquet of flowers in a crystal vase and set it in the center.

"Oh," she said, amused. "Augie pick flowers too?"

"No," James said, drawing the word out as though he were insulted. "I picked these flowers, each one just for you."

Mekinges reached into the basket, tore off a piece of bread and dipped it into the champagne. It made both taste better as far as she was concerned. "How long we stay down here?"

"About forty-eight hours, I figure."

"Two days of just you and me with nothing to do?"

James turned his head toward the cots with an impish smile. "Oh, I think we can find something to do."

Mekinges nodded. "Then I want to make new toast."

"Wonderful." He raised his glass.

She took a nervous breath. "Here's to the wind that blows and our baby who grows." She clinked her glass against his.

James was stupefied. "What baby?"

Mekinges leaned back and patted her tummy. "A brother or sister for Jake."

James was speechless but, Mekinges could tell, overjoyed.

CHAPTER 47

Across the field, Sol and Mary sat in the Hazelnut grove discussing their lives, how everything had changed so drastically for them after their move from Cahokia.

Mary wanted to build a fire but Sol explained that doing so would defeat the illusion of the farm being unoccupied. Besides, with the moon three-quarters full, he thought they could see well enough. "Can you see Augie on the porch over there?"

"Just barely."

"Good enough." He pointed. "Look. I can see a big old rabbit sneaking into Mekinges's garden. See him? Probably going for the lettuce. She'll be mad."

"It is a beautiful night," she said. "Look at those stars. Did God really make all those?"

Sol gazed up. "Jim told me the Bible says that not only did he make them, he knows each one by name."

"Pshaw," she exclaimed.

Sol shrugged. "Why not?

"There must be thousands."

"And . . ." Sol patted the top of her head, "he knows the number of hairs on your head."

"No. Really? Why would he care about that?"

"He's God. Why would he care about anything? You should know. Your father's a minister."

She shook her head. "He never preached about that stuff. Mostly grace and hell. Oh, and vanity. He hated vanity. I think he ended every sermon with, 'What use is vanity when confronting an eternal hell?'"

They were quiet for a while, listening to the chirring of the nocturnal insects.

"I think we're going to move, Mary," Sol said abruptly. "Would you like that?"

It was a surprise. "Move? Where? Into town?"

"No." He thought for a few seconds. "You've never been happy here, have you?"

"I wasn't at first but . . . really, we've got everything we could ever want here, don't we? Where do you want to go?"

Sol turned his chair toward hers. "This game of hide the silver, where's the silver is obviously over. I'm tired of it."

"All right," she drew the words out slowly. "What are you thinking?"

"Well," he said softly, "it isn't widely known yet but I hear there are mountains of gold in California just waiting to be claimed."

She stared at her husband, then rubbed her brow. "You're tired of silver, so now you want gold?"

"No, not like that at all. I just want us to start a new life together out from under Jim's shadow."

"Speaking of which, I hope we catch somebody tonight or he is going to think forever it was me who betrayed him."

"See? That's what I'm talking about. Who cares what he thinks?"

She nodded. "California," she said, trying to imagine such a move.

"Yeah." He got up. "Be right back. Got to relieve my bowels of an uncomfortable burden."

Mary laughed and reached down. From under her chair she produced a patch of sackcloth. "I came prepared," she said. "Here."

As Sol squatted, thinking about how well Mary had taken the news about moving, a blow to the back of his head knocked him unconscious.

Mary assumed the rustle from behind, was Sol. "That was fast."

A hand smothered her mouth, then pulled her chair over backwards. On the ground she got gagged and tied, then drug back into the trees where to her horror she saw Sol laying with a large dark stain in his silvered blond hair, his head turned away, unmoving.

She made an effort to scream through the gag but was silenced by a slap across the face.

"Be quiet, Missus Yoachum," Pogue said, "or I will ram this rifle butt into your husband's head again, and I don't think he'll survive it."

She looked up, terrified. Even by moonlight she thought she recognized familiar faces, men who had purchased peach brandy from her stand in the store.

"You're going to be guarded. One sound out of you or him gets his head bashed in. You got that?"

She nodded.

The invaders headed back into the trees to creep through the foliage around the clearing to get as close to the hill as they could.

Pogue figured there was no choice in how to deal with the black man without getting a white man shot.

Augie sat on the porch with two rifles, one against the house, the other across his lap. He was alerted by a covey of quail taking flight into the darkness. He assumed it was a fox but then saw a fox fleeing from the same point. Something wasn't right. He jumped to his feet and aimed the rifle toward that location.

A bullet entered his stomach the same second he heard the shot. Augie fell to his knees, then onto his belly, the rifle beneath his prone body.

"Got him," Howard Jones yelped with triumph. "Let's go."

As the prowlers neared the porch, Augie managed to get off a shot.

Howard 'Six-fingers' Jones fell, mortally wounded.

The rest opened fire and riddled Augie's head and shoulders.

August Winter, one of the few free Negroes in Missouri, died disappointed in himself, but excited by the prospect of meeting Jesus, face to face.

Clovis Pogue led the raid into the house.

CHAPTER 48

In the cave below, as James was about to lead Mekinges to bed and into his arms they heard the sudden noise of their bedroom stove being scraped across the floor. Mekinges froze. James reached for a rifle.

"What does this mean?" Mekinges asked.

James shook his head and pinched the bridge of his nose. "It probably means that Augie is dead."

To his surprise she grabbed the other rifle.

James couldn't help but smile. "You're going to shoot a gun?"

"I do anything to protect husband."

"Well, aren't you the sweetest thing?" He thought for a few moments. "It'll be all right."

When they heard the unmistakable sound of the bedroom floor planks being pried up, James felt less confident. "It'll take them awhile to break those locks. I doubt they can, but if they do, then we'll have them trapped. I'll be down here and Sol will be upstairs."

"I don't think Sol is coming," Mekinges said sadly.

James couldn't bear the thought. He shook it off. "Well, we'll be fine. There's another way out, you know. You go back to where the skeletons are and wait. Relax."

"No," she said. "Ejaja. If you stay here, I stay here."

James kissed her forehead, then nodded. "All right then. Ejaja."

237

y

Upstairs, Pogue was livid to see the locked lead floor, but not surprised. Whitestone said, "Well, mate, how do we get those bloody locks off?"

Five others in the room wondered the same thing.

Pogue spread his palms. "It's dynamite time."

Whitestone scratched his head. "We'll have to chisel a hole into the concrete. That could take a while."

"Three holes," Pogue said, patting the long leather pouch attached to his belt. He reached in. "A smithy's hammer and an iron rod." He pulled them out. "I've seen this trick before." He knelt to the floor and began.

"Three? That's too much."

"Better than too little."

The clanking of metal striking metal could be heard below.

James, now genuinely worried, was equally enraged. He couldn't wait to see whom it was that he would shoot first, coming down the ladder. He hoped it wouldn't be Philibert. He hoped that his brother and Mary were all right.

"Time to go to other end of cave," Mekinges asked.

"No," James seethed. "Not yet."

The gang took turns chiseling into the concrete, while wandering around the house pillaging and pilfering the dressers and storage pantries. They fought over Mekinges's jewelry.

At last Pogue said, "Good enough," and jammed three sticks of dynamite into the holes.

"Whoa, mate," Whitestone said. "One should be quite sufficient."

Was Pogue serious? His men began to worry. Three sticks? Did he not know anything about dynamite? One whistled a nervous tune as he and the rest nonchalantly began backing out of the bedroom.

Once the fuses were lit, Pogue said, "We'd better get on the other side of the wall, don't you think, Whitestone?"

Whitestone wasn't there.

He figured they'd gone out for air, or were cowards. That was probably it. Damned cowards, he decided as he ducked behind the wall and covered his ears.

CHAPTER 49

On the other side of the field Sol had regained consciousness. He pulled his mind into focus and gathered the probable circumstances.

Assuming that he was being guarded, he made as little movement as possible to wriggle free from the rope bindings. Since it wasn't that hard he presumed the men he was up against were odds-on idiots.

Moments later, with his hands around the dozing guard's neck, the man's eyes opened with moonlit terror. Sol strangled him to death.

He released Mary, and then grabbed his rifle. They ran from the grove into the field, their eyes scanning for Augie.

Was that him coming out of the house? They stopped. More men came out, a half dozen, Sol thought. The marauders, he was sure, and it looked as though they were running for their lives. Had James scared them off?

An explosion in the rear of the house blew the back roof into bits, high into the air.

Sol screamed, "No . . ."

Mary buried her face in his arm. "Oh my God."

"Come on."

As they crossed the field they noticed two bodies on the ground some thirty feet to their right.

On the porch Mary gasped at the sight of Augie's body. Sol bent to his knees and realized by the wounds to Augie's head that their black friend was gone.

In the front room a wall lantern burned revealing the back of the house to have been obliterated, now filled with rubble from the hillside – mud, limestone and pieces of cedar trees mixed with debris from what was once walls. The smell of explosives and wood dust filled the air.

"They're in the mine," Mary said. "They'll be all right, won't they?"

Sol looked to where the borehole had been. If it wasn't filled in, it was at least for now covered. "Yeah, they should be all right. There's a back way out anyway." He knelt to start pulling things from the pile that covered the entrance. "Bring some lanterns. Let's see if the lead cover door is still in place."

When he lifted away a nearly whole dresser drawer he was shocked by the sight of a severed head. By moonlight alone he recognized the face of Clovis Pogue. "Oh, Clovis, dear Lord, what have you done?"

Mary returned with two lanterns, only one of which was burning. She sat the other on a dislodged floor plank to light it but was thrown off balance as the floor shifted. They froze. It shifted again and then dropped several inches. A low rumble rose from the underground and then grew louder.

"Run," Sol said.

They ran from the house for a distance of fifty yards then turned. Nothing more seemed to be happening. Then it did. A landslide.

Sol and Mary watched in horror as the whole side of the hill slid down into the open bedroom, then pushed the rest of the house forward till it collapsed and was slowly covered by earth and tress. Limestone powder rose into the air.

Sol would remember later that he'd been surprised that the deluge had not seemed thunderous, but casual and smooth like a creature making an ordinary shift of its weight.

"My God," Mary said. "Should we go around the other side?"

"In the morning. It's a half-day's hike by daylight and rough even then. Lots of climbing." He thought for a moment. "I'll bet Jim and Mekinges will be at our house for breakfast by sunrise."

Sol put his arm around his wife. They turned away and walked home. There was nothing else they could do.

They couldn't sleep, and so sat on the porch waiting for dawn, hoping to see James and Mekinges walking across the field with grinning faces.

CHAPTER 50

By early light Sol and Mary walked back across the property to inspect the scene of the calamity. Here and there, parts of the house protruded from the rubble, barely giving evidence that a man-made structure was ever there.

An arm jutted up from the middle of the debris and a foot seemed to have floated on top the land flow to the outer edge. Were they parts of Clovis Pogue or had some of the marauders been as foolish as he? Sol had no idea how many men had been involved in the wicked work but he sensed that the survivors were long gone.

There was no sign of Augie's body.

The only reason he could muster for James not appearing by now was that his brother must be trapped. It would take hours to climb around the back of the hill and it would be a slog that he did not think his wife capable of making.

Hoof beats approached. Sol cursed himself for not having a weapon and then told Mary to hide.

Jake appeared on his horse and rode to the slide.

Sol stood, helpless. "Jake, so glad you're here. Your pa is trapped in the mine."

Jake, bewildered by the sight, knew better than to waste time with questions. "Let's dig him out."

"Can't from here. I'm going around to the other side. Get fresh horses. You and Mary go to town and tell Lum Booth. Tell him we need help."

Jake remounted and pulled Mary up behind him. As they sped to the barn Jake asked, "What happened?"

Mary cried into the back of his shoulder. "We got tied up and there was an explosion and a landslide and then . . . I don't know. Oh my God, oh my God."

y

The rescue group from town made it to the back of the hill around three o'clock. Besides Jake and Mary, there were only two others; Lum Booth and Joe Philibert.

They spotted Sol about a hundred yards up the rise, barely moving, clawing at rocks.

Jake and Philibert climbed up.

"Uncle Sol," Jake said.

Sol turned with the expression of a decrepit beggar hoping for morsel of hope. His hands were bloody, his face covered in dross. "Help me," he rasped. "My brother . . ."

Jake put a hand on Sol's shoulder. "Where's the entrance?"

Sol buried his face in his hands and wept. "It's gone. There used to be an overhang here. You could crawl up into a hole but . . ." He looked up. "It's gone. I don't know what to do." He looked into Jake's eyes for guidance.

Jake looked around and realized that with the collapse of the cavern, this whole billion-year-old Ozark Mountain had shifted, probably by only a few inches, but enough to be completely impenetrable. "Let me help you down, Uncle Sol," he said.

"We can't give up."

"No. We will never give up. Of course not, but there's nothing we can do here now. Come on." As he helped his exhausted uncle back down the hill, he said, "Remember, we're talking about James Yoachum. He'll find a way." In this world or the next, he thought, his heart once again broken by the leaving of his father.

Lum Booth wept unashamedly.

CHAPTER 51

Sol and Jake wrenched the remaining shards of the cabin from the rubble, stacked them into a pile and burned them. It was a week after the still unbelievable night of April 19th, 1843.

As they watched the fire Sol told Jake that he wanted him to have his house. He and Mary were leaving, but not because of the disaster. They had planned to do it anyway. "We're going to California."

"No!" Jake said. "What about the warehouse?"

"It's yours, dear nephew."

Jake stared disbelievingly.

"You going to marry that girl?"

"Alice?" Jake said, trying to shift to the new topic. "Well, she wants to."

"What about you?"

Jake sighed. "It scares the heck out of me."

Sol chuckled. "You'd be quite weird if it didn't." He put a hand on Jake's shoulder. "Fear is part of the thrill, Jacob. But, listen to me, once it's over you'll feel like it's the best thing you ever did."

Jake nodded. "Yes, I'm going to marry her."

"Then that big old house over there is a wedding gift from me."

"No!" Jake exclaimed, in disbelief.

"And the storehouse is a gift from your father. You should be very well off."

"I don't care about being well off."

"You want to come with us?"

"To California?"

Sol nodded.

Jake shook his head. "All of Alice's family is here. I don't think . . ."

"Of course you don't. You're rooted here. You belong here. I don't think the Ozarks could get along without a Yoachum." He brushed away an emerging tear as he began to rake pieces of charred wood into the rubble.

Over the next few days they chopped and drug juniper trees over the flotsam of the slide.

"When these dry," Sol said, "burn them, and then throw grass seed, or seeds of any kind, all around. Plant some saplings. Make it look like there was nothing ever here."

"Why?"

"You know why. Because of what's underneath. Blood silver."

"When are you going?"

"We start out in the morning."

"No."

Sol laughed and embraced his nephew. "I love you, Jacob. You're as fine a person as I or anyone else has ever met. I should know. I met you when you were five minutes old and you have amazed me ever since."

CHAPTER 52

Three weeks later Jake walked into the post store.

"Jake," Philibert said. "I didn't know you were in town."

He gave a slow nod. "Well, yeah, I am, I guess."

Perninia rushed from the back room to embrace him. "Oh, Jake," she said. "What happened out there? We heard there was an explosion. Did you find Uncle Jim?"

"Who'd you hear about the explosion from, Perninia?"

"Everybody. Please tell me Uncle Jim is all right."

"Not yet, but he'll turn up soon." He gave his smile. "You know my pa."

"You think he's still alive?" Philibert asked.

"Of course I do," Jake said.

Philibert nodded. "Hope so. How are things in Springfield?"

"Well, I don't know. I've moved back. Staying at my uncle Sol's place."

"Going to help him with the family business?"

"Guess so. We've got all that silver out there, you know, and people are still wanting to trade for it." He watched Philibert's eyes go wide. "Say, Joe, I've got a little card game going on over at the candle shop, but I don't trust the fellow. You got a card deck I can borrow?"

Philibert pulled a drawer open. "Sure thing." He shut it just as quickly. "I guess not. I thought I did."

"You do. I just saw it. Open the drawer. Let me have it."

Philibert's face went white as he handed the deck to Jake, and watched him count through it.

"Hmm," Jake said, "Fifty-one. You're missing one."

Philibert tilted his head with an expression that said, 'well, that's odd.'

"I bet you've got thirty pieces of silver though, don't you, Joe?"

Philibert flinched, his face reddening with shame. "No."

Jake pulled the rumpled fifty-second card from a pocket and tossed it on the counter. "Oh, look! There it is. Wouldn't want to start a game without the ace of spades. Might make me look like a man of poor character."

Philibert's stomach twisted into a sour knot.

"Let me ask you something else, Joe. Have you seen Clovis Pogue around town?"

His throat growing dryer by the second, Philibert answered, "No."

Jake looked at his cousin.

Perninia was bewildered.

He turned back to Philibert. "If you see him, tell him that with the Yoachums, scores do not go long unsettled." He turned to leave but stopped. "And Joe, if you ever cross my path without your wife . . ." He let the half sentence hang and started singing as he headed for the door. "Thirty pieces of silver, burns on the traitor's brain; Thirty pieces of silver! Oh, what a hellish gain!"

CHAPTER 53

Jacob married Alice Patterson October 29th, 1843. They had a laugh when they read the announcement in the Springfield Advertiser. Because of a typesetting error the date was listed as October 29th, 1834. "That's when we should have gotten married," she said.

That summer Jake bought two ox carts to carry as much merchandise as they could in one trip from the warehouse to Galena, where they settled down and had seven children not counting the first which was stillborn. Their children in order were Elizabeth, Jacob, Robert, Sara, Nancy Jane, Ruby and Mary.

In May, the following year, the tornado of '44 wiped Delaware Town off the face of the earth, reportedly taking twenty-seven souls up into its whirling throat.

The lives of Joe and Perninia Philibert were spared but they lost all their earthly property.

They made a trip to Galena where Perninia pleaded with her cousin for permission to stay in Uncle Sol's old house until they could get back on their feet.

Jake thought it was good idea. If the house hadn't already been ransacked and dismantled by looters, it was the solution to a problem that had been annoying him. He didn't want his Uncle Sol to return from California to find his lovely home abandoned and in disrepair. Furthermore, since Philibert

247

no longer had a store to tend, they should also take the warehouse property and see if they could do something with that. Jake took Philibert aside and told him it was his chance to make a new beginning with all debts wiped out. Joe said, "Thank you. You watch, I'll make you proud of us."

They did. Joe and Perninia went into the livestock business and made the back of the old warehouse a giant smoke house where Philibert regularly gave meat away to any neighbor in need.

At long last Perninia's father, Jesse Yoachum, arrived that year and moved in with his daughter and son-in-law. Under his management the livestock business grew bigger and prospered.

The Philiberts had nine children. Mary, August, John, William, Elvis, Sarah, Tom, Josephine, and Charles.

y

When the Government built Table Rock Dam, thereby inundating this land, they moved a cemetery they found there to higher ground and named it Philibert Cemetery.

Eighteen miles south of Galena, in that cemetery is a headstone inscribed 'Joseph Philibert, died 1884. Perninia Philibert, died 1852.'

EPILOGUE

Clint and Ruby Smith – his great-great-grandmother, whom he called Gramma Yoka – drove east past Silver Dollar City on Route 76, in his black Ford F-150.

The theme park, situated above Marvel Cave, was nearly sixty years old now, originally based on the concept of an 1880s Ozark Village but now attracting millions of visitors from around the world with its rides and festivals.

"Silver Dollar City," Clint said. "Makes you think, doesn't it Gramma?"

"It's a nice place," she said.

"You've been there?"

"Oh, a few years ago, when they made that TV show there, The Beverly Hillbillies. I got to meet Jed Clampett. That wasn't his real name though."

Clint smiled. "It's changed a lot since then."

In Branson, Clint took the bypass and went south on 76. Minutes later they drove through the gates of College of the Ozarks, down the hill to the back edge of the campus to the Ralph Foster Museum, perched on a high bluff known as Point Lookout.

Below the high, steep, rocky bluff was the White River and the beautiful valley beyond, these days crowded with condos.

Clint turned off the engine in the museum's parking lot, and looked at his great-great-grandmother. "Boy, are they going to be surprised."

She stared at the chamois wrapped disk in her lap and sighed.

"Okay. What are you going to tell them?"

She scratched behind her ear and tried to recall what she was supposed to say. "I am the great-great-granddaughter of Arnold Yoachum who passed the story of the Yocum trade coins down to me."

"Good. Now they're going to be skeptical at first. They'll want to get it tested and appraised and stuff, but I think they'll agree that we need to record your story immediately. You're going to be famous, Gramma Yoka."

She looked up, puzzled. "Me? I didn't do anything."

Clint said, "You are the only one alive today who actually owns a Yocum Silver Dollar. That's something. Think about it. I mean, generations of people have lived and died looking for that silver and you hold the proof that it really did exist."

Gramma Yoka pulled the coin from the chamois. She studied it. "Who does it really belong to, Jerry?"

"I'm Clint, Gramma. It belongs to you."

She looked at him with pale watery eyes. "Me? No. The Spaniards? The Indians? The Yoachums? No." She nodded. "It belongs to the truth."

Clint watched her think.

"It belongs to the history of the Ozarks. It belongs in a museum."

"I agree, Gramma Yoka. And here we are."

"Did you know this museum started up in the twenties?"

Clint shook his head. "No. Wow. Really?"

"Ralph Foster is a friend of mine."

Clint nodded. "Well, he won't be here today, but there'll be some really nice people in there, I'm sure. Are you ready to go in?"

She sighed and was quiet for a long moment. "Could I keep it just a little while longer?"

Clint batted a finger against his lips, and then nodded. "Sure." He decided that he could make the recording with his iPad back at her place.

He turned the key and started the engine.

On their way back to Lakeshore Assisted Living, they passed a Branson attraction called Lost Silver Mine.

"Did you see that, Gramma Yoka – Lost Silver Mine?"

She didn't. She had dozed off, but Clint noticed she kept a tight fist around her Yocum Silver Dollar.

Coins have a way of making a human hand behave that way.

Author's Note: In 1970, the United States minted its last circulating silver coin, the 40% silver John Kennedy half-dollar, marking the end of precious metal coins in America.

ABOUT WOODY P. SNOW

Author of the acclaimed short story, *The Boy Who Stole The Moon*, Woody P. Snow lives in Springfield, Missouri, with his wife and their dogs and cats.

He has achieved the highest awards for his daily nationally-broadcast radio show, screen-play writing, and songwriting including a Gold Record for *Rocky*.

Made in the USA
Charleston, SC
03 July 2015